Praise for *Sisters of the Undertow*

"With both humor and depth, Johnnie Bernhard probes beneath the superficialities of life in *Sisters of the Undertow*, revealing an unexpected hero. I read it in one sitting and thoroughly enjoyed it. Bernhard has some stuff!"

—Adair Margo, Member, National Council on the
Humanities and First Lady of El Paso, Texas

"Johnnie Bernhard has written a book of two sisters that is probably the most honest story of sisters that I have ever read. I could not put the book down and her book references scattered throughout the book speak to my booklover's heart. You know these women and you will embrace them as I fully plan to make this a 2020 Pulpwood Queen Book Club Selection! Five Diamonds in my Pulpwood Queen Book Club Reading Nation Tiara, my highest mark!"

—Kathy L. Murphy, author of *The Pulpwood Queens'*
Tiara Wearing, Book Sharing Guide to Life.

"Johnnie Bernhard pierces the soul of sisterhood, revealing the poignant paradox that familial love does not always come naturally, but it always comes. Sisters is a heart-wrenching yet triumphant story about conquering your fate and learning to play the cards you were dealt."

—*Galveston Monthly*

"Johnnie Bernhard writes with such humanity and genuine care for her characters that it's hard to leave them on the page. In her latest novel, Sisters of the Undertow, sibling rivalry between two very different sisters impacts the course of their lives, as storms swirl both inside and outside. I think we all feel swept up in an undertow sometimes, and Bernhard gives up something to hope for amid the wreckage."

—Erin ⸝ ⸝⸴ *Magazine*

"Johnnie Bernhard has an unusual gift of creating characters in *Sisters of the Undertow* who have such depth of personality which evolve in their lifetimes, it's as if it weren't a novel but a memoir. It's an amazingly captivating novel by an award-winning author; as you read it, you'll know the reasons."

—Margaret Barno, *The Daily News of Galveston*

"Johnnie Bernhard has a most unique way of creating the richness of family and stripping down a character—in this case Kimberly Ann—to her walled-off, vulnerable, afraid self. It's only then that we watch her reclaim a life she tossed aside. I loved watching that, cheering her on."

—Bren McClain, author of *One Good Mama Bone*

"There are so many ways to drown in this world, whether you are treading the dark waters in a family where one sister struggles to swim away from the burden of a sister with special needs, to those moments in life when being lucky or unlucky are simply a matter of fate. Noted novelist Johnnie Bernhard, shortlisted twice for the prestigious Mississippi Institute of Arts and Letters Award, takes us on a journey between the shores of the Gulf Coast to the high plains of a college campus in West Texas. Sisters Kimberly Ann and Kathy Renee each fight their own battles to keep from getting pulled into the undertow of life. From mean girls at school to male brutes bruising the innocents with their testosterone driven cruelty, Sisters of the Undertow will pull you into their current and keep you reading until the end. Sometimes those who appear weakest are actually the strongest, and sometimes the strongest are the most vulnerable for getting dragged under. If you love stories about sisters, families, and the human struggle to fit in, you will love this book, Johnnie Bernhard's third novel and her best yet!"

—Kathleen M. Rodgers, 2019 MWSA Mike Mullins Memorial
Writer of the Year Finalist

"Kim's the pretty one, the smart one, the lucky one. Still, she doesn't get along with her mother or her awkward, developmentally challenged sister, Kathy Renee. And then come the bullying boyfriends, the unsettling future, and Hurricane Harvey. Johnnie Bernhard addresses bold life challenges while creating a polka-dotted world, where romantic and familial love are filled with betrayal, regret, and ultimately compassion. Kim must lose everything to find out exactly what she's had all along. As personal and as heartfelt as a memoir, Sisters of the Undertow is one woman's story about redemption and the simple, healing powers of sisterhood, books, and a dog named Raul."

—Margaret McMullan, author of *Where the Angels Lived*

"*Sisters of the Undertow* is a beautifully written story focusing on two sisters close in age who launch their lives from opposite starting points. Johnnie Bernard's story will make you laugh and cry. It will touch the heart of everyone who reads it and will stay with you long after you've turned the final page. This is a must read, especially for anyone who has a sister."

—Marjorie Herrera Lewis, author of *When the Men Were Gone*

"Johnnie Bernhard has woven a vivid cautionary tale in *Sisters of the Undertow*, combining the beautiful language of literary fiction with a page-turning narrative. Following a family's story in Houston from the 1960s to 2005, she delivers the 'lucky' and 'unlucky' plights of a gifted girl and her special needs sister. Bernhard delivers on a deeply researched novel, writing with authority about the broken characters who face bullying, sexual assault, PTSD, homelessness, and limited intellectual capacities. She weaves complicated spiritual issues throughout the story, challenging her readers to examine their own views."

—Susan Cushman, author of *Friends of the Library*

"You'll ponder your own familial relationships as you turn the pages of this wonderfully realistic story. Sisters of the Undertow is an engaging exploration of the dynamic ties that bind two temperamentally dissonant sisters, written in the deep, introspective, unfiltered voice I've come to relish as author Johnnie Bernhard's trademark."

—Claire Fullerton, author of *Mourning Dove*

"An engaging novel that, at its core, wrestles at the struggle for personal happiness in the contemporary world. *Sisters of the Undertow* will resonate with anyone who's ever asked: 'How did I end up here?'"

—Cliff Hudder, author of *Pretty Enough For You*

"Johnnie Bernhard has Anne Tyler's knack for creating quirky, endearing characters with modest ambitions and big, beating hearts."

—Sharon Oard Warner, author of *Sophie's House of Cards*

Sisters of the Undertow

Sisters of the Undertow

A NOVEL

Johnnie Bernhard

HUNTSVILLE • TEXAS

Texas Review Press
Huntsville, Texas 77341

Printed in the United States of America

Library of Congress Cataloging-in-Publication Data

Names: Bernhard, Johnnie, 1962– author.
Title: Sisters of the undertow : a novel / Johnnie Bernhard.
Identifiers: LCCN 2019052155 (print) | LCCN 2019052156 (ebook) | ISBN
    9781680032109 (paperback) | ISBN 9781680032116 (ebook)
Subjects: LCSH: Sisters--Family relationships—Fiction. | Sibling
    rivalry—Fiction. | Hurricane Harvey, 2017—Fiction. | Houston
    (Tex—Fiction. | LCGFT: Novels.
Classification: LCC PS3602.E75966 S57 2020 (print) | LCC PS3602.E75966
    (ebook) | DDC 813/.6—dc23
LC record available at https://lccn.loc.gov/2019052155
LC ebook record available at https://lccn.loc.gov/2019052156

For our sisters, everywhere

and

*To those who volunteer with the Cajun Navy Foundation
and animal shelters across America.
You are the better angels among us.*

Wisdom is brilliant, she never fades. By those who love her, she is readily
seen, by those who seek her, she is readily found.
She anticipates those who desire her by making herself known first.
Whoever gets up early to seek her will have no trouble
but will find her sitting at the door.

Wisdom 6:12–14

Part I

1

S he was different. I knew this when I was just a kid. Not in the sense I know now, but rather as an uneasy feeling in my stomach, an anxiety I wasn't old enough to recognize. I was fair; she was a brunette. I was lucky Kimberly Ann, the pretty and smart sister whose name was always called for the correct answer. She was unlucky Kathy Renee, the plain and troubled sister whose name was never called at all. We were sisters. I loved and hated her.

We shared a double bed during our childhood. The only thing changing during those years was the bedspread. Sometimes it was purple and nubby, scratching our tender skin when we pulled it up to our chins. Sometimes it was a simple quilt, never a Dutch doll or star-flower pattern but one made from our worn-out clothes, sewed together without a clever stitch. For the longest, our bed was covered in a white chenille with fringe trailing on the hardwood floor. It changed with time, but my sister, the little girl I slept with every night, remained the same.

While I played the clarinet in the junior high band and won ribbons in track and field, she remained the same, a little girl with brown eyes, neither stunning nor intense. I think she always knew what people thought of her. She wanted to say something in return, and for many years I waited for her to say it, but I learned she was incapable of cruelty.

We were born sixteen months apart, of the same mother and father, yet our lives would become as different as two planets orbiting around the sun, never to fully understand each other, despite our years of circling.

But in those early years, before the doctors and the education specialists, we were happy in our ignorance of each other. She didn't know I was smarter and healthier, and I didn't know she couldn't do story problems or read beyond the fourth-grade level. Before I knew she would always be different, we were perfect little girls in our happy world. Our bedtime ritual was one of friendship and comradery, except for the nights I would inflict my privilege as the older sister. It began with a warning before the lamp clicked off.

"Stay on your side of the bed. Here's the border. Don't cross it," I'd say to her, drawing an imaginary line in the center of the bed with my index finger.

She met my challenge with confusion. Thinking it was a game, she'd toss her right foot over the imaginary border. This was returned with an elbow to her side. She then rolled to the far side of the bed, as far away from me as she could go without falling off the bed. All I could see was the wild mass of black hair, neither curly nor straight, just thick and coarse upon a pink and white pajama top, as her chest rose and fell in anguished sobs. Unlike her, I was capable of cruelty.

But on those perfect nights of my early childhood, we would jump into bed at the same time; no one wanted to be first. We only thought of the immediate; there were no regrets from yesterday or anxiety for tomorrow. All we knew was to jump on the bed, up and down, up and down, laughing and holding hands. It ended when my father knocked on our bedroom door, "Quit the monkeyshines, girls."

Those days were sealed tightly from the outside world. I didn't know what was fair and what was unfair. I didn't know about luck, that random toss of the dice determining who you will be for the rest of your life. I didn't know then my sister had an IQ of eighty-five. My dad didn't know either, but I think my mom knew all along and hid it from us. The one certainty I knew in my childhood was every day would end the same way, my sister lying next to me in our double bed.

"Light out, Sissy."

"Night-night, Kat-Kat." I'd click the light off between my thumb and index finger as perfect silence covered us, erasing any imaginary border that had come between us the night before.

2

Mom and Dad were lucky people, for a time. That time of boy meets girl, first dates, long kisses, and paisley pants in the Sixties. Not that the Sixties were such a lucky time, but that Sandy Barnes and David Hodges met and fell in love. They were born healthy, attractive, and somewhat athletic. They met in 1967, the year David escaped Vietnam, thanks to an erratic heartbeat discovered during his physical exam. A few months earlier, my mother dodged a bullet during a race riot at Texas Southern University, when Houston police fired three thousand rounds of shotgun and carbine fire into a men's dormitory. A rookie cop, on the job for fourteen days, took the bullet. He was unlucky.

Sandy never told anyone why she was on the TSU campus that day. I never thought to ask her until after she died. Breast cancer found her and her lymph nodes, a residual effect from inhaling the petrochemical plant air she breathed for sixty-four years. I never thought to ask my dad either. He might have enjoyed contemplating his wife as a civil rights protestor, open-hearted in the Third Ward of Houston. But that thought didn't occur to me until after he died either. The erratic heart that saved him from Vietnam eventually caused a massive stroke on his sixty-eighth birthday. He became bedridden and silent until his troublesome heart stopped.

Mom attended the University of Houston after high school and landed an accounting job at Todd's Shipyard near Green's Bayou. Her fondness for miniskirts paired with polka dot blouses never went unnoticed by Dad, a draftsman. Between designing barges and stamping paid in red ink on typed invoices, a relationship began at a Bunn's coffee station shared by the two departments.

"Morning, David. Coffee's fresh. Made a pot at eight," Mom called into the drafting department from the open door. She held a carafe of black coffee in one hand and a red coffee mug in the other. Mom had always viewed shyness as a fault and practiced acts of assertiveness each day to overcome her childhood affliction. She felt a sense of accomplishment when she realized her assertive task for the day was completed by 8:45 a.m.

The men in the drafting department turned and looked at my dad, and like a moth to the flame of a lime green miniskirt and a red polka dot blouse, he got up and walked toward the Siren's call.

"Thanks, Sandy. How are things?"

"Good, always good. And you?" She smiled her best smile, looking directly into his eyes. They both had green eyes. She believed the coincidence to be a sign of destiny.

"It's a paycheck Friday this week. Want to catch dinner and a movie? Maybe some barbeque?"

"That's right. Oh no, I just remembered, I'm behind in payroll." She blushed as she didn't want him to think she was careless. A careless accountant was unforgiveable and quickly unemployed. She made a mental note not to order ribs or wear white for the dinner date. "I'd love to see Faye Dunaway in *Bonnie and Clyde*."

"Give me your number. I'll call you tonight. You like barbeque, right?"

"Love it." She took the pen behind her ear and wrote her phone number down in the palm of his hand. The touch of her hand and the pen it held resonated through his body.

"Well, see you later, David." She turned quickly, and the little lime green miniskirt walked away. He returned to his drafting table, avoiding the eyes of the eight men in the room. He stood for a moment, transfixed by the stack of blueprints on his table; then, slowly, he opened his closed right hand. Seeing her phone number written on his skin, he felt the warmth of her again.

Glen Sproat, his fellow draftsman, spun on his stool, watching his coworker marvel at his hand.

"You're a lucky man, David Hodges."

Dad drove his 1962 Volkswagen Beetle—an immaculately kept red exterior with a red and white interior—to the intersection of Main and Southmore, where a two-story apartment complex of white brick and black iron lattice-work sat on the corner. The grounds were modest with a metal sign noting "The Orleans" nestled in a neatly trimmed boxwood hedge near the asphalt parking lot.

He turned the engine off, looked up to the second balcony, and saw my mother twirling a macramé plant hanger of ivy. She stopped the plant from spinning and removed several leaves, placing them in her purse. He got out of the car and closed the door. Startled, she looked out toward the parking lot and waved at him.

She spun quickly in her polka dot shift dress of pink and white, and pointing her white boots in the direction of the stairs, she hopped down each step, her blonde hair bouncing in the late autumn sky. She was almost running to him, he thought. He didn't want to stop watching the girl in the white boots; he wanted to stand there and stare at the pointed toes meeting each concrete step in the stairs, the last of the day's light in her face. He broke the spell and walked toward her.

She greeted him with a kiss on the cheek and a hug. He smelled Chanel No. 5 behind her left ear lobe. The scent distracted him for a moment. It was his mother's perfume. Expensive. Sophisticated. He almost felt afraid of her. Then he smelled the peppermint in her mouth. His shoulders relaxed as he held her longer than he thought he should have.

Where does she get all the polka dots? Such a funny girl, he thought.

Mom didn't want to be the first one to pull away from the hug. She didn't want to embarrass herself or her date. She held on to him, making a small fist in the green and blue plaid of his shirt.

He always wears plaid shirts, long sleeve. Always. Then there's the same brown loafers and matching belt. David's sensible. Reliable.

They both laughed, embarrassed by their own thoughts and longings. Swinging the car door open for her, he touched her elbow, guiding her into the seat next to his. He loved the idea of her being next to him; he had so often driven alone without anyone to talk to, but this evening, there she was—a girl, a warm, funny girl who smelled of expensive perfume and peppermint. Suddenly, the world seemed better than it ever could be.

They drove along in the Volkswagen in east Pasadena in 1967, cocooned within the red and white interior. All around them, young men went to Vietnam and died; race riots ignited cities and scorched souls, and little black girls were spit upon on their way to school and church. But within the interior of the 1962 Volkswagen, for a tiny moment, something singular and beautiful was happening for a young man and woman. Sandy and David fell in love.

Tom Jones sang "What's New Pussy Cat?" on the AM radio station and life in Pasadena, Texas seemed the best place to be on the planet. After a meal of barbeque chicken (she used a knife and fork to eat her chicken, an action not unnoticed by him), pinto beans, and coleslaw, the couple drove to the movie theater.

El Capitan Theatre, an 11,000-square-foot kaleidoscope of film and Hollywood twentieth-century glamor, featured an exterior marquee of a vertical neon tower of P-A-S-A-D-E-N-A. Above the lobby doors, multicolored neon flourishes of *Capitan* and the movie billing competed for the patrons' attention.

The magic of Hollywood ignited the backwater of Houston and gave Pasadena a new theater with exterior murals of a Spanish captain and a Spanish galley, sailing beyond the petrochemical plants east of town. Inside were oceanic-themed walls of Neptune on a sea horse, and Europa riding a bull among the dolphins; the lobby ceiling featured a giant mermaid and compass.

It was the pride of Pasadena until it succumbed to the porn films of the Seventies. Resurrected by the faithful, it became an evangelistic church, later abandoned and sold.

But before the rise and fall of east Pasadena, David Hodges opened the door for Sandy Barnes on an autumn night to the simple joys of popcorn and a movie. The couple waited for snacks near the strategically placed red velvet roped balusters on the seashell themed carpeting.

"I'll have a Dr. Pepper and a small popcorn, David." Her green eyes smiled at him. His eyes smiled back at her.

We both have green eyes. Square. Pi. Pi squared. Infinite. Perfect. Sandy, he thought to himself as he reached for her hand, walking into the dimly lit theater. Side-by-side they sat, watching Faye Dunaway and Warren Beatty make love in a cornfield.

"Do you think the real Bonnie Parker had cheek bones like Faye Dunaway?" was the only thing she said during the one-hour-and-fifty-one-minute movie. He stole that moment to kiss her. She kissed him back.

The couple went to the El Capitan Theatre every Saturday night until the Saturday they were married at St. Pius Church. It was the only time he didn't see her in polka dots that year. By 6 p.m., they were travelling east on I-10 toward Biloxi, Mississippi. It seemed like an exotic honeymoon destination full of gulf breezes and white-columned porches. It seemed far, far away from oil refineries.

They followed the coast road of restaurants, night clubs, and souvenir shops until parking in front of the White House Hotel, a nineteenth-century jewel nestled on an expansive green lawn of blooming azaleas and mythical oaks. A black and white polka dot scarf around her slender neck fluttered in the humid breeze.

"Are you happy?" She asked him, taking his hand and kissing it.

"Yes, crazy happy, beyond what any man deserves."

Until the day she died, my mother reflected on what Dad said that night. It helped her to rationalize her decisions and indecisions; the seconds, the minutes, the hours of not understanding why. It wasn't that God had punished her, she thought. Maybe they had simply used up all the luck any two human beings deserved on that night in Biloxi, Mississippi, all those years ago.

3

I was Mom's fourth pregnancy. The first three ended in their second trimesters. Vomiting and bleeding, she lay on the cold pink tiles of the bathroom floor as life seeped from her womb. With each miscarriage, she became smaller, and smaller.

She didn't wear polka dots anymore. She and Dad didn't go to the El Capitan anymore. When the swinging ivy in the macramé planter died, he threw the entire thing away. Mom never noticed its absence.

Before she carried me to full term, she spent her days watching television, staring at her stomach, and praying the Rosary. A devout Catholic, she attended Mass, recited her prayers, and believed Purgatory was full of practicing Catholics, like herself. With each miscarriage, her belief intensified. With one foot in Purgatory and the other in Pasadena, Mom resolved herself to a penance of daily Mass.

By the third miscarriage, my mother dreamed of her three babies in Limbo. Floating on little pink and blue clouds, one boy and two little girls, with heaven above and earth below, her babies neither smiled nor cried. They simply existed in a vaporous air, along with millions and millions of little babies on pink and blue clouds in Limbo. When Jesus came, she would see her little boy and two daughters again. She whispered that fact to herself each day. It helped her live through the next twenty-three hours and fifty-nine minutes.

Life became predictable for the girl who once wore polka dots. After morning Mass, she did the kitchen dishes, swept the entire apartment, and rinsed the bathroom sink free of toothpaste. By late afternoon, she crushed

Ritz crackers into a casserole dish, the recipe found while reading her favorite magazine the day before. Routine and hope were tender morsels she used to fill each day.

Her conversations with Dad revolved around her health. They began at sunrise and ended at sunset, a circle around the sun, day after day, year after year.

"How do you feel today?"

"Better than yesterday."

"How did you sleep?"

"Worse than last night."

The spell would break temporarily with a doctor appointment.

"Hope things go well with Dr. Selman today," Dad said before leaving for work. Dr. Selman's name would change intermittently: Dr. Cohen, Dr. McGregor, Dr. Davis, Dr. Abbott. . . .

"I'm sure it will be more of the same old, same old," Mom replied, while scrubbing dried egg out of a skillet in the tiny kitchen of the little apartment. Thrown over her shoulder was a gray dish towel.

"Any news?" Dad asked when he came home and sat at the kitchen table, waiting for dinner. By evening the gray dish towel doubled as an oven mitt, as Mom pulled a cookie sheet of breaded fish sticks out of the oven. Today seemed different from all the other days he had asked this question, he watched her move slowly from the Formica kitchen table, placing a white paper napkin next to his plate, then, seconds later, placing a fork on top of it. *Maybe she doesn't hear me.*

"Honey, did you hear me? What did the doctor say today?" She stopped at the stove, placing the dish towel over the cookie sheet. She looked directly at him with her hand resting on her left hip.

"I heard you. I just wanted to get my thoughts together before answering you. Dr. Selman was different, David. He seemed to know what he was talking about. He told me I had eclampsia, a cardiovascular condition." She sat down at the table, wiping away imaginary crumbs with a sweep of her open palm. "It's why I've lost the babies. But my swelling isn't as bad with this pregnancy. That's the tell-tale sign of the condition." She pushed her chair in front of him, placing both hands and right foot in his direction. "See, not that much swelling in the hands and feet."

He grabbed her hands, kissing them. "Baby, it isn't as bad this time. I can see that. We'll make it work. We'll have our baby."

"I've just got to keep my blood pressure down. Called Mama this morning and told her. She had the same thing. Lost two babies before I was born. Why she never told me, I have no idea." She got up from the chair and removed the dish towel from the cookie sheet. She stopped and turned around to face him. "Why do women think it's their fault when they lose a baby? Sometimes it's just bad luck or we get sick. This time will be different. Got to keep the blood pressure down."

"No more housework, just rest and read. I'll cook when I get home. Clean house, laundry on the weekend. Think only of you and this baby. Nothing else matters."

Mom did just that. She began her day on the couch with her feet up and the first prayer of the day on her lips. "Jesus forgive me. I truly don't know what I have done to deserve this. Women all over the world have babies every day, whether they want them or not. I want my baby." The white plaster walls within the little apartment said nothing in reply for a long, long time.

Finally, on Christmas night in 1970, I made my entrance. Kimberly Ann, a rainbow baby, born after all the dark storms of miscarriage. I had all my fingers and toes and could breathe on my own.

We began life as a family in a brand new three-bedroom, two-bath home near Almeda Mall. We were all happy in that house, in the perfect neighborhood, living as daddy, mommy, and baby, until Mom got pregnant again. Twenty-nine weeks later, bad luck found us again.

4

With high blood pressure, swollen feet and hands, Mom woke Dad up at 3:45 a.m.

"Something's wrong, David. Help me to the car. We need to get to the hospital."

"Honey, you're all right." He moved to his left side, checking the time on the nightstand by the glowing digits on the clock radio. "Lie down. Here." He padded the mattress. "Let me rub your back."

"No, get up, get up now. Take me to the hospital." With the added tension in her voice, a rush of bright red blood pushed down her leg. "No. No. Help me."

"Let me call your mom. I'll get Kim up. Dressed."

"Just take her with us. We don't have time."

Dad rushed into my room, rolled me in the bedspread, and carried me out the door. In the back seat of a 1971 Volkswagen Bus, I could hear my mother's moans. That's all I remember of that night. The heat from the bedspread and my mother crying.

"Sweet Jesus, stop the bleeding. Stop it. Please."

I don't remember anything else. The hospital. What my father said. I don't know who took me and where I went. Later, Grandma Jean would come and stay with us, watching me and taking care of Mom. She did that throughout all our crisis. Grandma Jean. She smoked a lot of cigarettes and made me macaroni and cheese with diced hot dogs.

"Here, honey. Granny made you some lunch." I'd watch her open a few cans and set a pot of water to boil on the stove. The hot dogs swam in the boiling water until they made a little pink broth.

That cigarette of hers never left her mouth. I wouldn't be surprised if a few ashes ended up in my food over the years. It didn't matter. I could never find fault with her, and she never found fault with me. I was her favorite, as she never quite warmed up to my sister. I'm sure she blamed Baby Kathy for ruining her daughter's life.

That's how it all began for my little sister. Everyone was always talking about her health, her aptitude, her future, as if she hadn't any say in the matter.

Kathy Renee was delivered by C-section sixteen months to the day of my birthday. She weighed three pounds and spent six weeks in an incubator on oxygen. A surgery schedule was put in place, and she began her life with repairs to her eyes, heart, and lungs. The hearing aids would come a few years later, along with Coke-bottle glasses. Modern medicine in the seventies did its best to recreate what nature didn't have time to do. At least, Pasadena Memorial Hospital was fit to give my sister one of the only prizes she'd get in life—a paper certificate proclaiming her the smallest baby born in 1972.

That's how life was for a long time. Grandma was either opening cans of food with the electric can opener or smoking cigarettes while reading a book with a shirtless cowboy on the cover. Those are shadow memories to me. Neither clear nor unfocused, just something in the back of my mind occasionally seeping through when I recalled my early childhood. I do remember the house was sad. The people were sad. The furniture was sad. Everything around me seemed sad, except for Grandma Jean's macaroni and cheese with hot dogs.

My mother never stopped blaming herself. Sandy, the polka dot–wearing blonde who skipped on sidewalks and charmed my father, was gone forever. I suppose Dad never quit missing her. They became dutiful people. Nothing more, nothing less. Baby Kathy never had the cognitive ability to know the difference. But I did.

I counted every deficit and disappointment by the time I was in junior high. I lived on a bitter moral scale of responsibility and anger. Most of the time I was angry. As children jumping in our beds each night, I loved her. In time, I loved her because she was pure, unlike me. God mercifully removed the concepts of anger and vanity from her psyche. Despite the wreck of her body and mind, she never blamed anyone or anything. She loved Jesus. She loved Mom and Dad and especially me, her big Sissy. Kathy Renee was a happy girl. The only one in our family.

5

I nearly drowned when I was eight. I could blame Kathy Renee if I wanted.
Technically, it was her fault. It was also her fault we never took another
vacation to South Padre Island or any other beach.

Mom was hopeful for a sunny day on the beach with her little girls. She
dressed us in matching red and white polka dot bikinis, white sandals, and
wide-brim straw hats. We took turns putting our head in her lap, as she
placed a drop of olive oil and a cotton ball in each ear.

"Now girls this is the best way to keep water out of your ears," she sang
to us, placing two drops exactly in each ear canal. I guess it worked; I never
had swimmer's ear, but Kathy did. Plastic tube after tube was placed behind
her eardrum to improve drainage. It didn't matter in the grand scheme of
things. She could barely hear out of them anyway. By the time she was ten,
she wore hearing aids in both ears. When I was younger, I visualized a terrible monster living in her ear, beating on her eardrum until it broke.

After our ears were coated with extra virgin olive oil, Mom lavished our
skin with suntan lotion. I loved this part the best, because of my mother's
beautiful hands and the smell of coconut-scented suntan lotion smoothed
over my little girl body of chubby thighs and boyish hips. Kathy Renee
laughed, running away from Mom's outreached hands. She was very tick-
lish. Even drying her off with a bath towel sent her running away, laughing.

"Come back here, Kathy Renee. You can't go to the beach without this.
Now, come on," Mom pleaded. Dad scooped her up and deposited her
on Mom's lap. Within minutes she was running and laughing from Mom's
outstretched hands covered in suntan lotion. It made Dad and me laugh.

We knew she enjoyed her little game but, somehow, Mom never had the patience for simple games. I guess she thought it was a waste of time to see her daughter run and laugh, when she should have been learning her ABCs.

We left the whirling hum of the A/C window unit in the cinderblock motel room. Crossing the asphalt parking lot, hand-in-hand, we passed through a small gate near the outdoor pool. I often felt like I was pulling my sister along. She was so much slower and smaller than me.

It was during that time in my childhood I noticed the differences in people and animals. I didn't like small things—small dogs, small cats, or small people. I didn't trust them. They were out of place in the world I knew. They didn't match the other cats, dogs, or people; they stood out and were alone in their smallness, tiny and shrunken from all the other normal cats, dogs, and people.

I began to associate small people with the Munchkins in *The Wizard of Oz*. Munchkins were frightful—strange, small things with too much make-up and exaggerated smiles and frowns, stubby hands, and neckless bodies.

In the same way, small dogs were peculiar with their shrunken heads and too-big eyes, yap-yap-yapping at little children, ready to tear at their meaty thighs with pointed yellow teeth. Small cats were sly, slippery, secret animals; they could not be trusted. A lovely, furry kitten may approach with a purr; its little tail touching the naked arm of a child's, coaxing, teasing for affection, then suddenly, a horrible strike of the paw. Unexpected blood and a scratch on a child's face—that was what you could expect from a small cat. I did not like small things, and Kathy Renee was small, smaller than all the other girls her age. I yanked her arm hard when I saw the beach, the Gulf of Mexico just a few feet away. Kathy tripped, but she did catch up to my pace. My sister was very small and slow.

"Girls, come sit with me and let your dad look at the water." Kathy Renee and I sat on a thin blue blanket while Dad dutifully walked to the water's edge. It was taking him forever, so Kathy Renee and I began exploring the beach just beyond Mom and the blue blanket. A discarded beer can from last night's reverie, a sand dollar, broken in two uneven pieces, and a hermit crab were our first finds. Kathy Renee placed them carefully on the blue blanket.

I watched Dad stare into the vastness of the Gulf with its rolling white-capped waves for a few minutes. I studied his back carefully, and I thought that, if I tried hard enough, I could make him say the water was perfect for us. I could force him with my eight-year-old mind to turn around, laughing and waving, "Come on, girls. The water is fine!"

But, he didn't turn around. Kathy Renee amused herself by lining up additional treasures on the blanket. A Styrofoam coffee cup and a piece of driftwood shaped like a fork sat next to the beer can.

"That's a living animal in that shell. Put him back or he'll die."

"Don't see animal, Mama."

"*An* animal."

"Look, no one inside." She held the hard-shell home of the hermit crab to her right eye, giving it a long, thoughtful look. Then placing the opening in the shell to her lips, she said, "Come out, animal. Come out."

Dad returned from inspecting the water and sat down next to the beer can.

"How does it look, Dave? Current very strong?"

"I'll go out with them. You rest here. Maybe get us some lunch going."

"Okay, girls, you can swim. Hold your father's hand. Kathy, Kathy Renee, leave that poor crab alone and go with your father." Mom sighed heavily, lying on her side with a magazine propped up by her right hip. Her hair was blowing about her, free from a hat or rubber band, wild and blonde in the sunlight. I looked at her for a long time. I thought my mother was the most beautiful woman in the world.

I reached for Dad's hand as he bent over Kathy Renee and her hermit crab.

"He'll be here when you get back. Let him take a little nap on the blanket with Mama."

The word nap must have given her some confidence to leave her friend, as Kathy Renee was a good napper. I hated naps. It was one more reason we were so different from each other. But today on Padre Island beach, we were linked arm in arm, as my father and his daughters walked to the shoreline.

I loved how the saltwater tasted and smelled, but I was afraid of what was unseen along the gulf's floor—blue crabs with long pinchers, jellyfish, translucent and poisonous, flounder sleeping beneath the sand. Maybe a sand shark. I had a book on sea creatures. Some had friendly faces, but most could paralyze you with just a touch of their tentacle. Kathy Renee didn't know about those things, so she never feared them. She broke away from Dad and me. Jumping into the waves, she never looked back when we called her name.

She bobbed up and down in the blue water, quickly above her head until she landed on a little sandbar. Dad was furious, screaming at her.

"Don't move. Stop. I'm coming to you."

I held his hand as we got closer to the sandbar. I was on tiptoes then. Kathy Renee laughed at us, launching herself off the sandbar, bobbing toward me in the water. I could see the water swirling in two different directions near her and the sandbar.

"Stop. Stop. Now," Dad screamed. He let go of my hand and reached for Kathy Renee. How could he let go? I was his daughter, too.

It was then I felt that current, pushing me away from them. I couldn't feel the bottom with my tiptoes. *What was underneath the water, staring at my feet, seeing my toes move? A hungry crab? A shark?* I screamed loudly, splashing the water with both my hands, trying to scare them away, the unseen things living near the undertow.

Dad turned and looked at me. "I'm coming for you, Kim." He picked up Kathy Renee and threw her toward the shoreline. She squealed with laughter, riding the waves closer to safety. A game to her. A silly game.

Dad swam to me. When I could reach him with my fingertips, I linked my arms around his neck and my legs around his torso. I clung to him, so there'd be no separation between us. No room for anything, not even the current, ripping me from him and carrying me below the surface.

Choking on tears and saltwater, I held on to him until we reached the shoreline. Kathy was there at the water's edge; beyond her, I could see my mother running toward us. We all held each other, crying. All except Kathy. She didn't understand why we were sad. The water was freeing, moving between her legs and arms. Buoyant, her crooked spine didn't ache. Her too-small hands and too-small feet didn't drop things or fail to hold a spoon correctly. Her body and the Gulf were one. She wasn't afraid, like me.

It was then I knew she was a survivor. Stronger than me. I would grow to clutch my vanity like a life vest, whether it be men or my looks. Not her. She didn't care about her looks, or the creatures living on the floor of the gulf. She didn't know about small dogs with pointed teeth, or nasty little kittens who scratched tender flesh. She simply lived, neither caring nor knowing enough to be afraid.

We had one last summer together before we began living in separate worlds. It was the summer of 1980, when Hurricane Allen pounded the Texas Gulf Coast. It was the last time I remember loving my sister without guilt.

We were in our shared bedroom the night the hurricane landed. Listening in bed, holding each other tightly, we heard the bent limbs of the pecan tree scraping against the side of the house. As the winds increased, objects we couldn't see but only hear pelted our bedroom window. Dad came into our room with a flashlight and told us to get our jackets and sneakers on.

"It's almost time for the eye of the hurricane to pass over. Come on, girls."

We put on shoes and bright yellow raincoats over our nightgowns then followed Dad out to the driveway.

"Funny thing about a hurricane is you don't know where the wind comes from. Could be from Cuba, Florida, even Africa. Hurricanes are like a big vacuum cleaner, sucking up wind from everywhere they've been," Dad explain holding each of our hands as the three of us stood together looking into the sky. Mom stood underneath the front porch light watching us.

The most brilliant calm passed over our neighborhood, the low clouds parted, and we counted the Seven Sisters, the Pleiades, above us. Those sisters of the brightest light were perfectly aligned, during that hurricane.

I never felt as loved or alive as I did then, though I couldn't comprehend the perfection and completeness of nature at that age. I knew without a doubt, I was part of something magical, as large as the universe, this earth. It was my family. I thought of all creation fitting together like measuring cups in a set, one inside the other, for a complete whole.

It was our brilliant calm, before reality found us in our little home near Almeda Mall. Soon, I would sail through adolescence, checking every box with a satisfying X of success, while moving farther and farther away from my sister. I had to. She choked the very life out of me.

6

Mom moved us from St. Pius Elementary School to Lincoln Public Elementary when I was in the third grade. St. Pius lacked the funding to provide Kathy Renee with the best teachers in developmental reading.

"Get your sister. We're doing our flash cards on phonetics." For an hour, once a day, we stood in front of three-by-five index cards and pronounced vowels, consonants, blends, the slippery slope of the schwa sound, diphthongs, and the silent e. Several times during our lesson, Mom would put her hand over her mouth and walk into the bedroom to cry. She emerged ten minutes later, red-faced with her hands plastered to her sides.

"Kathy, dearrrr, you remember the sound of the Long-O and the Short-O. You must round your lips like this," Sandy mouthed the words go, home, and show, slowly to her daughter. Short-O is in the word not."

Kathy stared at her with big brown eyes, completely lost.

"Okay, Mama. Nnnn-ooo-ttt. Hhhhooommmeee."

"Kathy, honeeeey. It's a silent e on home. We went over these yesterday. You did so well. Please concentrate."

"Concentrating, Mama." Kathy would furrow her brow and stand taller.

"Good girl. Now, what sound does this letter make?"

I was ready to poke both eyes out with Mom's knitting needles, sitting innocently on the coffee table.

When the death march was over, I retreated into my room, where I lapped up Beverly Cleary's *Ramona, Age 8* and *Ramona Forever*. Poor Kathy Renee, she had to sit at the kitchen table with Speak and Spell, yet another learning tool masqueraded as a toy.

"Let's buy her an Etch-A-Sketch for fine motor skill development," I overheard Mom tell Dad one night in their bedroom. I was up late, reading *Ramona*. I put my book on my stomach when I heard Mom's voice. I looked at Kathy Renee purring next to me, fast asleep, dreaming of another world, where index cards, vowels, and consonants didn't exist. I stared at the back of her head for a long time and concentrated. I was willing her a dream of white-capped waves, rolling, rolling endlessly to the shore. She was a rider of each wave; like Jesus, she could walk on water. The spell broke when I heard my father's voice.

"What about a doll? Why can't the kid just have a doll like other girls her age?"

"We can't give up on her, David. I need you to help me. I can't do this alone."

"I am helping you. Every day, every week, every year. We need a break from this, especially Kathy Renee."

"Okay then, I'll do it alone."

The room was silent next to mine. I heard the click of the bedside lamp. I heard my father cough. My mother and father retreated into indifference.

That Christmas morning, I got a Lite Brite and a collection of hardback Nancy Drew mysteries. I lined up my books on the windowsill, like a little altar. Kathy Renee got an Etch-A-Sketch and a book of paper dolls. I never understood why they bought her paper dolls, but Kathy Renee soon went to work on the paper dolls with a razor blade Dad carelessly left on the edge of the bathtub. Because Mom wouldn't let her use a pair of blunt scissors without her supervision, Kathy found a way. She didn't even cry when we found her in the bathroom, bright red blood on her thigh and slashed clothes of paper dolls with missing heads and legs on the floor. Mom never forgave Dad, and Dad, well, he did exactly what she wanted him to do from that day forward.

Every night after supper he and Kathy Renee would sit at the kitchen table and count coins. This is how my sister learned math. Mom would supervise from the living room couch, occasionally walking into the kitchen for a paper towel, a glass of water, a bite of cheese, in and out, in and out, making sure progress was being made. I followed the routine for a while, then retreated into my room with Nancy Drew. From the closed bedroom door, their voices would leak through.

"If I had a nickel and a dime, how much money would I have?" Dad asked.

"A quarter."

"No, baby. A nickel and a dime. Here they are. Look. Now, take from the pennies pile and count out how much a nickel and a dime are."

I could hear the coins scraping against the wood of the table. Some nights I'd put my book on my stomach and listen. Other times, I sailed away from all of them. I was on the Muskoka River with Nancy as she pulled the strap on her scuba mask tighter, silently entering the deep, black water where a mysterious shark was sighted.

"Okay, if I had twenty pennies and I took seven away, how many would I have left?"

"Twelve pennies, Daddy!"

"Oh, for God's sake, let me do this," Mom shouted from the couch.

I fled from the subtraction lesson by wandering into the lilac grove with Nancy late at night. We were both frightened by the ghost hovering in the lilacs.

As we changed grades each year, public school remained a nightmare for both of us. The latest experiment on children and their aptitude to learn was ability grouping. Apparently, the entire nation was experimenting. Proponents of ability grouping claimed it was the best way for students to achieve their perceived ability level. Perceived was the key word for the opponents, who argued such grouping segregated students along racial and socioeconomic lines.

I was in the Blue Bird group. My sister was in the Raven Group. As if we weren't smart enough to figure it out. Why didn't they just say crows, vultures, some ugly bird people didn't want to see or hear.

My reading class met right before Kathy Renee's. My reading teacher, Miss Andel, was the prettiest teacher in the entire school. She always wore peasant blouses with tasseled ties that swung when she walked. On her bare feet were Dr. Scholl's sandals with wooden heels and a bright red strap across her toes.

Miss Andel sang to the Blue Birds every day for an hour. She passed out work sheets individually, no sloppy handing a pile to the front desk for the kids to distribute. She handed you a work sheet as if she were offering you a trunk of gold.

The Blue Bird group was a miniature sorority mixer for upper elementary. We were smart and wore nice clothes. Our teeth were white and perfectly aligned. We did as we were told to the teacher's face, and only rebelled when Miss Andel stepped into the hall to blow her nose. That's usually when Tommy or Joseph would throw a spit wad at the ceiling or at the back of someone's head. Once Miss Andel stepped back into the room, Tommy and Joseph would smile at her and return to their SRA reading packets. Polite, diligent workers she wrote on their report cards. On my report card she wrote, "Kim is delightful!"

Once I looked up from my assigned reading and caught Miss Andel applying perfume to her naked feet then quickly pushing them back into the sandal. I thought it odd. She looked up at me, embarrassed. But Blue Birds didn't tell on people or say anything disagreeable to their faces. We did it behind their backs, until deciding they weren't Blue Birds after all. With reckless arrogance, we set a high expectation in the Blue Bird group.

Kathy Renee's reading teacher was a monster with an unassuming name, Mrs. Smith. This monster wore utilitarian dresses in various shades of beige with a polyester sash around her waist, every day. The dress matched the shoes or did the shoes match the dress? All of her shoes were small-heeled pumps that made her feet swell over the expanse of the shoe. Angry red feet. So unlike Miss Andel's feet, perfumed and dainty.

The Raven reading group was a sociology experiment for the learning disabled and emotional handicapped of upper elementary. Kathy Renee entered a treacherous sea with other urchins, confused and adrift.

"Mama, there's a girl in my reading class that said she had on her mama's panties."

"What?"

"Why'd she wear her mama's panties?"

"Oh, for God's sake. What's going on in that class?"

"Does her mama wear her panties?"

"That's enough of that talk, Kathy Renee. Eat your turkey pot pie."

Mom visited the school demanding answers. There were none to give in the Raven reading group under the direction of Mrs. Smith. Wielding self-control, Mom reinforced what was in her power. She added another thirty minutes a day study time in language arts development for Kathy Renee. The messenger is usually the first to be punished. Best to keep my mouth shut.

Kathy Renee continued to share stories of the Raven group during dinner, focusing on Rhonda Garcia, the girl who wore her mother's panties. As the year continued, and the temperature increased, with chubby, sweaty hands smearing the tops of the desk with black pencil lead, the battle between Mrs. Smith and the Ravens continued. The star soldier of that war was the mama-panty-wearing Rhonda, a biracial sprite who, with improper undergarments and questionable lineage, became the bane of Mrs. Smith's existence.

"Doesn't it smell like a Life Saver, Kathy Renee? Wintergreen flavor." Rhonda held the plastic pot of paste up to Kathy's nose. A picture of a smiling black and white milk cow was on the plastic pot with the words school paste in red block letters. Before Kathy Renee had a chance to take a whiff, Mrs. Smith ran to the two girls, whisked the pot of paste from Rhonda's hand, and threw it in the garbage. She then dragged a small chair across the classroom floor and placed it next to her desk.

"Sit here," Mrs. Smith screamed, pointing to the gray plastic chair. Rhonda approached the chair, pulled at the elastic at her waistline under her dress (wearing her mother's panties, again) and sat down. A low moan of frustration rose from Mrs. Smith's throat.

"Don't make a move, missy. That's enough out of you for the day."

But as soon as Mrs. Smith turned to face the other students, Rhonda picked up the black magic marker on her desk and scribbled all over her bare legs and arms. It was then I learned the sole expectation for the Raven reading group was to survive the hour.

The only remark Mom made after that story was "God help us" followed by the sign of the cross. She had the same reaction when receiving Kathy Renee's report card. On the back of the card was Mrs. Smith's snippy summary of my sister as her student: "Kathy Renee's grades are a reflection of her poor self-discipline and inconsistent work habits."

Things weren't much different for our religious training. Mom made us attend the same confirmation class, so I could look after my sister. Kathy Renee didn't say much during class, but thoroughly enjoyed coloring pictures of Mary, Joseph, Baby Jesus, and St. Therese the Little Flower. She chose St. Therese as her confirmation saint.

"She picks pretty flowers for Jesus," was Kathy Renee's discernment in choosing.

Almost a year later, we were celebrated in matching confirmation dresses of white. Forming a line of solidarity and holiness, our class gathered to receive Jesus' Body and Blood in a special Mass just for us. When the priest motioned to place the Host on Kathy Renee's tongue, she turned for a split second to look at Mom and Dad on the front pew. The Host fell to the ground. The priest frowned, covering it with a white cloth. Mom gasped and Dad put his head down. Grandma Jean got up and left. I'm sure she was smoking a cigarette in the church parking lot. That's how she dealt with Kathy Renee. She chained smoked. I looked at Father Nguyen and then at Kathy. I didn't know whether to stay in place or grab Kathy Renee and get back in line to do it all over again. We'd have to act quickly before we were turned into pillars of salt.

Father Nguyen touched Kathy Renee's shoulder. His touch was met by the clearest brown eyes. "I'm sorry, Father. I didn't mean to."

"Yes, now, come along. Look forward and put your tongue out." The Bread of Life was placed on Kathy Renee's small, pink tongue. She chewed it, closed her eyes, then quickly returned to the pew, where she buried her face in our mother's lap.

That ceremony was the end of my religious training. Mom never forgave me for that, and I never asked for her forgiveness. Kathy Renee continued. Throughout my sordid adult life, she let me know she said a Rosary every day for me.

7

Dad called Parks Junior High a seven-hour holding tank for preteens. "I pity the teachers. They're basically teaching hormones with legs," he said, watching Mom peel potatoes at the kitchen sink.

"Is that really where we want our girls?"

"There's not a private school in the area that can compete with the extracurricular programs at a public school. Not to mention science labs, language arts, career education. Nobody's gonna pray for you in a public school, but at least you'll learn to march to a Sousa tune in band."

"David! This is exactly what drives me crazy about you. Can we have a serious conversation about our daughters' educations?"

"I'm being serious. I just don't see this period of their lives as make one mistake and their future is doomed forever. You either get a mediocre education at the Catholic school, because the money isn't there for teachers and curriculum, or you take a risk with the kid's well-being at a better funded public school. You can't have Jesus with you all the time."

"This conversation is over."

"Oh, come on, Sandy. You're putting way too much pressure on us."

"I got this one, too. Don't let it worry you again, Dave."

Two weeks later, my sister and I enrolled at Parks Junior High. Our Lady Academy was never mentioned again. Economics won that fight.

The only class I shared with my sister was band. In no time I was first chair of the clarinet section, despite being constantly challenged by the second chair clarinetist, Riley Hammonds. Her upper registry notes shrieked, but I had control. These were the beginning years of mastering control and competition for me.

Kathy Renee began her years of social isolation. On one hand, Mom's singular fortitude to have her daughter competent in reading and math jettisoned Kathy Renee to regular education classes. No more Ravens and glue-sniffing classmates for her daughter. But there remained the one thing she could not change. Kathy Renee was different. A shadow clung to her like a social burial cloth. You could just feel it. Everyone felt it. Those were the years of embarrassment for me. Embarrassment followed by red-faced shame of hating her and wishing she'd simply evaporate into thin air.

She was last in everything, including last chair of a huge flute section divided into three categories: excellent, good, and bad. The bad category was composed of six girls with mousy hair and thick glasses. Their clothes were either wrinkled or ill fitting. Nothing worked for them. The band director would stop at least three times during class to tune them. All eyes were on three red-faced, habitually flat, flutists.

"Pull the mouthpiece out, Kathy Renee. Out!" My heart froze every time Mr. Darshan screamed her name. He'd then grab the flute from her. "Like this. Look at me, Kathy Renee. Like this."

"Oh, I see Mr. Darshan," again that same, mousy reply she had for everything.

I was literally sick to my stomach, counting the seconds until the class ended, when I could escape with my friends, the same Blue Birds I'd known since starting school.

Lunch was the same exercise in humility. I made sure I sat a comfortable distance from her. Oh, I could see her. A drift in a cafeteria buzzing with kids, boys spitting loogies on the ceiling, giving the room a cave effect complete with stalagmites. Mean girls wearing too much make-up with too much cleavage prowling the perimeters for nasty boys and scared little girls. Girls unlike Kathy Renee. Kathy Renee wasn't scared; she was just unassuming, which made it even worse. There she sat with the other third-tier flute players, nibbling at the crust of their bologna and American cheese slice sandwiches.

I could have sat down with my parents and told them the reality of our days. I could have demanded they separate us. "Send her to Our Lady. She loves being Catholic." But I didn't. I was too busy forming my own social consciousness. Most importantly, Kathy Renee never complained. She loved Parks Junior High. She loved band. She loved eating in the cafeteria. She even loved physical science. She thought the pulley and fulcrum lesson was interesting. She had Dad set up an experiment in the garage testing the phenomenal strength of the humble pulley. That girl just loved everything. It seemed the more I hated and withdrew into pretension, the more she loved and grew in sincerity. It was maddening.

Our litmus tests in surviving junior high was starting our periods and the end of year school dance. Kathy Renee started her period six months before me, although I was a year older. My mom blamed it on hormones in chicken.

"It's the crazy hormones and artificial garbage in the food we eat."

Dad and I met this new outrage with fear of eating kale and tofu for the rest of our lives, as we sat shackled in Mom's kitchen.

"It's just not fair. It's not," Mom sobbed in bed one night. I laid a copy of *Pet Sematary* on my stomach and listened. My best friend, Jennifer, third-chair clarinetist and Blue Bird, stole her mom's book for me. Jennifer's mom was from Pittsburgh. She smoked long, skinny cigarettes and read everything Stephen King wrote. She was an entirely different species from my mom.

"You should be happy about this, honey. She's maturing. She's healthy."

"Should we get her tubes tied?" Mom said faintly.

"You've lost your mind. I can't believe you said that?"

I strained to hear them. I didn't know what that meant. *Tubes tied?* I had sex education, where they divided the boys and girls into separate groups. We saw a film of swimming sperm. The teacher showed us a condom then opened the package and put it on a frozen banana. Ms. Wells was fired for that little demonstration. But we never talked about tying tubes. I put my ear against the wall separating my room from my parents.

"She's just so accommodating. Always trying to please, all of us, everybody. Some stupid boy will talk her into it. It will ruin her life forever."

"Sandy, trust her."

"She doesn't need to know what the surgery is. We can tell her it's her appendix."

"She'll know. I'll know. We'd never forgive you. Leave her alone. All you're saying here is not to embarrass us by getting pregnant. Why can't you trust her? Why?"

Mom didn't say anything else. Neither did Dad. I walked to the hall bathroom, pretending to wash my hands and get a glass of water. The light underneath their bedroom door was gone. The next day at school I told Jennifer everything. I also returned her mother's book.

"That plot was dumb. I predicted weird things would come from the pet cemetery after the first few pages. Just gross."

"Better stick to Beverly Cleary," laughed Jennifer, a chestnut brunette, green-eyed, perfect Blue Bird. She retied the knot securing the massive hot pink T-shirt tied at her hip.

"Whatever, Jennifer. Look. I need to talk to your mom about something. It's important. What are you doing after school?"

"No dance practice on Monday. Come on. Mom picks me up by the band hall after school."

"Okay. I'll ask to use the phone in the nurse's office at lunch. I'll tell Mom we have a group project in history. She can pick me up about five."

"You can stay for supper."

"No, Mom likes everyone home for meals."

Jennifer's mom, Leah, picked us up near the band hall. Her signature foot-long cigarette hung out the window of her red Mazda RX-7. Stephen King's *Christine*, split in half and dog-eared, was resting in the dashboard.

"Hey, girls. How was your day?"

I folded myself into the back seat. I thought of Jennifer riding in that matchbox whenever the family would go anywhere. Dad's Volkswagen van had two bench seats in the back, but we were a family of four. Jennifer was an only child. My dad was a shipyard worker. Jennifer's dad was an aeronautical engineer with Lockheed at NASA. Her mom wore spiked bangs and acid-wash jeans. My mom wore her hair in a ponytail, day-in and day-out. She didn't even own an off-the-shoulder sweatshirt or a crop top. That's why I was here today—to get the truth. To get some wisdom from an older woman in the know. Jennifer was lucky to have a cool mom.

After eating a Little Debbie cupcake and drinking a Coke, a real Coke, not a Kroger version of a Coke like my mom bought, the three of us sat at the kitchen table. Wise older woman and two girls on the verge of being women.

"Mrs. Braden, what does tying your tubes mean?"

"It's Leah, Kim." Leah Braden took a long drawl from her cigarette and looked me directly in the eyes.

"Sorry, Mrs. Leah. What does tying your tubes mean?"

"I can see you're never going to drop this Mrs. Leah thing. Fine with me. Tubal ligation is surgery women can get to "tie" their fallopian tubes. It's a form of female sterilization. It prevents eggs from traveling from the ovaries to the uterus, so you can't get pregnant."

I didn't say anything. I knew some of the words she was using from the sex education class. I immediately thought of that film again. The one with the swimming sperm, and the monthly visit of the eggs, depicted as marching suitcases carrying eggs into the ovaries. It was then I knew I would be haunted by that film for the rest of my life.

I didn't say anything else to Mrs. Leah. Jennifer and I went into her bedroom and watched reruns of *Laverne & Shirley*. At exactly five o'clock, I heard Mom's station wagon in the driveway. Then I heard the doorbell. *Why do you need to come inside? Please don't try to have a conversation with Jennifer and her mom.*

"Hi, Leah. So good to see you."

"Sandy. Come in. Would you like a Coke?"

"Oh, no. Got supper going. Kathy Renee's at the house."

Then Mrs. Leah called my name. Jennifer followed me to the front door, opened wide with one mom in and one mom out.

"Thanks, Mrs. Leah. See you tomorrow, Jennifer."

"Hi, Jennifer." Mom smiled.

Jennifer looked at my mom. The same way Mrs. Leah did. They thought she was weird. I guess that's okay, since Mom thought they were weird, too. We got into the car. I didn't say anything on the ride home.

"Have fun?"

"It was okay."

"Something wrong?"

"No." Of course, everything was wrong. I didn't trust her anymore. My responsibility to Kathy Renee just increased by a million. I didn't want to talk about it, especially with my mother. She didn't deserve a chance to explain herself. I learned not to trust anyone with my body from that day on, except Grandma Jean. She knew what I had to live with. She knew, but never said a word. She'd look at me when I told her the latest story about my family and would light another cigarette. It was her sign of understanding, our comradery in a shared burden. I planned on calling her as soon as I got home. I was moving in. I wondered if the Villa Maria Retirement Home accepted minors as residents.

My sister never had a baby. Whether or not it was her choice or my mother's, I'll never know. Mom's lips were sealed about a lot of things.

8

The school cafeteria was aglow in the shimmering light of a mirrored ball. The anticipated end of the year school dance had arrived. The PTA moms outdid themselves. Little paper hearts dangled above tables loaded with candy and chips. Ice buckets held cans of Coke, Dr. Pepper, and Sprite. In the back of my mind, I could hear my mother's voice, "Do you realize the educational products that could have been bought instead of junk food and cheap decorations? Those PTA women got their last donation from this family."

At least the woman didn't skimp on clothes for her children. The reason was simple. Mom saw us as a direct reflection of her. Her self-worth was rung so tightly around us she wore it as a cross and a crown. My mother, the martyred queen. Kathy Renee was her cross to bear, and Mom was determined to save her from the world. Saving Kathy Renee also required my help. Protective big sister and doting little sister in coordinated outfits chosen by a loving mother was what Mom showed to the world. It lasted for a while.

For our first school dance, I wore a red and black dress with massive shoulder pads and a black vinyl belt at the waist. When I climbed on the toilet seat in the bathroom to get a full view, I resembled an inverted triangle with red shoes. Kathy Renee wore a yellow, off-the-shoulder sweatshirt with layered pink and purple tank tops underneath. That confetti disaster was coupled with a denim, three-tiered ruffled skirt and purple jellies on her feet. Mom insisted on the big purple bow in her hair. She thought it would hide the hearing aid Kathy Renee wore in her right ear.

Once inside the cafeteria, I looked for Jennifer. I had moved my social position slightly to the left, not completely abandoning the Blue Birds, but infusing my impressible youth with those who chose to French kiss boys and smoke cigarettes we purchased with our lunch money. There were a few in our select group who read *Flowers for Algernon* and wrote their own poetry. They were smart enough at fourteen to never write anything with an A-B rhyme scheme. Blue Birds learned how trite that was in the sixth grade.

I spotted Jennifer near the DJ. A potpourri of junior high girls surrounded her, dressed in hot pink, lime, purple, and tangerine. We hugged tightly, squealing each other's names as if they were anthems. Forming a circle against the losers, teachers, and PTA moms, we danced to every song the DJ played, until our sweaty circle advanced toward the girl's restroom.

At least fifty girls were stuffed into the four-stall, two-sink gym restroom. Hair spray and Love's Baby Soft perfume coated the air in a sticky-sweet vapor. The patrons were a mixture of Blue Birds, Ravens, and that large, aggressive group known as Red Birds, code for average. I spotted the group's leader, Amanda Rogers, standing on the toilet seat of the last opened stall, holding court with a hairbrush in her right hand and a tube of glittery lip gloss in her left.

"Hey, Kim." I turned quickly toward her just to make sure she wasn't talking to me, but unfortunately, she was. "Miss Goody Two-Shoes. Yeah, you." I froze in the sea of girls near the first sink. "I catch you kissing Ronnie Garrett again, I'll kill you."

Amanda's minions laughed. I recognized them from band. None of them were first chairs or section leaders. They were all loud troublemakers, especially Janie Wiggins, Amanda's best friend. She waited to see if her friend had another threat, then she walked directly in front of me, taking her drumsticks from the back pocket of her black pants covered in cat hair. The tight white shirt she was wearing had perspiration stains shaped like ovals under each arm.

Janie held the distinction of being the only female drummer in the drum section in band, as well as the girl with the largest boobs in the entire junior high. She flaunted both by always carrying her drumsticks in her back pocket and always wearing tight shirts. My mother didn't like her. At every band concert she'd make a remark about "that girl" in the drum section. When I'd remind her Janie had a right to play drums, because girls can do anything, Mom would roll her eyes at me and snort, "Mark my words. That young lady is starting an early career of running wild with boys."

I thought about my mom for a second, then I looked at Janie and her drumsticks.

"What's the matter, Kim? Don't have anything to say to us?"

"Not really. Just came in here to wash my hands."

"Well, don't let me stop you." Janie then moved directly between me and the sink.

"Janie, did she ask your permission to use the sink?" Amanda called down from the toilet, where she remained standing on its closed lid. Everyone was laughing and staring at me. I froze where I was standing, never taking my eyes off the drumsticks in Janie's hands.

From nowhere, a Coke can sailed through the air, spraying us with brown, sticky froth until slamming against Amanda's head. She fell sideways off the toilet seat. Then a large cardboard package of JuJu Bears bounced off Janie's right hand, knocking her drumsticks to the floor as little red bears flew in the sink.

Everyone looked behind them toward the bathroom door. There stood Kathy Renee with a smile on her face and that stupid purple bow in her hair.

"Leave my sister alone. She didn't do anything."

We were all in shock, as no one moved, staring at her standing in the opened door.

"Come on, Kim. Let's go home."

I walked toward the door and took her hand. No one said anything. I turned around once to make sure no one was following us. Silence. No movement. They probably couldn't get over the fact that the smiling, stupid girl they'd made fun of since elementary school had stopped them in their tracks.

We left the gym after calling Dad from the phone in Coach Moran's office. It took me forever to get permission to use the phone. All those nosy PTA ladies wanted to know why we were leaving the dance. "Aren't you having fun, girls?" I told them I ate too many Cheetos and was sick to my stomach.

Kathy Renee and I sat on the concrete steps outside the gym, staring straight ahead into the thick humidity of a South Houston night. Neither one of us said anything for a long time. Then she touched my knee.

"Don't be mad at me, Sissy. I didn't want that girl to hurt you."

"I'm not mad." I touched her hand still resting on my knee. "I hate those girls anyway. The dance was dumb."

"You were dancing."

"I danced because my friends were dancing. Did you dance any?"

"No one asked me. I had fun watching, though."

I squeezed her hand on my knee and thought of the day at South Padre Island when we were little girls. I nearly drowned because of my fear of the water, but not my sister. Technically, I was stronger and should have been able to swim back to the shore, but my fear of the unknown stopped me. Not her.

Kathy Renee was the smallest girl in her class, slow moving, slow thinking, but fearless. Was this God's mercy? Giving the least likely hero the tenacity to slay lions in a junior high restroom? She sensed fear and saved me from a hoard of girls bent on evening life's score. Those girls hated me because I was middle class and pretty, everything they wanted to be but would never be.

Neither one of us said another word to each other as we sat on the concrete steps waiting for Dad. My hand lingered in hers, our sign of sisterhood and its intense loyalty. I heard the sound of Dad's Volkswagen in the dark, then the headlights appeared before us.

"Hey, girls, how was the dance?"

Kathy Renee looked at me before speaking. I smiled at her, then climbed into the back seat.

Sitting next to Dad, the rightful place of our mother, Kathy Renee began to laugh.

"We had the best time, Dad. The best time of our lives."

9

"Kathy, there's no need to drive with both feet. You've either got it on the brake or on the accelerator. Take your left foot off the brake." This was how Saturday morning began the year Kathy got her driver's license. Dad shouting and Kathy Renee laughing. Mom stood peering from the miniblinds in the living room. For some reason, Kathy could not master pulling into the garage. Dad even hung a tennis ball on a string from the center of the garage ceiling to guide her. I sat at the kitchen table, eating a soggy bowl of cornflakes listening to the circus.

"Brake! Brake! Stop the car. Stop! I'll pull it in myself." Dad screamed from the driveway. I abandoned the bowl of cereal and went back to my room. I got back in bed and decided to spend most of the day reading. Pat Conroy's *Prince of Tides* was just released. Jennifer bought it for me. I'm sure her mom was a few blocks away smoking Kools and reading Stephen King as I devoured Conroy's southern angst until Mom started beating the bedroom door with her fists and demands.

"You are not spending another weekend in bed. Get dressed and get outside."

I put the book down on my stomach and replied to the closed door. "What's outside?"

"Flowerbeds that need weeding. Sweeping the sidewalk. Get out of bed and help. No one is allowed to be royalty in this family. We're serfs together. Now, get dressed." I could hear her heavy breathing on the other side of the door.

"Mom, I need a dress for homecoming. Can't we go this morning?"

"After the yard work and lunch. And yes, we're eating here. There's no reason to pay $10 for a hamburger at the mall, when we've got food here. Your sister needs a dress, too."

Why did every activity involving me include her?

"I'll call Grandma Jean. She'll take me. Besides, Kathy Renee isn't in the Homecoming Court. I was elected by the junior class to be in the court. The sophomores don't even know she exists. Why does she need a dress?"

"You've got a smart mouth this morning. Don't you dare bother your grandma. Your sister has a date. She's getting a dress, with you, at the same time. Now, get dressed and get outside."

I didn't respond to the door again. I read another chapter then got dressed and went outside. The driving lesson was over, and Kathy Renee was dutifully pulling dollar weeds out of the lawn.

I knew my sister had a friend who happened to be a boy, but I didn't think she had a boyfriend. Sometimes I'd pick her up on Wednesday night at the Catholic Teens for Jesus meeting. Matthew Ramirez was always standing by her. They'd tell each other goodbye with a big hug, like they'd never see each other again. I didn't think anything of it until Jennifer made her point known at school the following Monday.

"Your sister's dating a wetback."

"He's not a wetback, Jennifer. The Ramirez family has been in Texas longer than yours. Isn't your mom from Pittsburgh?" I took a bite of my bologna sandwich then wadded the entire thing into a mushy white ball.

"What does Pittsburgh have to do with it? If your sister wasn't such an idiot, she wouldn't date a Mexican or even think about going to Homecoming with someone like that."

I threw the white wad of bread and baloney in her face.

"Is that white enough for you, Jennifer?"

"You're just as weird as your sister. My mom said your whole family is weird. Weird Catholics. You think you're the only ones going to heaven. Well, you're wrong. The Pope isn't the vicar of Christ. The Pope is the devil."

I stood up from the table without another word, realizing it was probably my last interaction with Jennifer, the bluest of the Blue Birds.

During halftime at the Homecoming game, I was escorted to the center of the football field by a brute of a boy, Ben Mullin. He was the jock of all jocks in the junior class. Six feet, two inches tall, weighing in at two hundred pounds, Ben was on a direct path to a full ride to A & M.

I suppose I was lucky to be standing next to him. After all, he was going to be an Aggie. My future kept the same title it had in the past, sister of the weird girl. Ben stunk of sweat and dirt as we stood together along with maids and escorts from each class underneath the glare of the stadium lights. Janice Gaston was chosen Homecoming Queen. A senior with a pouty mouth and a tiny waist, Janice had long been the "it" girl of high school. Groomed for SMU, she had begun the plans necessary to be the "it" girl there by winning the coveted tiara tonight on the football field.

After the Homecoming game, Ben met me at the school dance.

"You look good in that dress," he offered, throwing both arms across my shoulders to slow dance with me.

"Thanks, Ben." He still stunk from the football game, and I tried to hide the look of disgust on my face by resting my head against his outstretched arms. I didn't know much about romance. My mother's talk about the birds and the bees was a two-minute expository speech given the day I started my period at twelve years of age.

"I will keep these in the towel cabinet for you. Keep yourself clean and don't let a boy get into your pants." She then demonstrated how a Kotex pad worked by pulling off the adhesive strip and applying it to a washcloth. "This will keep it in place on your panties. I didn't have this when I was a girl. We had to pin them."

I watched her the entire time, wondering how, at the tender age of twelve, a boy was going to get into my pants—both of us wouldn't fit. When I got older, I realized it was the game I'd play as a female for the rest of my life. I certainly understood it was the game Ben Mullin wanted to play. This slow dance was the pregame activity.

"I like this song. Let's dance this one, too." Two slow songs in a row, with his animal sweat smell against my pink dress, and we were back out in the parking lot in his father's truck.

Leaning back from the stirring wheel, Ben Mullin unzipped his pants. I didn't know whether to laugh at him or jump out of the truck. The one clear thought resounding in my head was how much he stunk.

"Hey, Ben, let's . . ." I looked at him, searching to find the words that would make him zip his pants up. I didn't know what those words were. My mother didn't teach them to me. I never read them in a book. My father never demanded I act or say something for his own gratification. I didn't know. But Ben knew what to do. He pushed the back of my head with his right arm toward his lap as if he were holding a football, aiming it toward the goal post. I jerked up.

"No. Let go of me." I pushed my hands against him to create a space between us. In the dash light, I could see sweat glistening on his forehead. He grabbed my head again.

"You creep. Let go of me." He let go of my head, reaching against the bench seat for the door handle, then pushing the truck door open, he screamed at me.

"Get out."

My heart stopped. What would happen when I got out? Would he run me over? Beat me behind the truck. I didn't know.

"Get out, I said." He then kicked me out of the truck with his right foot. I landed on the asphalt parking lot, scrapping my hands on the pavement as I tried to break my fall. He backed the truck up, with the tires screeching at my head. It was a wonder he didn't run me over. Then, the truck was gone. I lay on the cement, bleeding hands and knees, watching the truck taillights grow faint in the dark. I stayed in that position a long time with my face against the asphalt, struggling to steady my breathing, as my mind struggled to understand what had just happened. I got up slowly. I couldn't see much, only the awareness of bleeding hands and knees. I walked toward the school gym. Inside, I saw a reflection of myself in the glass trophy case lining the gym lobby. Ben Mullin left a black footprint on my pink dress. A size twelve shoe was imprinted across my right hip. I went to the bathroom, walking straight into a stall with my head down. I lifted the dress where the shoe print was marked and saw the purple bruise spreading across my hip.

I stayed in the stall, until I knew there was no one else in the bathroom. When the last girl left with a flush of the toilet, the sound of running water in the sink, the grind of the wheel offering a brown paper towel for her wet hands, I emerged from the stall and looked in the mirror. My chin was bleeding, too. The hem in my dress was torn where my shoe heel caught it while trying to break the fall. The shoes were scuffed, tattered leather, never to be angel white again.

I wanted to go home, but the only way home was with my sister and her date. I was blackballed from the Blue Birds, thanks to Jennifer. I didn't want to explain the shoe print on my dress, the ripped hem, and my bleeding face to anyone. I needed to deal with this alone, but I wasn't old enough nor wise enough to know how to do that, so I hid in the bathroom stall, embarrassed and ashamed.

Who would believe Ben Mullin kicked me out of a truck because I wouldn't kiss his crotch? I danced with him. I followed him out to the parking lot. He didn't force me to do those things. But I didn't know it would lead to that. I thought we would kiss, and kiss, and kiss some more. I knew how that worked with boys. I learned that on my own and from talking to Jennifer. But I didn't know about unspoken expectations. I'd eventually learn those rules, like all the unspoken rules girls learn; it was our rite of passage.

I washed my face, then I tried to scrub away Ben's shoe print from my dress. The brown paper towel left a soapy mush against the black stain. I sat in the stall again and waited. Waited, listening to girls come and go, some laughing, some angry, some silent. Finally, I realized it was dark in the gym. No one would see the ripped dress or my face, if I stayed within the darkened perimeters of the gym. Slowly, I walked toward its double doors. I saw Kathy Renee and Matthew dancing underneath the disco ball. They were the happy couple on the dance floor, sparkly and perfect. Everything I wasn't.

10

Grandma Jean got her oxygen tank on my eighteenth birthday. She called it an early Christmas present. Her years of smoking and eating hot dogs caught up with her and delivered chronic obstructive pulmonary disease and high cholesterol.

Mom and Dad moved Grandma Jean into the Villa Maria, an upscale assisted living community, that same year her health began to decline. Granny liked the Villa and her studio apartment. There was a daily Mass service in the commons, a cafeteria featuring chocolate pudding accented with a candied cherry, and endless rounds of Bridge, Canasta, and Skip-Bo. The oxygen tank didn't slow her down. She wheeled it alongside her wherever she went in the Villa.

I visited her, alone, every Saturday afternoon at two o'clock. It was our time, without Mom or my sister. Granny loved those visits as much as I did. I could tell her the truth, and she could smoke in front of me. Something neither one of us could do in front of my mother. Occasionally, I'd buy her a pack of cigarettes with the assurance she'd never tell mom or smoke with the oxygen tank on. Our shared secrets created a sacred bond.

The residential pool at the Villa featured a hot tub with an adjoining pool. Lining the pool were chaise lounges in tropical colors of lime green and hot pink, where residents sought sun-drench heat for arthritis-riddled joints. Granny and I spent a lot of Saturdays in the chaise lounges, wearing our matching leopard-print swimming suits, one bikini and one tank. We wore huge sunglasses in black frames, peering into paperback novels amid the chatter of the hot tub crowd.

I had discovered Isabel Allende and escaped into the mysticism and passion of a South American country and its characters of poverty, lust, and crime. Granny remained a loyal fan of cowboy fantasy romances. I used to be embarrassed by the book covers of ample breasts stuffed in corsets and the rippling stomach muscles of bare chested cowboys. But, in time, like most things, it didn't bother me anymore.

We sat poolside for hours; I'd occasionally jump in to rinse the sweat from my body, returning to the chaise lounge and Isabel Allende. Granny only interrupted her reading for a cigarette. I loved our routine. The outside world seemed miles and miles away.

It took me almost a year to tell her about Ben Mullin. I hid his smell, touch, and voice somewhere deep inside me. The only thing that would bring it to surface was seeing him in my economics class my senior year. Fortunately, most of my classes were AP and Honors, which merged me in with the remaining Blue Birds, but excluded people like Ben. He never looked at me in economics; he'd occasionally glance over to where I was sitting, but there was no real recognition of me in his eyes. I was just another girl, a thing he could either like or dislike, depending on his mood. What happened between us was long forgotten by him, but I would never forget it. It set the curve of what I expected from men—not much, except for my father.

I waited until Granny took the first long drag of her cigarette, before coaxing her to the flowery love seat near the bay window. This was our place to exchange truths and secrets.

"I need to tell you about a boy, Granny. A boy who really hurt me. It happened last November, but I didn't want to upset you about it. I just can't keep it to myself anymore." I told her without looking at her face. In my peripheral view, she put out the cigarette in her coffee cup and turned the oxygen tank on. Closing her eyes, she inhaled through the tiny plastic veins inserted into her mouth and nose as the machine hummed in response. She touched my knee with her hand, but I didn't look at her. I concentrated on the mean red cuticle on my index nail. The oxygen tank continued to purr.

After a few minutes, she removed the mouthpiece.

"Honey, I just knew there was something wrong these past months. You just seemed so far away in our visits, but I didn't know if it was school or home. I felt like you'd tell me when you were ready."

"I don't know if I worked it out, Granny. I got into a truck with a boy. I could have said no. I knew what I was doing at that point. That's my own fault. But when I wouldn't let him do what he wanted to do, he got really mad at me. Kicked me right out of the truck. His black footprints were all over my Homecoming dress. It was hateful. Today, he acts like he doesn't even know my name. Like nothing happened." I didn't look up at her but began chewing at the long red cuticle, eventually ripping it from my finger with my teeth. Grandma pulled my hand out of my mouth.

"Now, listen to me, Kimberly. You got into the truck with a bully. He's a bully boy and will probably grow up into a bully man. I imagine he's watched his father disrespect his mother most his young life. He doesn't know a girl, a woman, is a human being. You didn't do anything wrong. You just got to learn some hard lessons about life. When something bad happens, and it will, that's just the world and that's just who we are as people, but when it does happen, you've got a choice to make. You can either fold or bid when you get a bad hand but, honey, you never, ever win if you fold. Don't be a victim. Fight it. Fight it until your last breath.

I leaned into Granny and started crying.

"Now, now, it's gonna be okay. Sure wish I could tell you you're the only one this has ever happened to or even, it won't ever happen again. But there are no guarantees in life, baby. Now, hug all that ugliness out of you. Hug me tight. Good. You're my girl, Kim. You always will be."

I sat in the luxury of my grandma's love for me until I stopped crying.

"I love you, Granny."

"And I love you, now let's go on down to the cafeteria and get something to eat. I feel like having a banana split for supper. Four o'clock isn't too early for dinner?

"No ma'am. Let me call Mom and tell her I'm eating with you."

"Now don't tell Sandy I'm feeding you junk for dinner. Tell her we're having steak, potato, and a salad. That should make her happy."

I used the phone hanging on the kitchen wall. Turning back to look at

Granny, I watched her apply lipstick using a compact mirror she kept in the pocket of her sweater. Until the day she died, mauve was her color for lips, fingernails, and toenails.

My obedient, responsible sister picked up on the third ring.

"Kathy, is Mom there?"

"She's outside."

"Tell her I'm having dinner with Granny. I'll be back in a few hours."

"Okay, if you'll tell Granny hi for me. Guess what? Matt and I are going to the movies."

"Whatever, Kathy. Just tell Mom."

"You can go to the movies with us. Double date, even."

"I don't want to go." I hung up. It was just like her to suggest a double date when I wasn't dating anyone.

"Ready, Granny?"

"Let's go; grab my walking stick at the front door just in case."

We rode the elevator to the ground floor, sharing the stale air with Margaret Olson, Granny's neighbor and her yapping, shaking Chihuahua, Poco. When the elevator door slid open, Margaret and Poco emerged first.

"I'd be a nervous wreck, too, if I had to live with Margaret Olson," Granny whispered. "Poor little dog, just shaking to death."

In the cafeteria, Granny and I sat near the row of fake palm trees near the exit door to the pool area. There was no need to talk. We were in silent expectation of our meal. The cafeteria worker placed a banana split in front of each of us in a glass dish.

"These look wonderful, Patty," Granny smiled, while slipping a five dollar bill in the woman's smock pocket.

They were perfect: ripe bananas expertly cut, mile-high whip cream sprinkled with crushed peanuts, cherries on top with a slightly bent stem, chocolate syrup, strawberry and pineapple filling, all nestled on top of three rounded mounds of vanilla ice cream. We ate only whispering the occasional, "This is good." "Mmmm." "Delicious." When I finished, I looked out at the pool area, watching the sun move lower in the horizon, casting shadows on the seamless pool water and Granny's oxygen tank near the patio doors.

It was the last meal we had together. She died a month later when her lit cigarette fell on the flowery love seat. The synthetic material created a noxious smoke, quickly filling the little apartment. It was bad luck Granny's oxygen tank was in the bedroom. She died in the lavender snap-front duster I bought her for her birthday. In the pocket was her compact mirror and a tube of Mauve Magic lipstick.

Part II

11

I graduated that May, landing a tuition and board scholarship to Texas Tech in Lubbock, a West Texas city where tumbleweeds blew across the road and scorpions were unexpectedly found in shoes and salads. They were the cockroaches of the West.

I chose library science as my major. I made the decision years ago when I fell in love with Nancy Drew and the mystery series I received as a Christmas gift. The books remained, in numerical order, on a window ledge in my room, like a sacred altar to Carolyn Keene. Years later I discovered the true author was Mildred Wirt Benson, who remained true to her genre by using the name Carolyn Keene as a pseudonym.

Majoring in library science was one of the easiest decisions I ever made. It was as natural as breathing, because I preferred books to people. If I could be a librarian, I'd create a group of patrons far superior to the Blue Birds. Instead of a homogeneous group of predictability bent on perfection and efficiency, the patrons of my library would be a cool collective of readers, as diverse as the authors who feed their addiction.

My library would be unique, hosting reader events throughout the year with an annual event featuring a sleep over. Patrons would arrive in their pajamas. An array of couches, futons, and overstuffed chairs would provide comfort in late-night reading. Families with book-loving preschoolers would receive a pup tent with a full-size air mattress and assorted pillows for lounging with books. Conveniently located lamps with soft, enduring light would shine upon the patrons reading nests.

An endless supply of snacks—chocolate-covered peanuts, Switzels, pretzels, lightly salted popcorn, and individually wrapped moistened towelettes would be offered, along with a gentle reminder not to soil a book page while snacking. Of course, no talking was allowed, so patrons could eat and read without being disturbed. I was offering complete escapism from the trials of life. Clearly, my goal to be a librarian was more important than a career choice based on economics.

My mother was hounding me all summer about a *real* college major. I heard her, and I really thought I had answered her many times, but I became so used to living in my head since Granny died, I just assumed Mom heard the very loud thoughts in my head. I was sucked into the undertow of self-absorption and isolation, where everything I heard and said seemed muted. I viewed the world beneath six feet of turbulent water, aloof and distant. When I cared to surface, pushing my head above the water, I told my mother, "Library science is the life for me."

My mother's negative response was immediate. After all, her sense of playfulness and imagination was spent years ago in her martyrdom for Kathy Renee. It was if her long sighs and marked frustration with any conversation she had with me was the final breath of energy she had to offer. Her presumption of Dad and me as healthy orbs in another galaxy, needing neither her light or energy, allowed her to concentrate solely on Kathy Renee without guilt.

"Surely, you know reading is a hobby, something to kill time when there's nothing else to do."

Dad was sitting in the recliner, watching the news before dinner. He didn't turn around to look at either one of us. With his last bit of energy, not robbed from AutoCAD and the shipyard, he clicked off the television and spoke to its blank screen, "Do what you love, Kim. It will make life much more tolerable."

Mom's long sigh followed her husband's comment with the conversational finale, "Do what you want. Looks like you and your dad decided a long time ago what was best."

Dad clicked the television set back on.

That night I dreamed of Granny. I dreamed I was working as a librarian at the Pasadena East Library, located next to the Villa Maria's swimming pool.

Granny was in a chaise lounge, wearing her leopard print one-piece bathing suit with a wide-brimmed straw hat on her head. A romance paperback featuring a bare chested cowboy rested on her lap.

"Hi, honey, come sit next to me and tell me what you want for lunch. Maybe a BLT with chips?" She patted the chaise lounge cushion next to her.

"No time. It's the paperback exchange party at 1 p.m. Just a second for a Coke and a hug."

"You're a busy girl, and a happy one, at that. Those books are like your own babies." Granny smiled at me, then motioned for the aide with the lifting of her index finger, unashamedly manicured with a bright red, pointed fingernail.

"Patty, bring us two Cokes in bottles with straws. Thank you, ma'am."

We drank our Cokes, looking at the sun reflecting in the swimming pool.

"Why don't we start a book club just for romance readers?" And that was the last thing she said to me, before my sister's alarm clock went off. My grandmother was gone forever.

The dream gave me a clearer vision of my future. I would be a librarian, and I would have a separate life from my mother and sister. Lubbock was the first step. In my mind, I developed a card catalogue called Adult Lessons with an orderly numerical system for filling the lessons I learned so far: Ben Mullin and the Blue Birds.

The ritual habits of my mother and sister disappeared behind me when Dad and I drove 520 miles to Lubbock in late August. We took Mom's minivan, since she and Kathy Renee were on a pilgrimage to Our Lady of Guadalupe in Mexico City. After that, they planned on distributing Spanish editions of the Catechism to the locals. I imaged a dusty, noxiously hot donkey trail with a lot of complaining from my mother. Of course, Kathy Renee would be laughing and singing all the way. So, it didn't bother me too much to dodge that bullet disguised as a vacation. It bothered me even less that they weren't part of my bon voyage to college. I did ask them to pick me up a sombrero and a bull whip as souvenirs, though.

The farther Dad and I drove from Pasadena, the livelier our conversations became, while through the windshield Texas became flat and arid with an occasional plateau or lonely mesa in the distance. I was leaving the Blue Birds' judgment, Ben Mullin's footprint, and Kathy Renee's shadow far behind me. It was freeing; I'm sure my father felt it, too. No one knew me in Lubbock, and I loved everything about that.

Dad moved me into the dorms, carrying cardboard boxes of clothes, shoes, and books in ninety-five degree heat up four flights of stairs. There were elevators, but the line of red-faced mothers, fathers, and college students kept the wait at the elevator at least an hour or more.

"We'll climb the stairs, Kim. I can take two boxes at a time. Hey, your nose is bleeding." Dad held the cardboard box on one knee, reaching into his back pocket for a handkerchief. "It's the low humidity here. Drying out your sinus."

We were miserable, but we were not alone. Hundreds of students and parents looked as bad as we did.

"Last box. Let's take a break before getting your schoolbooks." Dad placed the box on top of a wooden desk in the corner of my dorm room and sat in the chair in front of it.

"Where's your roommate? If you're lucky, she'll never show."

"I'm sure she'll show, Dad. We did start at seven this morning. Most normal people wait until after breakfast."

"Yeah. Let's get some food."

Before going back to the motel for a shower, Dad stopped at a convenience store. He came out with a six pack of beer in a paper bag.

"Here. Let's make this our little secret, Kim. Don't call your mom and tell her I got you drunk your first day in Lubbock." He reached for a bottle of aspirin in the cup holder and chased two with a sip of beer. "I'm feeling my age today."

"You're good with me, Dad." I pulled the tab on the beer can and slowly drank it, trying to leave the impression it was the first beer of my life. I felt happy, because Dad was treating me like a person, not a responsibility. We were friends that day; it was one of our best days together. When he left for home the next morning, I felt a terrible sadness. It was the same sadness I felt for Granny. I knew I'd never get the chance to be with just him again.

From the fourth-floor window of my dorm room, I watched him get into the minivan.

"Bye, Dad. Thanks for everything," I yelled at him from the window. He turned around and smiled, lifting his right hand into the air, waving. Then, he was gone.

That night I dreamed of Granny in her lavender snap-front duster, wearing mauve lipstick. We didn't talk in my dream but sat together on the love seat by the bay window in her apartment, a lit cigarette resting in a glass ash tray on the coffee table. The dream was so vivid I woke to the smell of cigarette smoke, but it wasn't Granny Jean smoking the cigarette. It was my roommate, Rachel. Rachel was from Dallas, cut her own hair, and wore black eyeliner to match her two wardrobe essentials, black leather pants and a black T-shirt.

"Good morning," I offered.

"Hey." She took a deep drag from her cigarette, exhaling the smoke from her nostrils.

That was the only word Rachel said to me. Street drugs replaced her school career a month later. Her parents moved her and an assortment of unopened textbooks back to Dallas.

12

I began the life of a single female on a university campus realizing there was a hierarchy in dorm life. My building was coed with the first floor dedicated to male athletes, the second floor dedicated to female athletes, with floors three and four serving as a bull pen for liberal arts and science majors. I made a mental note to never, ever go near the first floor.

My routine was simple that first semester. I began my library science classes in the morning, since I had placed out of the core requirements classes my senior year in high school. I didn't have a car, so the rest of the day was spent in the cafeteria, dorm room, or library. The library was shaded by two large cottonwood trees. I spent a lot of time under those trees, reading. I never felt lonely. I guess it was because I had spent so much time with my sister or a group of girls; the solitude was welcoming.

Under a cottonwood tree, I met Brian Ladner. It was late October, a dry seventy-degree day. He sat down next to me on the summer burnt grass, uninvited.

"What book are you reading?" His skin was dark from years on the water and in the sun. Brown-eyed, black hair, he could have been from Galveston, except he was more withdrawn than someone from the Texas Gulf Coast. I could tell he was nervous. I could also tell he was lonely.

"Anne Rice."

"The writer from New Orleans. I don't live far from there."

He was drawing me in, and I was easily led by his smile and wide-open, intelligent eyes.

"Where you from?"

"Ocean Springs. It's on the Gulf of Mexico. Actually, the Mississippi

Sound. Lots of brown water until you make it out to the barrier islands in the gulf. I wasn't born in Ocean Springs. I just graduated from there. Military brat. I've lived a lot of places. "I'm from the Texas coast, between Houston and Galveston. What got you here?"

"Football scholarship. I'm a safety. My mom didn't want me going into the SEC, because it would have been too easy for my high school girlfriend to follow me."

"Guess your mom didn't like your high school girlfriend, Mr. Football Player."

"You don't have to call me mister or even football player. I do have a name. But you're right about my mom. She thought my girlfriend was only interested in a Mrs degree. Her life goal was to build a home a mile from her parents' and make babies."

We both laughed, and he sat down next to me.

"Brian, Brian Ladner."

"Kim. What dorm do you live in?"

"Hulen Hall."

"Me, too. I was just going to walk back and get something to eat in the cafeteria," I said, putting *Interview with a Vampire* in my paperback and standing up. "Are you hungry?"

I nearly bumped his head, because he jumped up as soon as soon as I stood up.

"I'm always hungry," he said, swinging his backpack across his right shoulder. We talked all the way to the cafeteria. I guess I was a little lonely, too.

Our first *official* date was at Lake Henry, about sixty-five miles southeast of Lubbock in early November. I quickly learned if you wanted to do anything in the vastness of West Texas, it took time and gas. It wasn't unusual for people to drive two hours for a change of scenery.

A mild wind from the north, about fifteen miles an hour, made the day perfect for flying a kite, Brian assured me. The Hata kite, bright yellow, orange, and blue with a fourteen-foot nylon tail rested in the back seat, next to Raul. Raul was Brian's mixed-breed dog. With markings of chocolate brown on his head and a white body, he was mostly bird dog. The alliance between the boy and the dog was so perfect the dog nudged me with his nose every time I tried to walk between him and Brian. I'm sure Raul resented me sitting in his front seat.

"Raul isn't going to bite me, is he? He's been growling at me since I got into the car."

"Don't pay him any attention. He jealous. Like that with everyone. I only had him for a week when he was hit by a car. Sewed him up myself. We've got a special bond."

"You did surgery on your own dog?"

"Look, Kim. My folks are frugal people. We didn't spend money on vets, except to get the vaccinations. The military teaches you how to take care of stuff."

"I don't think I'd have the guts to do that, much less keep a dog in the dorms. How do you get away with it?"

"You'd be surprised what you can do if you had to. I sneak him around the dorms. My roommate helps me out, besides Raul isn't a barker unless threatened. We've been tight, since he got hit. Been sleeping with me ever since then, not letting me out of his sight. You're new to the pack. He'll get use to you."

I nodded and looked back at Raul. Holding a paper bag of peanut butter and honey sandwiches and two cans of Coke on my lap, I realized there were a lot of people, even dogs, who wanted Brian's attention. He was special—kind, intelligent, athletic. I didn't know what box to put him in. I knew the Blue Birds, Red Birds, and Ravens, labels nicely attached to others, so there was no need to second guess or fear the unknown. Brian lived in a land I was unfamiliar with. I'd never known a boy like him. Maybe Ben Mullin was an anomaly, and the goodness of Brian would erase everything I knew before I met him.

He smiled at me, placing his hand on my knee as he turned the car into the entrance of the park. Raul's wet nose and open mouth were inches from my neck. I still was convinced he'd bite me as soon as Brian was out of sight. I placed my hand over Brian's as added dog protection. Brian squeezed my hand, as we pulled into the parking lot near a row of cedar picnic tables.

"Let's get her in the air while the wind is good," Brian said, taking the kite out of the car. Raul jumped out after the kite. "I've got 300 hundred feet of line, so we can get her up high."

I watched him walk toward an open field, then, running, he let out the line of the kite. Higher and higher above the blue of the lake it floated in a cloudless sky.

"Come on, Kim. Take the handle. Hold it tight."

I took the kite and it immediately nosed-dived into the lake.

"I can't believe I just did it."

"Not a big deal. Hey, let's swim out to get it."

"In our clothes?"

"That's up to you." Brian took his T-shirt, socks and shoes off, then ran toward the water. I didn't follow him. I watched the sun reflect off his brown hair, the grace of the repetitive motion as he raised each arm in and out of the water, the methodical movement of his head, turning left and right, as he swam toward the kite. It didn't take him long to grab it, then turning around, he faced me, shouting, and waving with his free hand.

He swam back toward me, then ran to where I was standing on the shore, laughing, with drops of water dancing off his bare chest. I loved him. I loved him with all my heart that very moment, more than I loved anyone my entire life.

"You nut. There's a big sign in front of the lake saying no swimming."

"I don't care. Felt good, the water felt so good." He reached into the back of the Corolla wagon and pulled out an old beach towel. He dried his hair looking at me, then rubbed the towel his wet chest and back. When he was done, he threw it on the hood of the car to dry.

"You're a good swimmer. Were you on the swim team in high school?"

"No, but my dad and I swam once a week to Deer Island from Front Beach. That's in Ocean Springs. We had a house near the beach."

"You swam to an island?'

"It couldn't be more than a mile. I loved it. It's not like we had to fight monster waves; in the Sound, it's flat, flat like this lake."

He grabbed the towel off the car hood, rolled it tightly from end to end, and looped it around my waist, pulling me close to him. I could feel every ocean in the world rise and fall within the inhale and exhale of his breath, upon my skin. I laughed when he kissed me.

"Are you laughing at me, Kim?"

"I'm laughing because I'm happy." Raul nudged the back of my leg when Brian pulled me in for a second kiss.

That night when we got back to the dorm, I walked to the student union to check my mailbox. There was a letter from my sister. Sitting on the tile floor, against the wall of student mailboxes, I read it beneath the artificial blue of fluorescent lights.

> Dear Kim,
> How are you? I hope you are happy. I am happy. I'm almost done with high school. Mom and I have been visiting nursing programs around Houston. I want to be a CNA. That is a Certified Nursing Assistant. I have to go to school for six months after high school. I want to work at the Villa Maria, helping people like Grandma. I miss Grandma a lot. I miss you, too. Please write me a letter. I pray for you all the time. Here's a holy card from Our Lady of Guadalupe. At the church, it was hard to see her. We rode on a conveyer belt that moved right through the church. It was crowded with people from all over the world.
> Your sister,
> Kathy Renee

Folding the letter and placing it back in the envelope, I stuck it in my jean pocket as I walked back to the dorm. I didn't read that night, thinking only of Brian, wondering where this would all lead. Turning out the light, I rolled onto my side, facing the cinder block wall of the dorm. I missed my family, but I didn't want to go home. I couldn't understand what type of person that made me. Not as good as my sister, I believed.

Through my fault, through my fault, through my most grievous fault . . .

I delivered three heavy blows to my heart as I confessed indifference to my flesh and blood.

13

The following weekend Brian asked me to the movies. *Hair Spray* was a big hit with the college crowd. A cult mania followed with students dressing in miniskirts and loud shirts, girls teasing their hair into beehives. Dorm parties with dance contests to Chubby Checker's "Limbo Rock" were a part of every weekend. "How low can you go" echoed in the hallways.

I met Brian in the parking lot in front of the dorm for our movie date, our first date without Raul, so I immediately relaxed when I realized I was second in line in the Brian pack.

Once we got to the theater, we stood in line with other students, waiting for our tickets. It was an opportunity to show off dance moves before the show. Brian started singing "The Fly," moving his hips in unison to waving his arms in the air. I watched him, laughing, while around us a little crowd formed, encouraging him to continue. He bowed when done, and the crowd loved it.

"Where'd you learn to dance like that, not to mention knowing all the words to the song?"

"My mom. Whenever Dad deployed, Mom refused to give in to fear. We'd have a fun dinner, like Frito pies or pizza, and we'd spend the rest of the night dancing to all her forty-fives. My little sisters loved it. Watching "American Bandstand" and "Soul Train" was how we learned the latest. Mom, no matter the circumstances all around us, lived for the music and dancing. It kept us all going. There were times we didn't know if my dad would come home."

"Your mom sounds amazing. We didn't do too much dancing at my house, just a lot of phonic flash cards and math worksheets."

"The best thing Mom taught me about dancing was how to hold a woman. How to approach her with confidence. The art of conversation during a slow dance. Being the only son in a house full of girls, it was a great lesson in getting along with the opposite sex. Basically, it was respect for women 101."

He paid our tickets, then grabbed my hand.

"Want some popcorn?"

"No, I got candy in my purse. Now, that's what my mom taught me. How to be thrifty."

"Smart mom."

We sat in the dark, holding hands, as the big screen brought us to the world of chubby teen Tracy Turnblad and the "Corny Collins Dance Show." Neither a pretty girl nor a Blue Bird, Tracy could dance, but her true gift was her heart of gold. She used that perky heart to speak out against segregation. I couldn't help but think of my sister, passionately making the world a better place, one holy card at a time.

"Hey, want a Hot Tamale?"

"You've got tamales in your purse?"

"Not wrapped in corn husks tamales, but a cinnamon-spiced, sug-ar-loaded tamale. Like a Mike'n'Ike. Try it. I love 'em."

I handed him several pieces, placing them in his warm hand. He turned toward me and kissed me. My heart swelled in the dark theater.

"Didn't know you had such a sweet tooth, Kim."

"I'd rather have candy in my purse then money. It makes me feel good, knowing I've got instant happiness waiting for me anytime I want it."

"Hey, quiet down over there. We're trying to watch the movie," rang out from a male voice in the dark.

Brian kissed me again. "Better be quiet, Kim."

Where did this wonderful, sweet boy come from?, I thought to myself, grabbing his arm and squeezing it in mine.

When the movie let out, we walked back to the car, talking about where we should go next.

"I feel bad you bought the movie tickets. I don't expect you to spend all your money on me. We're both broke college students."

"I've got an idea and it won't cost any money. I just don't want you to think it's too weird."

"Don't worry about that. I'll let you know if it's weird right away."

He opened the car door for me and I sat down, hoping he wouldn't suggest anything too strange. I hardly knew him, but what I knew, I was in love with. *Please be the guy I think you are, Brian. You're the only thing I have hoped for in a long, long time.*

"A lot of people in Lubbock visit Buddy Holly's grave as a way of paying their respect. It's a local thing with Holly being from here. I've never gone, but I heard about it from some of the guys in the dorm."

"What are we going to do when we get there? It's dark and it's a cemetery. It's creeping me out."

"Nothing you don't want to do, Kim. I swear. Trust me."

We drove in silence to the City of Lubbock Cemetery, which was incased in a chain-link fence. My heart was beating so fast, I knew he could hear it. Shadows of windblown cedar trees stood across the cemetery, as sentinels to the dead. He kept driving deeper into the land, marked by acres of tombstones and humble markers. He stopped, reached across me, and took a flashlight out of the glove compartment.

"Nothing to be afraid of. Now, come on."

I took his hand when he opened the car door and walked into the darkness. He shined the flashlight on a simple cement marker.

In Loving Memory
of Our Own
Buddy Holly
September 7, 1936
February 3, 1959

"He was just a few years older than us when he died. How sad."

"Buddy Holly was my mom and dad's favorite. Called him the original rocker everyone copied. A special man who made a lot of people happy with his talent."

Brian placed the flashlight near the gravesite and pulled me closer to him.

"I want to be the first man to dance with you to a Buddy Holly song."

I had no response. The words wouldn't come, I was thrilled and afraid at the same time.

He pulled me closer, gently taking my hand in his and resting it against his heart, as we swayed from side to side against each other.

"Brian?"

He began singing with my face pressed close to his.

As we danced, the wind blew through the cedar trees, the quarter moon casting their shadows against the loneliness of the tombstones. I felt his heart against my chest, his words in my ear, then he lifted my chin with his one hand and kissed me.

"I want to keep dancing with you until I'm an old man, Kim. I'm a lucky man to be with a girl like you."

We kissed again, then without words, he walked me back to the car, opening the door, making sure my jacket, all fingers, me, were tucked safely inside before closing it. We drove home, singing to the radio, unconscious of the world outside the interior of the car. When we got to the dorms, he walked me to my room.

"Good night, Kim. I'll see you tomorrow."

"Good night."

There were no dreams that night, only an elysian peace, where those who are in love are the luckiest people in the world.

14

The night before Christmas break, Brian and I sat in his car in front of Whataburger on University Avenue. I watched snow fall on the windshield, while Brian ate his hamburger. He bought one for Raul, who devoured it in one bite.

I wasn't hungry. The thought of flying back home and leaving him left me empty. I didn't even want to talk about it. I just wanted Christmas to be over, so I could fly back to Lubbock, and we could pick up where we left it here, tonight. He wasn't himself, either. He ate in silence, occasionally turning to look at me, smiling with those huge brown orbs. When he threw the hamburger wrapper on the floorboard, he turned to face me.

"There's something I've been keeping from you, Kim."

I didn't say anything. I felt my heart drop into my gut. I kept looking out the windshield, hoping something would appear in the dark, reassuring me this was all a dream, and I'd wake up and start my day by walking to breakfast with him.

"I've flunked this semester. No, the grades aren't in, but I was smart enough to figure out exactly what I needed on the exams to squeak through. Didn't happen. My chemistry and calc professors couldn't wait to deliver the news. I'm embarrassed. The scholarship is gone. I'm a dime a dozen safety in football. I just didn't do the work, Kim. No excuses."

"So, we're saying goodbye tonight? Just like that. What do you expect me to say after the delivery of all this good news?"

"No, this isn't goodbye. I . . . I want you in my life, Kim. College just isn't for me. I come from people who have served this country for generations, and I'm a punk safety at a mediocre college in the middle of nowhere. I don't feel very proud of that."

"What are you saying? What? You're joining the Peace Corp? What?" I felt my blood pressure rise with my voice in each word I spoke. Raul felt the tension in the air and began barking.

"Stop, Raul," Brian shouted then grabbed my left hand on the car seat. "Kim, I'm going home to enlist. I need to earn the right to go to college."

I started to cry. "Principled people are the first people to die in a war. If you need to be a hero, go volunteer at the SPCA."

"You don't mean that."

"I do mean it."

Raul had his mouth on the back of my neck—hot, wet breath combined with the smell of onions from the hamburger he ate made me nauseous. Nothing about this night was going to be good.

"I want to come back and marry you. I knew I loved you that day at the lake. I just didn't want to tell you. I was scared. But I do know this without any doubt, you're the reason I want to be a better man."

"You can't put that one on me. You don't even really know me enough to talk about marriage. This hero thing you've come up with is a substitute for your failure here. I don't want to hear it. I won't be responsible for what happens to you."

I wasn't giving in, and I would not make it easy for him. Accepting bad news was not the role of a Blue Bird. I deserved more. I was entitled to more. I didn't care about service, duty, and country. I cared about me. Me, without him.

He reached across the car seat to kiss me and I pulled away, hugging the cold glass of the window. We drove back to the dorms in silence.

"I'll write you, Kim. It will all work out," Brian offered, turning off the ignition.

"Yeah, right." I got out the car and slammed the door. I didn't look back.

My first week back home I slept twelve hours a day. I'm sure my parents thought I was either depressed or pregnant. In the coin toss of life, which was worse: a depressed daughter or an unmarried pregnant daughter, definitely depressed? Kathy Renee was in and out of my room, leaving glasses of orange juice, a prayer card, and cherry-flavored cough drops. I ate the cough drops like candy, while the orange juice and prayer card remained untouched. My sister's cure-all in the world of good and bad was sugar, more sugar, and the Church—the perfect cocktail for human suffering.

"You'll have to join the living, Kimberly Ann. It's Christmas Eve." Mom sat on the side of the bed, stroking my hair. "Your sister has invited a special friend. It's important to her that you like him.

I heard her, but I didn't respond. I opened my eyes and stared at the empty box of cough drops.

"Mom, can you do something for me? "

"Sure, honey."

"Don't call me Kimberly Ann. I'm not that little girl anymore." I rolled over and pretended I was going back to sleep.

She didn't reply. I heard her walk out of the room, quietly closing the door behind her, something she had never done before. I turned the lamp on near my bed, reached for my backpack on the floor, and pulled out *Fried Green Tomatoes at the Whistle Stop Café*. It made me think of Brian, even though he was in Mississippi, and the novel was set in Alabama; somehow, I felt close to him in the fictional cosmos. That's what desperation is. You're willing to bet your entire existence on a shred of hope that doesn't exist in anyone else's mind but your own. Any slim chance to be near him, no matter how far fetched, was better than nothing at all. I imagined our souls united in a cloud of fictional characters in the Deep South. There were lots of good things to eat, and we spent the day talking. His mother wore an apron.

I eventually joined the family for Christmas dinner, sitting across the dining room table from Kathy Renee's date, Elie Sabagh. A twenty-five-pound roasted turkey sat between us, making it difficult to get a full view of him. In many ways he looked like Matthew Ramirez. My sister liked dark men. She liked men a lot of white people hated. But Kathy Renee was that pure; everything she did was out of a blind love for others. She wasn't a slave to people's opinions or social norms.

I did what was considered popular, even successful in the social norm, and I continued to hate and distrust men and preferred the company of books to people. At this rate, I was guaranteed a place of acceptance in a commune in the West with a shaven head and a shapeless dress of flax and hemp.

I sat cross-legged at the dining room table, a deliberate move to upset my mother. After popping a brussel sprout in my mouth, sans utensils, I addressed our dinner guest.

"Where you from, Elie?"

"League City."

"What I mean is, where were you born?"

"Kim, please pretend you have manners," Mom warned. "Let's start again with a blessing of the food. David . . ."

Dad shot me a pleading look, before saying the same prayer we'd been praying since beginning any meal in this house.

We bowed our heads, including Elie. Dad delivered his prayer with the same emotion and intonation he always delivered a prayer in. We all heard his unspoken thought at the table. *Now, that's out of the way, let's eat.*

"You were telling us where you were born, Elie." I prodded, putting a napkin in my lap to appease my parents.

"I'm from Damascus. Syria. We moved to the states, so my father could go to school here. He's an electrical engineer with Lockheed at NASA."

I thought of Jennifer's dad. He worked there, too. Would I ever be away from the Blue Birds?

"I met Elie at the 7-11. I'd go there every day after school for a mixed Slurpee. He makes the best," Kathy Renee said. She and Elie locked eyes and smiled at each other.

"I work there and go to school at the University of Houston, Clear Lake campus."

"Elie, I'm sure you know we are a Catholic family by the number of crucifixes in the house, and my father's rote-memorized prayer. I mean it is the day we celebrate Christ's birth. Is that uncomfortable for you as a Muslim?"

"Now, that's enough, young lady."

"It's a legitimate question, Mom."

Kathy Renee reached for Elie's hand and looked at me with tears in her eyes.

15

I received my first letter from Brian during the spring semester. I still don't understand why everyone insisted in calling it the spring semester. February in Lubbock was ice, snow, and a cold north wind blowing off the flatlands of West Texas. That wind blew right through me, rattling my closed heart. The letter remained unopened in my dorm room for a week before I got the guts to open it. The return address was the Parris Island Recruit Depot in South Carolina.

I woke up Saturday morning to the institutional silence only found in dorm rooms and hospitals. The silence, echoing a cough or footstep, reminded you of your loneliness and hopeless within that institution. I put a coffee cup with instant coffee into the little microwave Dad bought me for Christmas. Its cheerful chime encouraged me to eat the cellophane-wrapped Twinkie on top of my desk. Maybe I'd get that same yellow glow of the Twinkie if I ate it. Ripping it open with my teeth, I took a bite, then opened the letter from Brian.

> *Dear Kim,*
>
> *I made it to boot camp in South Carolina. I eat, sleep, and work. Not much time or energy for anything else, except to think of you.*
>
> *The guys here are mostly from the South. They sign up for different reasons. Some are running away from their mothers, their wives, or their pregnant girlfriends. There's a few like me who come from military families. They're okay guys. I don't spend too much time talking or going out.*
>
> *I know you are hurt by my decision to leave Lubbock, but my word is true. When this is all over, I can offer you a decent life as my wife. We*

won't be rich, but I will love you and our children. It's worth waiting for.

  Send me a letter, and I'll know it's okay to call you. It would mean a
lot to me.
Love,
Brian

I placed his letter inside my Library Science and Information Sources textbook and stared out the dorm window. The sun wasn't coming out and neither was I. I got back in bed and began chapter 8 of Barbara Kingsolver's *The Bean Trees*. The main character, Taylor, was avoiding exploding tires and sex with boys to escape small town life in Kentucky. Despite her efforts, she winds up in another small town, a mother and an employee at a tire shop.

I pulled the comforter closer to my chin, as the window near the bed frame rattled against the blowing north wind. My heart rattled in unison. I'd never write Brian back. Never. I was going to be a librarian. That's why I moved to this flat-land purgatory. I got up, found Brian's letter in my textbook, and threw it in the metal garbage can under the desk. Climbing back in bed, I returned to my book and, suddenly, life seemed manageable.

"Open up, Kim. Time to eat."

That twang followed by her fist against the door was a clear reminder of why I preferred books to people. Cindy Jones was a clear-eyed, tall blonde who wore her Wranglers like indigo snakeskin. This might have been part of her duties as the reigning Rattle Snake Queen of West Texas, a beauty pageant title she coveted like the Cherry Coke lip gloss on her big-as-Texas mouth.

Growing up on a cattle ranch outside of San Angelo, Cindy was well cared for by good-natured, doting parents and Mexican cattle hands since the day she was born. She was a pretty girl with the intellectual depth of a mud puddle. Most of her conversations were about the wonderful world of boys, anecdotes from the Morning Star Ranch, and her duties as a reigning queen.

Our first conversation was in the hallway, where she accosted me returning from the library. In an effort to impress me, she told me the size of the ranch: "It's not measured in acres, but in sections. Do you know what a section in land is?" To prevent a headache, I simply nodded my head yes. She then explained her beauty queen title, followed by the number of people who attended her high school graduation party, all delivered between chews of Dentyne gum. The smell of cinnamon was overwhelming.

"My dad bought a keg of Coors, and the ranch hands made cabrito. I had more people at my party than anyone else in my senior class."

"What's cabrito?"

"Barbequed goat. It's awesome."

"I don't think you should share that with a lot of people. The visual of a goat on a spit covered in barbeque sauce makes me want to vomit."

She didn't reply, either because she didn't know what a spit was or she was desperate for a friend. She kept hanging around, inviting me to eat with her in the dorm.

So here was Cindy at high noon pounding on my door. She did everything by the clock – breakfast at eight, lunch at noon, supper at five, and lights out at eleven. I guess ranch life teaches you punctuality.

"I heard the first pound of your fist, Cindy. Give me a second. I'm not dressed."

Since the cafeteria fed the athletic teams, as well as the rest of the dorm inhabitants, you'd see the same people at almost every meal. Cindy and I always sat near the athletic team tables. It was a free show.

Today's meal featured chicken-fried steak with mashed potatoes and gravy. The football players were in a fried carb coma, as they positioned their heads close to their plates, rarely coming up for air. Some of them held on to their plates with their left hand. I never figured out why they did that, unless it was to keep their balance while eating, or they were afraid someone would steal their plate.

The breaded steaks lopped off the sides of their plates. Next to the fried beef, sat a mound of mashed potatoes, delivered by a metal ice cream scoop. In its center was a small indention holding white gravy, resembling a volcano on the verge of erupting. Big boys. Big eaters. Big deal.

Cindy left the security of our table to navigate the salad bar near a feeding trough of football players.

"Hey you?"

Cindy turned around quickly. A dark-haired, brown-eyed specimen of brute force with his fork in his right hand and a dinner roll in his left, stood up and approached her. I was impressed to see he had the good sense to wipe his mouth with his paper napkin before speaking.

"Don't I know you from somewhere?"

I pretended to eat as I swirled my hamburger goulash, wondering how Cindy would manage this aggressive stance.

"Oh, I don't know. Where'd you graduate from?" She asked, playing with her ponytail, twirling the end of it around her index finger.

"I remember now. You were that girl with a baton, both ends were set on fire. It was at the Rotary Beauty Pageant. Wore a silver one-piece thing with tassels."

"That was me. I won the talent show and the pageant."

"Yeah, I remember."

The football player leaned toward Cindy, making it difficult for me to hear what he was saying. I found myself leaning in, too.

"Name's Josh. How come I haven't seen you round here before?"

"I guess you weren't looking too hard, Josh."

They both laughed, and I was immediately mad at myself for coming with her. I could be eating a sandwich in my room and reading a book. Now, I was being held hostage by two mental neophytes, ogling each other's bodies.

"Why don't you meet my friend? We both live in Hulen Hall."

Now, she's telling him where we live. This was only going to get worse, as the six-foot-long table of football players turned around to watch Cindy and Josh approach me.

She gingerly placed her salad swimming in French dressing on the table in front of her empty seat, then placing her hand on Josh's left arm, she directed him to the empty chair near me. She was a pushy minx.

"Hey, Kim." I was thankful he didn't extend a bear paw for me to shake.

"Hey." That was all he was getting from me.

"You two ladies ought to come to a party we're having."

"We'd love to," Cindy chirped.

That's when I looked down at my plate. I would not encourage this with eye contact.

"You got something to write on?"

"Sure do." She pulled a bright pink pad of paper from her purse with a matching ink pen attached to it. "Here."

"The alumni association gives us a barbeque right before spring break. It's a while off, but I won't forget to call this number."

"How sweet of you, Josh. We looove barbeque." Cindy gave Josh a perky little kiss, standing on one leg, tiptoed, while the other leg was bent at the knee, daring to touch her left buttock. Not only did Josh appreciate it, but the entire cafeteria was amazed by her acrobatic feat. I surmised Cindy had been practicing that act since the day she was born. By the tender age of nine, it was a natural reflex.

I turned again to the swirl of food on my plate, waiting for her to sit down and shut up. She did in a whirl of breathless plans and predictions.

"Can you believe this? What should I wear? I forgot to ask his last name. My daddy might know his family. And you can come, too."

I stood up, grabbed my cafeteria tray, and looked her in the eyes.

"I think I'm busy that day."

She grabbed my arm. "What? We've just been invited to a very important party. Josh was trying to be nice to us."

"I hate football players." I jerked my arm free and left the cafeteria.

A light snow began to fall, reflecting in the glow of the large campus streetlights lining the sidewalks outside the cafeteria. I took several deep breaths, letting the cold, damp air fill my lungs. A long, tired sigh escaped from somewhere inside me. Cindy made me tired. People just exhausted me. I decided to walk to the student union to check my mail and get a package of stale, tasteless cookies from the vending machines. I knew what to expect from the cookies. They were always stale and tasteless. A sort of yellowish, vanilla color in clear packaging. I had no expectations that would ever change. But people, oh, they can change who they are in a split second, and that slap of disappointment across the face will smart and shock every time.

I peered into the open mailbox. Inside was a letter from Brian and a holy card disguised as a post card from my mother. I threw both of them in the garbage, ripped the cookie package with my teeth, and placed them in my coat pocket.

As I walked to Hulen Hall, the snow began to fall heavier on the shoulders of three girls and a couple walking hand in hand in front of me. I stared at their coated backs, thinking about the expectation each held for the other. *He will kiss me goodnight. She will say she loves me. Susan will give me her lab notes. Shelly will laugh at my joke.* All that expectation fluttering in the February night as airy as the assumption we all deserved more than we got. Not me. It was just like eating these cookies I knew were stale the minute I opened the package. There was a lot of satisfaction in not having an expectation for anything better. I never expected Brian to come back to Lubbock and marry me, just like I never expected my mother to love me the way she did my sister.

16

I received another letter from Brian in late April. It sat on my desk unopened, until the phone rang in my room on Saturday morning. For someone to call that early meant it was either my sister or my parents. I ignored it. Looking up from my bed, I watched the gray phone hanging on the wall crying out for attention. By the seventh ring, I picked it up, anxiously.

"Kim Hodges?"

"Yes."

"We haven't met, Kim. I'm Brian Ladner's mother."

My heart stopped, and my eyes fell immediately to the unopened letter on the desk. Why I kept this one when all the others had been ripped in two and thrown away, I didn't know. Maybe I did know. I kept it for this day. The day his mother would call me.

I didn't say anything, waiting for her to deliver the sledgehammer. It wouldn't be good news; I knew it as every nerve in my body tightened, waiting to hear it.

"I'm calling with bad news."

"I know you are." That was the only thing I said to her during the phone call.

"Brian talked about you. He had your address with his things, when we picked them up last week in South Carolina. He drowned. My baby drowned, and it took them three days to find him. He was my only son."

I immediately thought of that day not so long ago, flying the kite with him and Raul. How we turned to look at me, his wet hair pulled back, the rescued kite in his outstretched hand. Perfect and forever that day.

"Are you there? Kim? I thought you would want to know. The funeral service is this Monday. I don't expect you to come."

The phone went dead in my hands. I hung it up on the wall, sat at my desk, and stared at the unopened letter. I picked it up, ripped it in two and threw it in the waste can underneath the desk. It didn't matter what it said. I went back to bed, staring at the phone hanging on the wall until I fell asleep. I dreamed of Brian swimming off the shore of Parris Island, South Carolina, not far from the barracks, where he left the young men sleeping in their bunks, in the chill of a gray spring morning.

He walked through the palmetto palms lining the sandy path to the ocean's edge. The first rays of the sun's warmth touched his face and bare arms. Pulling a white T-shirt across his back and shoulders, over his head, he welcomed that warmth to his chest and shoulders.

Where the sand met the shore of the Atlantic, he kicked flip-flops off his feet and placed a well-worn towel and the T-shirt on top of them. He stared at the vastness before him with his hands on his hips, as if that body of water with its rip currents, the undertow had been waiting for him, its whispering at his neck, its breathe within his ear, "Come."

But the Atlantic was not the Gulf of Mexico Brian knew. It was cold and dark that morning, mighty in its singular capacity to end lives. At low tide, Brian Ladner walked into the ocean until it enveloped his bare chest, then jumping into the air, he dove into its enormity. The waiting rip current found him, pulling him further into the ocean's depths. Each stroke of the arm, each beat of the heart, each thrust of the leg against that current, took him deeper into the current's control, until exhausted, he never resurfaced.

I woke up, only because I was hungry. By the early shadows outside the window, it was late afternoon. I had slept most of the day. Since the cafeteria wouldn't open until five, I made a bowl of Ramen noodles in the microwave, then, sitting cross legged on the bed, I sprinkled the packet of flavoring and MSG into the cloudy mixture and ate it.

I thought of Raul. Because I was so selfish, thinking only of hurting Brian for leaving me in Lubbock, I didn't know if the dog was here or in Ocean

Springs. I wanted to think of him in Ocean Springs, with Brian's mom and dad, walking the waterfront every morning and night or running just along the surf's edge, then shaking the Mississippi Sound off his body, as Brian's dad whistled for him it was time to go home. I wished that dog was mine, and I wished more than anything Brian Ladner was mine, again.

I placed the empty bowl, crusted with yellow powder from the flavor packet on my desk. Pulling the covers over my head, I cried, because I had so callously rejected a tender boy who said he loved me. Just as I had so cruelly disregarded my sister's love for me. *Through my fault, through my fault, through my most grievous fault.*

The ethereal hour, between the smallness of 4 a.m. and the expectation of a new day, I awoke to the smell of a cigarette in my dorm room. At first, I thought it was my old roommate, Rachel, fresh out of a Dallas rehab, but when I opened my eyes, I saw Grandma Jean. She was playing solitaire at my desk with Poco, Mrs. Olson's Chihuahua from the Villa.

"Morning, baby," Grandma offered between a puff of her cigarette smudged with Mauve Magic lipstick. She placed the Queen of Hearts face up, laughed and looked at the dog in her lap. "Do I fold or keep playing, Poco?"

"Keep playing, Granny. You'll never know what will happen if you quit now."

"Grandma, Poco is talking to you, saying your name like he's human. Am I dreaming this?" I sat up in bed and turned toward them. My knees touched my grandmother's knees. She smiled and patted my thigh. Rising on his hind legs, Poco licked my grandmother's face.

"I'm here. Nothing more than that has to be understood. Poco's here, 'cause we play a lot of cards together. He's a darn good bridge partner." She looked down and rubbed the dog's head. "It's true what they say about dogs going to heaven. Makes sense, when you think about it. Dogs love unconditionally, even people who don't deserve that kind of love. You folded on Brian. Don't fold on your sister, too."

She reached into her lavender duster pocket and pulled out a dog biscuit shaped like a mailman, with a bulging mailbag anchored to his side. "He just loves these things," she said, as Poco nibbled from her outstretched hand. "Have you thought of getting a dog, Kim?"

Before I could answer her, she and Poco were gone with the sound of the toilet flushing in the dorm room next door.

Maybe Raul wasn't in Ocean Springs? Maybe he was still in Lubbock. I've got to find him. Brian would have wanted that.

17

Eight o'clock in the morning and that nut Cindy was at the door, jiggling the knob to let herself in, oblivious to the fact it was locked.

"Breakfast. It's the most important meal of the day," she sang out in the hallway.

"The door is locked for a reason."

"It wouldn't hurt you to be nice. Doesn't cost anything."

Suddenly, I remembered she was my only connection to the football team, Brian's last contact on campus, so I decided to be polite, which was completely against my natural instincts in the morning, but I needed her, especially if Raul was still in Lubbock.

"Good morning," I offered, opening the door to her Dentyne-chewing, tight-jean queenliness. Cindy was wearing blue mascara to match her blue eyes. On her it wasn't garish; it was a "Big Howdy to the World" sort of fashion statement. She was one of the few who could pull it off, making girls jealous and boys lustful.

"Ready? I'm starving."

"Sure. Let's sit near the football players again. Did that one guy call you?"

"Josh? Such a cutie! No, he didn't that devil. I hope he's there. I'm going to let him know he hurt my feelings."

Off we went. I was on a mission to resurrect a boy by finding his dog, and Cindy was set to play an injured sex kitten with blue eyelashes.

"I'm gonna love me some pancakes. Do you mind if I sit here by you and the syrup?"

She did it. She sat down at the table with the entire football team. I took a seat next to her. On my right was the cornerback, weighing in at 190 pounds, barely six feet tall. He had unfocused eyes; actually, the right eye was lazy, pulling slightly to the right, with the left eye focused dead center. I didn't know whether to look at him in the direction of the right eye or the left eye. It was awkward, especially since the two unparalleled eyes swept over the length of my body in the split second he deviated from mopping up egg yolks with a piece of toast. No wonder Brian wanted to get out of here. He never belonged in that group. Football players. When that mental alarm sounded, my homecoming date and all its sordidness cast a dark hue over the breakfast table.

I ate my cereal in silence, making a wide berth for Cindy's sassy-girl routine. All she needed was a little lasso and horse whip in her hands to get those boys corralled and tamed.

"Josh, I know you didn't lose my number. Why didn't you call me?"

This was met with a roar of laughter from the other boys and an offer from the cornerback next to me.

"Josh doesn't know how to treat a woman. Give me your number. I'll call you."

More laughter from the team. I stared at my cereal, searching for deliverance in the soggy mix of sugar-coated raisins and wilted bran.

"You behave yourself," Cindy offered with a gentle slap to the cornerback's hand wrapped around his fork.

"Don't listen to him. He's still pissed about being a cornerback, especially since the only decent safety we had left," Josh offered.

"That jerk abandoned the team. Gave his mongrel dog to my roommate until he could come back for him. No one's heard a word from him. He'd better not show his face around me. Loser."

Raul's here. I knew then I would have to face another Ben Mullin, but this time I'd do it with the tenacity of a Raven and the cunning of a Blue Bird. No man was leaving a rip or stain on my person ever again.

With the allure of feminine warmth, I placed my hand on the cornerback's bent arm, giving it a little squeeze of affection and familiarity.

"What kind of dog is it? I'm a big animal lover."

He looked at me as if someone had offered him a treasure chest of opportunity. The possibilities would only be limited by his imagination, while somewhat stunted, still remained a powerful resource for adolescent entertainment.

"My roommate Seth and the safety were roommates first semester. I guess that's why he left the dog with him. We live in a rent house with a yard, now. Dog craps everywhere. Sick of picking it up."

"Oh, that's too bad. Maybe I can come over, help you out. Cook dinner. Nothing for me to whip up some enchiladas with verde sauce."

I threw it all out there, the possibility of sex, a hot meal, and someone to pick up the dog crap. What man could refuse this?

I glanced over at Cindy. She was in her element, laughing, tossing her hair, and touching shoulders, hands, whatever body part was close enough to her and above the dining table, marking her territory like the aggressive female she was groomed to be. After all, not just anyone can be a Rattle Snake Queen of West Texas.

While Cindy was busy, I took the opportunity to tighten the noose around the cornerback.

"What do you say. . . . I can't believe I haven't asked you your name. I'm Kim."

"Kyle. From Corpus."

There are no coincidences in life. My mother and sister lived that fact every day. For Kyle to be from Corpus Christi, not far from where I first learned of undertows made me shudder. For him to be a slightly different version of Ben Mullin panicked me; but this time, I would be completely in charge. Kyle, and any other guy who was like minded, brutalizing young girls and playing dirty on the field, would never hurt me again.

"Come over Thursday, after seven."

It was Holy Thursday, a day my mother and sister spent in prayer and reverence. For me, it was a poignant reminder of the treachery of people and the precarious nature of love and friendship. Jesus sat at a table, breaking bread and drinking wine with his best friends. Twenty-four hours later, the brotherhood collapsed in betrayal delivered with a kiss and the crowing of a cock. My conscience didn't bother me in misleading Kyle; it was part of my DNA.

"Yeah, no school on Good Friday. Works for me," I giggled, squeezing his arm again.

"Baylor, 2203, northwest of here. Black Mustang in driveway."

"Looking forward to it," I kissed him on the check, right below his lazy eye, and picked up my breakfast tray. I left Cindy to her own devices.

18

The Llano Estacada was a geographic pie carved up by demographics made from the Bible Belt, Texas Tech, the landed gentry, and poor blacks, whites, and Mexicans in the red, white, and blue of Lubbock, Texas. Two areas anchored those demographics: the cattle feed lots ripe in the heat with stench and bugs, and the Strip, a portion of Highway 87 outside of city limits lined with liquor stores. The Bible Belt enforced its own prohibition with keeping Lubbock County patricianly dry, making Pinkie's the Disney of liquor stores, the hottest spot in town. It not only boasted a special, *Pinkie's Wine of the Week*, but managed to serve up a well-loved, local cuisine in fried chicken gizzards. Pinkie's as a sommelier and gourmet trek was disturbing, but not surprising. Those people ate barbequed goat.

I folded my Lubbock County map and placed it in my backpack. Night had fallen, and I was proceeding as planned with Kyle. I wore an acid-washed denim jacket with red pumps and a black unitard, borrowed from the dance major next door. I told Janice I was invited to audit a jazz class as a PE elective. She didn't pause to reflect on the request, leaving the door open and flinging the slinky black polyester/spandex cloth at me. I figured she was saving every calorie for dance, since she survived on black coffee, Marlboros, and sunflower seeds. If I ever saw her in the cafeteria eating, it wasn't for very long. She'd gorged on cafeteria food, only to be out of sight ten minutes later, purging in the hall bathroom. The telltale sign of eating quickly then leaving, followed by the sound of tap water running to drown out the vomiting was never hard to detect, especially on a university campus in the eighties. Everyone wanted to look like the girl on the cover of

Sports Illustrated Swimsuit Edition. For me, it was just another reason to hate sports.

I took the bus to Baylor Street. It was a short walk to Kyle's, but I was terrified of twisting my ankle in the red pumps, losing my physical prowess once I was there. The bus made two stops to pick up white-uniformed maids coming home from their day jobs in Tanglewood. All the working women in this town wore white nursing uniforms: waitresses, maids, and nurses. Put a woman in white and she's either getting married or cleaning up, sometimes both. I felt a little dirty in my cat woman costume next to these women. They were going about it honestly, while I relied on the oldest trick in the book. What was Raul worth to me? My self-respect was never measured by what someone thought of me. We all had to serve somebody at some point in our lives. This was Kyle's moment. It would be brief.

I walked about a block, barefoot on the sidewalk with the red bullet shoes in my hand, until I spotted the Mustang in the driveway. In the lawn of dollar weeds and dead grass, a late model truck was parked. I prayed the driver wasn't inside the house with Kyle. He was all I could handle.

I put on my heels and shifted the weight of canned tomatillos and diced chicken, a block of Velveeta, and a pack of corn tortillas in my backpack. I bent slightly to the reflection of the Mustang's side mirror and reapplied my lipstick, then approached the front door, giving three firm knocks.

Kyle appeared shirtless, performing that God-awful guy trick of lifting one arm then latching it at the top of the door, exposing all that disgusting armpit hair entangled in white, caked deodorant. It was an unspoken message immediately letting me know he was in control and this rent house was his castle.

I tottered in my heels underneath the testosterone threshold he provided, not offering a kiss, but a quick reminder of why I had come and what was in my backpack. "Where's the kitchen? Got everything I need to get some Enchiladas Verde going."

"First left. I got some tequila for the enchiladas."

At an orange Formica counter bar was a bottle of tequila, a saltshaker, a lime cut in quarters, sans a cutting board, and one large kitchen knife. I tried to take the combination kitchen and den info full view, but I was stopped by the sound of a dog barking. There was Raul, scratching and jumping on the glass patio doors, while tied to wrought-iron patio table that moved whenever he lounged forward.

"Shut up," Kyle screamed at the patio door. "I hate that dog. I'd let him roam the streets of Lubbock until he got hit by a car, but my roommate wants him." He opened the bottle of tequila and filled two shot glasses.

My initial instinct was to hit Kyle over the head with the bottle and cut Raul loose with the kitchen knife. I didn't think the getaway would be clean and easy with the red high heels and the roommate in the house, though.

"Where's your roommate?"

"Watching TV or sleeping. He doesn't come out until about ten to party." He handed me a shot glass.

"Salúd."

Our glasses and eyes met at the same time, at least his centered left eye did. I downed the tequila and grabbed a lime to put out the fire in my throat and stomach. I looked at him again when I put down the shot glass, this time focusing on his lazy orb, swimming haphazardly in an increasingly red sea across the white of his eye.

"You don't need to cook. We can just hang out in here and listen to music."

"Sure. I'm really not that hungry." I sat on the couch near the patio door. Raul stopped jumping and followed me with his eyes. I was sure he remembered me, just as I remembered him. "Can we let the puppy inside? It's starting to rain."

"He'll jump all over you."

"I don't mind. Get us another shot, and I'll let him in," I squeezed Kyle's thigh next to mine, so he'd know my request would be worth it to him. "I'll get comfortable here. First, off with the shoes." I slipped out of the heels and opened the patio door. Raul met me with wet kisses on my hands, neck, and face. I buried my face in his fur, welcoming his affection, knowing this dog remembered me, me when I was a part of Brian's life. For a tiny moment, I could feel Brian standing above us, the warmth of his brown eyes and crooked smile.

"Shut the door, it's raining," Kyle shouted from the bar, pouring two more shots for the Saturday night event. I decided then there'd be no event. He wasn't getting anything from me, and I was obviously taking something he didn't want. Why play this out?

"Coming." The knot in the rope tied around Raul's neck was tight. I used my teeth to loosen it, which took longer than I wanted it to. Once he was loose, I put my arms around him in case he bolted. I was cold, wet, and covered in dog hair. When I looked up, Kyle was standing at the patio door with the shot glasses.

"What are you doing? I don't want that wet dog in the house."

"I know you don't. I'm taking him home with me. We're both going. This was a bad idea to even come here. I knew Brian and I knew this dog, way before I met you in the cafeteria. I came here tonight just to get Raul."

"That dog isn't yours to take." He downed both shot glasses and threw them above my head. I heard them hit the six-foot fence in the back yard.

"Okay. I'll buy him from you."

"He's not for sale."

I realized I was kneeling with Raul, directly in front of Kyle. It was a vulnerable position to take next to a bully, but I was afraid to let go of the dog.

"What's he worth to you, then? Go ask your roommate. I'll wait right here. Neither of you really want this dog. He doesn't even have a water bowl out here."

"I don't have to ask permission from my roommate. I know what I want from you." Kyle grabbed my hair, yanking me up from Raul and the patio floor.

"Don't touch me. Don't touch me." I pulled in the opposite direction. Raul began growling, a low, menacing sound came from his throat. I held him tighter, even when I looked up to see a wad of my hair in Kyle's fist, I didn't let go of that dog. I concentrated on Kyle's lazy eye, that was the bad eye, the eye that didn't see the world as I did. I was beginning to lose consciousness, when he grabbed my hair again and jerked me toward him. I kept staring at that lazy eye and holding on to Raul. I wasn't going into the undertow, I wasn't letting Kyle take me there to drown.

"Let go of that dog."

"No. He's mine. I'm keeping him."

That was the last thing I remember saying, before Kyle put both hands on my head, squeezing tightly until the tears came, blinding me with pain. I couldn't feel Raul anymore. All I could feel was the tightness on my head, the pounding of my heart in my ears. Raul was barking. I thought of his roommate. I had to get out of here.

"Raul. Raul. Come on, boy." I stumbled toward the opened patio door and Raul.

"Take the stupid dog, then. You aren't worth the trouble."

Kyle kicked Raul. He kept kicking him until the dog returned his blows by jumping on him, biting his hands and face.

"Raul, come on, boy. Come on." I grabbed Raul's neck, pulling him off Kyle. Kyle moaned in pain; his hands reaching for the lazy eye, its eyelid torn and bleeding. It was just bad luck Raul bit that eye, that bad, lazy eye, as if the dog knew instinctively this was Kyle's Achilles' heel. It stopped him cold.

From my peripheral vision, I saw the roommate standing in the doorway, watching. I pushed Raul toward the front door and we ran, past the Mustang, past the street corner, through the neighborhoods of families eating dinner on the day marking Christ's last supper.

I saw our reflection in the bay window of a home at 2208 Baylor. We were nothing like the girl and the dog who sat in the Corolla station wagon in front of the Whataburger four months ago. My scalp and ears were bleeding and Raul was standing on three legs, the other leg, crooked and pushed up against his backside. He was a far cry from the dog that ate hamburgers in one bite, while eyeing me and licking Brian's neck. I wasn't the same girl, either. Standing in the rain with mascara and eyeliner coating my face and neck black, I was barefoot and bleeding. I suddenly remembered I left the backpack and red shoes on the floor of Kyle's rent house. It didn't matter. I hated them, anyway.

"Raul. We'll get better. I promise." I bent down and rubbed his head.

We walked back to the dorm in the rain, cold and beaten. I didn't bother checking if a RA was prowling about looking for rule violators; Raul and I entered the elevator liked we owned the place. Once in the room, I peeled off the wet bodysuit that felt like a dirty rubber glove, dried off Raul, and put him in bed. I put on a nightgown and a pair of knee socks. Climbing into bed next to Raul, I pulled the covers over both of us. He released a low moan, shaking the entire bed. I patted him then reached for the paperback on my desk.

In that twin bed with Raul and Gabriel Garcia Marquez's *Love in the Time of Cholera*, humility and pain were replaced by the warmth of a living creature and the genius of a Nobel Prize winner, as Marquez took me to a twentieth-century homestead on the Magdalena River in Columbia. Underneath the covers with Raul and a book in my hand, I was buoyant.

I dreamed of Granny and Brian that night. They were playing Canasta, sitting at a poolside table at the Villa Maria. Smoke rings rose above Poco in the chaise lounge near the card table centered with an ash tray, two lit cigarillos, and two empty cocktail glasses. Granny smiled at me then raised her jeweled hand for another round of Old Fashioneds, "Don't forget the orange slices, hon."

My dream ended with the sound of someone pounding on the door. For a second, I panicked, thinking it was Kyle. I looked over at the clock on the desk, 8:00 a.m. Cindy was right on cue. I got up and looked back at Raul. His eyes met mine, but he didn't have the strength to lift his head.

"Kim, breakfast, the most important...." Before she could finish her usual proclamation, I opened the door and let her in, pointing to Raul on the bed.

"When did you get a dog?'

"Last night."

"As soon as he barks, the RA will be in here. Hey, let me look at you. What happened last night? Cindy turned my head from side to side with her hand, examining the holes in my scalp.

"Your friend, the cornerback of the football team did this to me and Raul." I pointed to the rope burns around Raul's neck and his swollen eyes and jawline.

"Oh, Kim. I've got to get him to a vet, and you to a doctor. Let me take you to the student clinic. Meet me out front with the dog. I'll get the car."

"No. They'll take him from me, plus I don't have any money for a vet. Don't you know anything about animals? You grew up on a ranch."

"Yes, I do, I was the FFA Sweetheart and won the top calf award at the county fair. My dad's the real expert, though. I'll call him then go by the cafeteria and get you some food. Be back in thirty minutes. Back to bed, you two." She was gone in a cloud of efficacy and cherry lip gloss.

Just like boy hunting and fulfilling her duties as a queen, Cindy was off on the latest mission. That's what growing up with money did for you. You never stopped to worry about getting caught or being cheap. You just did it. She was back in thirty minutes with a Styrofoam container of scrambled eggs, bacon, and biscuits, with pats of butter between tiny cardboard sleeves, two packages of grape jelly and two packages of strawberry jelly. I guess she couldn't decide what I liked best, so she brought all there was to offer. Those rich girls, confident in the assumption that if it was offered, it was theirs for the taking. There were no hang-ups about only taking what you absolutely needed. That was only for the children of martyrs, like my mother. There's nothing gained by being carefree and spontaneous was her golden rule.

Raul ate the bacon and I made egg sandwiches with the biscuits. We slept soundly, until awakened by an erotic version of Florence Nightingale in a leather fringed halter top with blue-jean cut-offs. The pockets of the jeans were longer than the length of the shorts. Cindy.

"How did you get in here?"

"I took the door key when I put your breakfast on the desk." She placed a small first aid kit on the side of the bed. She dotted a cotton ball with hydrogen peroxide and moved toward me.

"I think this is going to hurt a lot." I began to shrink away from her outreached hand.

"Most things do when you have your hair pulled out in chunks. Let's at least kill the germs. Don't want this getting infected. It would be a real shame to shave your head, so the scalp can heal."

"No, we're not doing that." I allowed her to apply the cotton ball to the areas where my hair was missing. Tears squeezed their way through my clinched eyes as I squirmed beneath her touch. "Okay, that's enough, Kim. Just take care of Raul, now." I stood up and started getting dressed.

"Hey, now. You really should let me finish."

"I'll be all right. Help me with Raul."

"Dad told me to use a little sulphur powder on the open wounds and burns. Works great on dogs. Back on the ranch, we used it to control fleas for the outside dogs. Natural product. A mineral." Cindy made a paste of sulphur mixed with tap water. She smoothed it over the rope burns on Raul's necks, then applied it to the cuts around his face and ears made by the tip of Kyle's boots. Raul groaned.

"Maybe you should be a vet instead of a teacher."

"Are you kidding me? That's a lot of work, examining cow and horse paddies, delivering dogs and sheep, house calls in the middle of the night. Besides, I'm gonna get that ranch when my daddy dies, so I can play with all the animals I want without working like that. Right, sweet boy," she whispered in Raul's ear. "Girl, you need a shower. I'll sit with him. Go on, now." Cindy lay next to Raul, gently scratching between his ears with her index finger.

I let the steady stream of hot water pour over my head and body, washing away the night and any residual of Kyle on my skin, underneath my fingernails, and in my hair. But there wasn't enough water and soap in the world to wash that stench away.

Tomorrow was Easter Sunday. I hadn't spoken to anyone in my family for at least two weeks. I'm sure Mom sent a card. The thought of checking the mail at the student center exhausted me. Maybe I'd call home. I can tell them about Raul, but I wouldn't offer anything beyond the simple fact I got a dog. I'd talk about the virtues of rescuing a pound puppy. Kathy Renee would love that. She'd probably light a candle at church for us. Despite the lie, Raul and I could use a prayer or two. I'd call them tonight, after I ate. The cafeteria seemed like a lot to manage, maybe Cindy could arrange food for Raul and me.

I'd call my family tonight for the simple reason I missed them, all of them. Mom and Dad would accept the collect call, just like they accepted all my deficits. Kathy Renee would want to talk first, laughing and shouting into the mouthpiece.

I stayed underneath the stream of warmth and goodness, thinking of home until the hot water ran cold.

19

Cindy found it for me, the one-bedroom garage apartment behind Mama's Pizza on University, east of campus. She lent me the down payment for 205 Seventh Avenue, complete with a bent rattan settee, a yellow aluminum table with two chairs, and a rattling AC unit in the window. Raul and I had a home. Now, I needed a job. My dad sent me a check for $500, but it was gone in a day with the purchase of groceries, a used ten-speed, utilities, and phone service. I bought a mattress and frame on credit with 21 percent interest. Cindy and Josh delivered it.

Josh, from the football crowd at the cafeteria, had earned a new title, main man of the Rattle Snake Queen. An affectionate couple, Josh and Cindy travelled together, entering each new adventure with Cindy shouting Josh's moniker, "O my gosh, Josh," like an anthem, delivered with a quick kiss on the mouth. Josh thanked his lucky stars every day for the first sighting of his future wife at the Rotary Beauty Pageant, where she danced to a disco song by the Bee Gees with flaming batons and a fringed, sequined leotard. They would never be lonely. They had each other for the rest of their lives, together, forever, BFFs.

Cindy was a loyal friend and, someday, she'd make Josh a loyal wife with access to a working ranch with thirty sections of land surrounding it. *That's thirty square miles, Josh, write that down and take it to the bank!* For an average football player with an average intellect, he showed no higher aspirations other than being Cindy's man. He happened to be in the cafeteria at the right time, eating pancakes on the morning Cindy decided she loved pancakes more than anything. I benefitted from their union. Not only were they generous friends but they were my only friends in Lubbock.

But luck wasn't going to pay my bills. I needed a full-time job for the summer. My first interview was at a sports bar, a new phenomenon among the Redneckeck Nation of chicken wing-eating and beer-drinking guys and dolls. Wild Wings was about a ten-minute bike ride from the apartment. I arrived ten minutes before my interview with Mr. Hank Martin, the manager of this establishment that which featured an all-female wait staff wearing red checkerboard skirts and white blouses tied in a square knot below the bust line.

Hank, the manager, sat down next to me with a big smile to match the size of his mustache.

"Miss Hodges, can I get you something to drink, while you fill out the application?"

"Water, please."

I took a full view of Hank in his red checkerboard slacks and white sports shirt with a red embroidered circle on his heart, marking the strategically placed company logo. It featured a blonde with teased hair holding a chicken, with the name of the restaurant, circling the blonde and the chicken. The chicken and the blonde also had big red lips. *Wild Wings. Was the designer of this logo suggesting you could get chicken and blondes when you eat here?* Just as I signed my name at the bottom of the application, Hank returned with a red plastic mug of water with an oily sheen floating near the straw.

"Great, the application looks complete. Do you have any questions about the restaurant?

"I don't think this job is about selling wings and beer."

"The job is about making customers happy."

"Really? If your food was decent, you wouldn't ask young women to push your business plan on their sexuality, by exposing their breasts and legs in those ridiculous uniforms."

"Who do you think you are?"

"Well, I'm more than my breasts."

"You're crazy." Hank ripped my application in two even halves, which was a bit impressive, making me think he had a lot of practice destroying job applications.

"Yes, that may be true, but at least I'm not dumb." I pointed to the logo over his heart. "Chickens don't have lips; they have beaks."

I left the glass of water untouched on the table and left without another word. For a second, I thought about turning around, calling the wait staff to attention, alerting the women to the dangers of sexual exploitation, maybe even burning those horrid uniforms in a sacred fire pit we'd construct in front of the restaurant. But it was hot outside, and I was flat broke. It just wasn't worth it to spend any more energy at Wild Wings.

I rode my bike home from the interview, spotting the Mama's Pizza sign before turning into the gravel driveway of the garage apartment. I ran up the wooden stairway, let Raul out for a quick run on the side of the house in front of me, then back up the stairs. I decided to walk to Mama's. It was exactly seven yards from my front door to the restaurant; I counted my steps, as I thought how I would approach the manager. Waitress. Cook. Dishwasher. I could do it all, leaving no doubt as to why someone wouldn't hire me.

The lunch crowd of students and office workers had left several hours before. A few girls sat at a table, talking, with one employee dutifully refilling their glasses of iced tea. He'd be lucky to get a quarter for a tip. The three girls didn't look up from their conversation to acknowledge his and the tea pitcher's presence.

He came back to the counter, when he saw me standing there.

"Is the manager in?

"I'm the manager."

"Hi, I'm Kim." I reached for his hand to shake it, and he smiled.

"What can I do for you, Kim?"

"I need a job. I can start now."

"Ever worked in a restaurant?"

"Yes." I lied, and he knew I was lying.

"It's minimum wage plus tips. We do it all here. Cook, serve, and clean. Be nice to the customers or you'll be fired. It's that easy."

"When can I start?"

"Here. Take this home and fill it out. Come back tomorrow morning at 9:30. You can help me prep for lunch. You'll also need to clean the dining room and restrooms. Never know what the evening crew is going to leave me until I open in the morning."

"Sure. Thanks. See you tomorrow."

"Kim. I'm Lionel."

"Lionel, I appreciate this. Oh, I almost forgot. Is there a uniform for this job?"

"Jeans and a T-shirt. Comfortable and clean. A good waiter is in the background; the customer doesn't want to know your name, what your major is, and how you pay tuition. Your job is serving food and making the customer happy."

"Makes perfect sense, Lionel. I can do this."

We shook hands again, and I think it was the first time in my life I shook hands with a man who looked me directly in the eyes, instead of an overall view and assumption of what the next move would be. Maybe this was my imagination working in overtime after the Wild Wings interview. Maybe I willed this interaction to be better, because it had to be.

Walking back home, I counted the steps again, affirming it was exactly seven yards from door to door. I checked my mailbox, nailed to the bottom railing of the stairs. Inside was a holy card from Kathy Renee. The front image was of seven angels in white robes, their wings touching, creating half a circle. Their arms were raised toward the sun, within their hands were golden trumpets. The back of the card read, "Then I saw the seven angels who stand before God, and seven trumpets were given to them. Revelation 8:2. "Beneath that were the words "I miss you, Sissy," followed by her neat signature and an xo.

I stood on the stairs for a long time, looking at the card and thinking of her. Still praying for me, still so sure of what she believed was undeniably the truth, a perfected truth. The universal church. Apostolic. Holy. I wished I had her faith. I learned the prayers, I followed the rules, doing everything

I was supposed to, but it didn't change me or how I viewed others. She saw the light of Christ in everyone, whether they deserved it or not.

That night Raul and I shared the bed, with the single window A/C unit rattling a lullaby for us through the night. I thought of my sister and the holy cards she continued to send me, despite the fact I never wrote back. *Kathy Renee, patron saint of lost sisters.* I slept without dreaming that night.

20

Lionel and I became fast friends. It was the first friendship I had with a man since Brian died. Reading was our common denominator. While he had no aspirations to base a career on it like I did, his true calling was art. And like all artists, his insight was birthed from the gift and pain of being sensitive in a world of Blue Birds, Red Birds, and Ravens.

Lionel was a thirty-two-year-old black man from White Columns, deep in the Piney Woods of East Texas. Between mopping the floors at closing to making pizza dough and prepping together at Mama's Pizza, we talked about books, art, and Lubbock.

"I haven't met a single person who moves to Lubbock for the climate or culture. People come here to escape something, then spend the next twenty years trying to get out of here. Lubbock could be the vortex, sucking us all in. It's the halfway point to California when people start in Beaumont, near the Louisiana border. It's the middle, man. The middle of nowhere."

Lionel was kneading the dough, gradually adding flour, a simultaneous process, until that perfect blend of water, flour, salt, and yeast became glossy and tacky. I stood next to him, slicing onions and bell peppers.

"I always felt that way about South Texas, where I grew up," I added, placing a plastic container of black olives in the fridge near the prep station. "The coastal plains, Galveston and Corpus Christi, are port towns that never recovered from hurricanes. Just layers and layers of history, founded on hurricane statistics of the people who drowned there. Too easy to be sucked underneath, thinking that's the best life can be.'

"Best to avoid Scylla and Charybdis." The joy I felt at hearing literary illusions from this man was beyond reasoning. After painstaking conversations with Cindy and the football players, I was savoring every bit of our time together.

"Have you read Carlos Castaneda's *The Teachings of Don Juan*?"

"Never heard of him," I answered, and it embarrassed me to do so. That's how much I admired him. He was smart and didn't have to tell you how smart he was, nor remind you of how stupid you were.

"Castaneda wrote a series of books on a shaman he met, Don Juan Matus. He submitted it as his master's thesis in the school of anthropology at UCLA. The books ended up selling millions of copies, translated in seventeen languages. He's like a spiritual guru, of sorts. The fact he became a celebrity doing this tells you how hungry people are for spiritual answers. Just hungry for the basic answer of why we're here. I'm not going to give the stories away; you should read them, but a lot of people claim what he saw and heard in the deserts of Mexico were true. Others say he did too much peyote."

"I don't know much about mystics, except the mystics of the Catholic Church. I admired St. Teresa of Avila. Read and reread *The Interior Castle* many times. It's profound. She's a saint if there are truly saints. How else could she have produced such a work, an uneducated woman from the Middle Ages?"

Lionel stopped kneading the dough, covered it with a clean towel, and placed it near the oven, so the yeast could rise.

"Am I boring you?" I asked him, as he sat on a bar stool in the corner to rest.

"No, go on. I'm curious."

"St. Teresa imagined her soul as being on a spiritual journey from the outside of a crystal, global castle into the interior of the castle, where the king lives in the center room. Outside the castle, it is very dark. Perfect light is where the king resides. The soul's journey to the center, the quest to be close to God, takes it through seven rooms. Suffering, detachment, humility, and especially prayer are part of the soul's journey. That's what we're working on as Christians. To be like Christ. Can you imagine the guilt associated with that?"

"I was raised in the Baptist church. We weren't so concerned with being like Christ, as much as we were about staying away from the devil. No saints or martyrs, either. The only one who comes close is John the Baptist with his locusts and honey. The Virgin Mary was reduced to an image on a Christmas card, never a saint but just a holiday image."

"Don't know much about Baptists."

"There's all kinds of Baptist churches. There wasn't much about the communion of saints in the East Texas church. It was the most segregated place I knew, although the preachers kept telling us were all brothers and sisters in Jesus' eyes."

The entire time Lionel was talking the song I learned as a child in vacation Bible school kept playing in my head. *Red, yellow, black, and white, we are precious in His sight. Jesus loves the little children of the world.*

"Kim, you still with me?"

"I was just thinking of what you said, and the things told to me as a child. Same lines but a different delivery."

"My delivery came from the all-black congregation of the Mount Zion Baptist. The whites went to Calvary Baptist. They had a gym for Wednesday night basketball games and church dinners. We had a parking lot, next to the railroad tracks. Even the public schools were more integrated than the churches. I learned early people were mean, growing up in that community. What you saw wasn't always what you got. Just because someone drove a new Oldsmobile and had a nice suit, didn't make him a Godly man. I believe there is a God, but it was the Holy Spirit and the Moonies that got my mama and me out of White Columns, Texas."

The hair on my arms rose when he used the words Holy Spirit and Moonies in the same sentence. Holding the paring knife firmly, I began slicing a five-pound container of tomatoes for our margarita pizza, the house specialty with fresh basil.

"My mom was a domestic, working for the same family since she was fifteen. She had me at sixteen. She worked for the Gibbons seven days a week, cooking, cleaning, babysitting, butt wiping, you name it. To make themselves feel better about paying her $1.50 an hour, they'd brag about Mama being a part of their family. 'We even take her on vacation with us,' they'd say. Their kids would chime in with how much my mother, the woman who gave birth to me, was just like a mama to them, too. They thought of themselves as generous people, 'cause they gave her the leftovers to take home every night. I ate those leftovers most of my childhood. Grandma filled in a lot, since Daddy wasn't around."

I gave Lionel a side glance to make sure he wasn't crying. He wasn't, but I was as the tears fell onto the sliced tomatoes, laying innocently on the chopping block.

"The times Mama was off, we'd go to the library, though she couldn't read. We'd check out coffee-table art books, like Cezanne's landscapes and still life, Gauguin's beautiful women of Tahiti. Mama was amazed a French man could lovingly paint a dark-skinned woman with full lips and a wide nose. We studied those artists and the places they painted, dreaming of France and Tahiti as future homes. About as far as we got was San Antonio. One day she came home from work, said she was tired of mopping floors and getting beat by Daddy, so we packed our suitcases and walked to the Greyhound bus station, inside the Texaco.

Met a nice Moonie lady playing guitar at the bus station in San Antonio," Lionel said, looking up from the pizza dough. "Don't know if you're old enough to remember the Moonies, Kim. They're the followers of the Korean spiritual leader, Rev. Moon and his Unification Church. We were basically homeless and hungry, and they took us in. Mama was never afraid. She'd tell me the Reverend and his people were chump change next to a redneck racist in the Piney Woods or a mean man in your bed. She eventually got her GED, then took some accounting classes at the junior college. She retired with a full pension from Lackland Air Force Base. Those military folks loved her, and she loved them. Still volunteers with Lackland Fisher House, organizing the weekly Bingo games."

"What were you doing all that time?" I asked, while refilling the parmesan cheese and red pepper shakers for the dining room tables.

"Kid stuff. Went to school. Helped my mom with her studies. Other kids lived with us at the Moonie house, so there was always someone to play with. Started drawing and taking art classes. Left San Antonio after high school, came to Tech on an art scholarship." He looked at the clock on the wall. "We got another thirty minutes before we open. Check the paper products on the tables and in the bathrooms."

"Sure."

Although I'd never seen his work, the other employees said he was very talented, especially with watercolors of the West Texas desert. His name was well known in the local art community, with several installations at the Ghost Dance Gallery on Texas Avenue. As soon I could afford it, I was buying something of his.

"Hey Lionel," I hollered from the supply closet. "We're down to the last six rolls of toilet paper."

"On the list."

It wasn't long before Mama's Pizza became my home and the employees, my family. I was just like everyone else who moved to Lubbock, I forgot about leaving, and I forgot about everyone I left behind.

That first summer of my friendship with Lionel was the best as we shared our love of pizza and books. We made a pact to read a book a week. It was an affordable challenge with Lou's Used Bookstore, a mile from the restaurant, selling paperbacks for fifty cents apiece. It was tip jar money well spent, plus a good walk for Raul and me.

Our first book was *Into the Wild* by Jon Krakauer. Based on the short life of Christopher McCandless, a college graduate, hiker, and wanderer who said goodbye to his family following graduation, the book focused mostly on McCandless' adventures on the American open road. In 1992 he hitchhiked to Alaska, where he followed an old mining trail with few supplies and the goal to live off the land. A short time later, he was dead. His decomposed body was found by a hunter in a converted bus. That slap of fate brought back my anger and grief. I was mad at Christopher McCandless for throwing his life away, just as I was mad at Brian.

Did Brian and Christopher make poor decisions? Maybe it was arrogance, thinking their reasoning skills were a match against nature's brute force. The answers didn't matter. The only thing that mattered is they were gone. Forever.

I thought of my mother's words over the years, the danger she associated with spontaneous living. It could cost a life to live in one carefree moment, never weighing the ifs, never absorbing the fear.

I should write Brian's mother a letter, some sort of communication acknowledging the loss of her son. After a week of indecision, I never found the right words for that letter. They never came, only the image of Brian, young and far brighter than a Blue Bird, golden next to anything I knew in this world. So I purchased a greeting card with a ready-made sentiment conveniently provided in the calligraphy script of a greeting-card maker. The image on the front was of a single cloud suspended in a blue sky. Inside I placed a Polaroid of Raul. He was sitting in front of the living room window in the garage apartment. The morning light showcased him in gold and white rays. I wrote a few sentences inside the card.

> *Dear Mrs. Ladner,*
> *This is Brian's dog, Raul. I don't know if he ever told you about him. He lives with me in Lubbock. I couldn't ask for a better friend.*
> *Sincerely,*
> *Kim*

I did not leave a return address on the envelope.

Reading, writing and sleeping was how I spent my first summer in Lubbock. I lived for my time at Mama's Pizza, especially if Lionel and I had a new book to discuss. It made the loneliness I chose much easier to live with.

I found my boss in the same place, most mornings, sitting at his desk, writing checks to vendors and making a grocery list for the White Swan delivery truck. I tied a red apron around my waist and began washing ten heads of Romaine lettuce, drying the individual leaves on a white towel next to the sink.

"I've got one question for you about this week's book. I finished it on Sunday.

What was the point? A beautiful, intelligent boy dies of starvation in a bus along the Sushana River in Alaska. It was a wasted life, total arrogance on his part, never considering the dangers of the wilderness."

Lionel looked up from the paperwork, "Kim, I haven't finished the book."

"I'm sorry. I . . . I was really disturbed by it. We can talk about it later."

"What I've read so far doesn't give the indication McCandless was arrogant, maybe naïve. He wanted to experiment with Thoreau's concepts of living on the land and in the moment."

"It's dangerous. Nature is a force man can't control. It's arrogant to think man has domain over nature. People jump into rivers or oceans and never come back."

He gave me a thoughtful look, then returned to his paperwork. I prepped the salads and pizza toppings, then made sure the bathrooms were clean. At eleven I unlocked the front door and went back to the prep station to slice lemons for iced tea. I looked up when I heard his voice, recognizing the tone and mono-syllable responses. Kyle. I peered around the corner and saw him and a brunette sit down at a table.

Lionel was standing next to me. "Okay, Kim. Customer up."

"Sorry, I just don't feel well right now. Would you be disappointed if I just went home?"

"You're kidding, right?"

"I'm really sick. I might throw up." I peered around the corner, again. Lionel watched me.

"Who's in the dining room, Kim?"

"No one special. Guy and a girl. Oh, Lionel. Please don't ask me about that guy out there. It's bad. Don't make me wait on them."

"Are you embarrassed to be a waitress in front of those two? Is it the guy or your ego keeping you from doing your job?"

"No, it's not that. You know I love working here. It's him. I just can't face him."

"You got to face him. He may come in here to eat for the next four years or even longer. Face him or quit the job. That's the choice. You skirt around it, it will never go away. I'm back here watching if you're afraid of him. Give them the menus. Now, go on."

I approached the table with two large glasses of water and menus. I placed both in front of Kyle and the girl. Neither one of them looked up at me.

"I'll be back to take your order in a few minutes." I practically ran back to the kitchen.

"Well, I didn't hear anything."

"Neither one of them looked at me. They were staring at each other."

"Exactly. Most people live each day going from point A to B, rarely thinking about the past or what's in the future."

"Not too long ago I had a bad experience with that guy. He probably doesn't even remember."

"Get over him, just like he has you. Now, get their order and let's get on with the day."

I went back to the table, where they sat, smiling at each other and holding hands. She was a pretty girl with thick, brown hair worn off her shoulders. She was wearing a navy tank top with a glittery red heart in the center. *Better guard that sparkly heart. He'll walk all over it with cleats.*

"May I take your order?"

He answered for both of them, looking directly at me. "Large pepperoni pizza, two Cokes." His eyes did not deflect a memory or even a slight reconnection of me. Just like Homecoming Ben, Corpus Christi Kyle didn't know I existed. I wrote down the order and walked back to the kitchen, feeling hot tears roll down my face.

"Kim. Come on. Don't let him steal today or tomorrow. He doesn't get any more of your time." Lionel hugged me, then began filling their order by placing a ladle of tomato sauce in the middle of raw dough.

"I really hate men. I do. Creeps, all of them. They're either mauling you or breaking your heart. It's like they're too lazy to scratch the surface of a girl, a person behind the eyes, the face, the body."

"You don't hate me."

I didn't say anything. I served the pizza and refilled their glasses before they asked. When they left, I cleaned up Kyle and his date's table. It didn't surprise me there wasn't a tip.

I worked the rest of the shift, quiet and sullen. When I punched the clock, Lionel handed me all the money in the tip jar and a paper napkin with a drawing of me and Raul, sitting on a mountain with rays of sunshine dancing off our bowed heads.

"A weekend in the Davis Mountains would do you a lot of good. It's a special place. Very healing. Maybe you should plan a trip in the fall. Too hot in the summer."

"Is this Carlos Castaneda speaking?"

"No, not at all. I've spent a lot of weekends there, clearing my head. It's a dangerous thing if you do all your living there, in your head, I mean. It disconnects you from others."

I knew he was referring to me. I didn't care.

"Kim, you won't starve to death like the kid in the book if you spend a weekend with nature. There's a cool lodge built in the mountains, white adobe building with handmade furniture. There's even a cafeteria if you get hungry. Indian Lodge. Dirt cheap."

"I'll look into it. 'Night, Lionel." When I left, I looked back on the lights still burning in the restaurant. I could see Lionel drawing. He was always drawing on napkins and pizza boxes, these beautiful images few people realized were right in front of them, but Lionel saw them, every single one of them.

21

I didn't make it to the Davis Mountains until the spring of my senior year. Kathy Renee was the reason why. She was visiting for a week that spring, and in order to fill those long, long days, I scheduled a trip to the Indian Lodge for us. If we were lucky, the healing power of nature, the antidote Lionel pushed over the years, would mend our fractured relationship. Kathy Renee probably thought of the Davis Mountains as a Texas version of the Camino, a pilgrimage through the Pyrenees to the shrine of the Apostle James in northwest Spain. I never visualized the French Pyrenees when considering the arid terrain of cactus and Ponderosa pines rising above the Chihuahuan Desert of the Davis Mountains. The only thing French we would find in West Texas was a french fry. And that would be covered in gravy.

If my sister and I were unlucky, this trip would be another disaster, like the vacations of our childhood—Kathy Renee riding waves, while I choked on saltwater. Besides, we were too old for family vacation and functions. My responsibility to those traditions was an annual Christmas trip to Pasadena. They reciprocated by coming to Lubbock on my birthday. I loved them, but I didn't want to be around them. Time only deepened that sentiment.

Kathy Renee graduated from a certified nursing assistant program at San Jacinto Community College, two years prior. With a steady paycheck and the independence of living in her own home, she changed in many ways, but one thing stood steadfast in her character, the unwavering faith. She continued sending me holy cards and stating her prayer intentions on my behalf.

I haven't changed much over the years, either. I remained in Lubbock, working at Mama's Pizza. For recreation, I participated in the exclusive book club Lionel and I formed. In between those times, I attended class. On rare occasions, I'd see Cindy and Josh, who were soon to be husband and wife. My life was the perfectly carved pie; there wasn't room for portioning out any additional energy and commitment to anything other than Raul. I was comfortable, not necessarily happy, in my self-absorbed world.

Now with my sister coming for a week, I would have to adjust my world. I didn't want her disrupting what I had created. When I picked her up at the Preston Smith Airport, my mind set was neither genial or hospitable. I was driving a used Ford Ranger I bought from one of the guys who worked at Mama's. It was cheap on fuel and got me where I needed to go. I left Raul at the apartment. There wasn't enough room for all of us in the cab of the truck, especially since Kathy Renee was travelling with her portable Mass kit and boxes of holy cards.

I was forty minutes late. She was standing right outside the airport, matching luggage, carpenter jeans with a tapered ankle, red T-shirt tucked in with coordinated red Ked tennis shoes. A wide red ribbon circled her waist, bow tied at the belly button. I immediately thought my mother was still dressing her. They probably shopped together every Saturday.

I didn't get out of the truck to hug her or pick up her luggage. I saw the immediate hurt on her face but shrugged it off and rolled down the driver's window.

"No money to park in the garage. Just get in. Hurry before a cop gets me."

She threw her luggage in the truck bed, opened the door, and slid over to me for a hug.

"Oh, Kim. It's so good to see you. It's been too long."

She smelled like Love's Baby Soft cologne. I was surprised it was still on the market. Giving her a polite pat on the back, I released the clutch and we jerked away from the airport.

"We'll be here for just the night. I planned a little side trip for us," I explained, pulling into the grass in front of the garage apartment. "Thought you might like to eat at Mama's Pizza tonight. That's where I've been working all these years."

"Of course, I would. How fun!"

I let her carry her luggage up the stairs.

"Hope you don't mind sleeping on the couch. It's a small place," I offered, unlocking the door. Raul jumped off the couch and greeted her like a long lost relative with wet kisses and a wagging tail. From the first time they met, a bond was established. With dogs and babies, Kathy Renee won every time.

"There's linens on the couch. Put your suitcase on the coffee table. Just don't have much stuff." I pushed the coffee table against the wall.

"I love your little house, Kim," she said, rubbing Raul's back.

"Make yourself at home. I need to study." I closed the door to my bedroom and let her and Raul enjoy each's company; kindred spirits they were of affable personas and positive thoughts. I found my own comfort between the pages of Anne Patchett's *Patron Saint of Liars*. It wasn't a selected read from the book club with Lionel. A professor had mentioned it in class. My hair rose on my neck when she said the title. Now, I was lost in a home for unwed mothers in Habit, Kentucky, a million miles away from my sister and my lifelong resentment of her perfected soul and the effect it put on my mother and father. And me. I was an afterthought. After her. Always.

I didn't emerge from the bedroom until it was time for supper. It's not that I didn't care about her. I would cry if she died unexpectedly, so there's some assurance my heart wasn't completely black. I just really didn't want to talk; I wasn't used to being around people, and I certainly wasn't used to talking about the past. I was determined to manage every conversation to exclude the Church and our parents.

"Do you need to shower before dinner?"

"I'll wash my hands but, first, Mom got you something. Here." It was expertly wrapped, as only my mother would do. I folded the gift wrap and placed the yellow ribbon on the coffee table. Inside the box was a silver bracelet with holy medals for St. Mary, St. Christopher, and St. Jude. Mom had my soul protected with these patron saints of everything, travelers, and lost causes. But that was my mother, covering all bases with everything she did. I put the bracelet on the coffee table.

"Don't you want to wear it?"

"No. I don't. I don't go to church anymore. The reason why is none of your business."

She didn't say anything, but my words took the light out of the room. Raul sighed on the couch. Kathy Renee got up and walked into the bathroom. I surveyed the living room, noting she had redecorated with icons and crucifixes. A clear methodology was demonstrated.

She had unpacked her suitcase, lining her clothes neatly on the coffee table, even though I told her a few hours ago we'd only spend one night here. She never listened. Next to her colorful array of shorts and matching T-shirt was a miniature altar, a small statue of Our Lady of Lourdes, and a Saint Raphael prayer candle.

When she returned from the bathroom, I was inspecting the prayer candle.

"Do you really travel with an altar?"

"I do. Mom hasn't been feeling well, so my prayer intentions have been for her healing."

"What's wrong with Mom?"

"She's tired all the time. Just not herself." Kathy began refolding the neatly arranged shorts and shirts on the coffee table. I made her nervous. That was clear.

"Mom's going through menopause, Kathy. Normal process. No need to conjure saints and the Virgin Mother of God to make her feel better."

She didn't look up at me when I said it. For a moment the room was silent, and I was afraid she'd start crying. I needed to be kinder—where was my sisterly love? This is how I always felt with her, guilty and angry.

Since I was a kid, the perpetual weight of being her sister choked me. I resented all of it, the special shoes, hearing aids, the flash cards, all of it, because . . . she took my mother from me. When I lashed out in anger, she'd return every cruelty with kindness. I couldn't control the monster in me, the jealousy, the rage, so I hid within the pages of a book or ignored all of them. It was best to stay away. *Mea culpa, mea culpa, mea maxima culpa . . . in my thoughts and in my words, in what I have done, and in what I have failed to do.*

Rationale begin to creep in between the awkward silence between us and Kathy's averted eyes. This was the first day of our vacation together. It was up to me to make it better, so I touched her shoulder.

"Let's go eat. This is on me."

She looked up and smiled at me.

We walked to Mama's Pizza together, talking and laughing every step of the way. It never took much to make her happy.

I reserved a special table for us, so we could enjoy a leisurely meal without the need to rush with the constant noise from college students guzzling pitchers of beer and talking with their mouths full of pepperoni and cheese. Lionel insisted on serving us.

"Welcome, Kathy," Lionel offered, pulling a corkscrew from a bottle of Chianti and pouring two ample glasses. "Compliments of the house."

"Thank you so much, Lionel." Picking up her wine glass, Kathy Renee reached across the table, clinking her wine glass against mine. "Cheers to the best sister."

Lionel looked at me and our eyes locked. He saw it. He knew immediately I was jealous of her and gave me a disappointing frown.

"I'll come back for your order in a minute. Enjoy the wine."

We decided on a large Margarita pizza, between sips of the warm, full-bodied Chianti. Flush with wine and simple happiness, something I never quite developed, Kathy Renee talked me into the classic Caesar salad with anchovies and crushed pods of garlic. Just like her taste in men, my sister's choice was based on pure instinct, not what others would think or improve of. My litmus test for the male species was based on the Blue Bird standard. It obviously wasn't working for me, but at least I knew what to expect. I measured my disappointment in how easy it was to forget each kiss, each touch, each nameless boy I met as an undergraduate in college. Meaningless, but safe.

"Are you still dating that Arab?" The second glass of wine encouraged me to go for the jugular.

That look. Confusion. Pain. I'm sure she questioned herself, *Did I hear her correctly?* She touched the back of her ear lobe to adjust the hearing aid.

"Elie? Elie from Damascus? Gosh, Kim, it's been so long since we've had a real sister talk, I was sure you forgot all about him."

"Guess it's the Gulf War going on that has me thinking about him. What ever happened to him or Matthew, the guy you dated in high school?"

"Matthew's married. Has three children. I still see Elie. We are good friends. I see him at church, but I am not the type of girl he wants to marry. He will marry a Syrian girl. That's better for the family. I'm not hurt by that."

"Don't you think about getting married?"

"No. I don't. I have a job and church, my family. I'm happy. What about you?"

"I'll never marry. Haven't met a man I respect enough to even like."

"Oh, Kim. There's lots of nice men. I don't want you to have a lonely life."

"Too late, little sister. It's the life I want."

Lionel served our food on that last bit of conversation, frowning at me as he placed the pizza in the center, and squeezed a fresh lemon over the salad.

"Always one for light dinner conversation. Huh, Kim?"

I didn't look up but served my sister the first slice of pizza as a form of penitence for my rudeness. We ate our meal in civility, laughing about our breath after anchovies, following the melted cheese as it trailed from the pizza slice to our opened mouths. Two cannolis stuffed with mascarpone and studded with chocolate chips ended the meal. Lionel refused to bring the bill.

"Let me tip, Kim. Let me tip him," sang my sister, pulling a $20 bill from her wallet and anchoring it underneath the candle holder on the table.

We walked home, linking arms, slightly drunk and very full. I unlocked the door, grabbed Raul's leash behind it, then turned on the living room lights.

"Go on in. I've got to walk him. I won't be long."

When I came back, she was already in bed, making a nest out of quilts and pillows on the couch. She smiled at me.

"Want to play cards or something?"

"No. I'm going to bed. Tired. We'll get up around six and leave. It's about a five-hour drive to the Indian Lodge."

I couldn't make myself lean over and kiss her or even wish her a good night's sleep. Something that simple. I just couldn't. I would not allow myself the luxury of affection and a relationship. I had to make it to graduation in this town. I couldn't soften my heart until I was out of here.

I undressed in the dark bedroom, then stood near the closed door, listening for any sounds she would make. I heard them, whispers in a well-known rhythm, a lyric she had sung all her life. *Glory be to the Father, and to the Son, and to the Holy Spirit. As it was in the beginning is now, and ever shall be, world without end.*

I found myself crying, craving the touch of her hand, the warmth of her hug, the sweetness of her love for me. I hesitated at the door. I was afraid. Afraid to leave the security of the bedroom. Afraid to open the door and say, "Good night, sister. I love you. I'm glad you're here. You mean the world to me." Too much vulnerability in that kind of emotion. I'd be drowning in the undertow, never to return to shore, fighting the currents of Brian, Ben, and Kyle. I needed a rationale thought to buoy myself upon. I couldn't open that door without a reason; my love for her was not enough. Then I remembered. I had bought her a gift a few days ago. I did have a reason to open that closed bedroom door. I purchased a book at Our Lady of Perpetual Help Gift Store near campus. Turning the light on, I dug it out of my backpack. It was still inside the paper bag.

"Kathy Renee, I forgot to give you something," I said, opening the bedroom door.

"Hold on. I got a flashlight." A beam of light shone in my face.

"I hope you like it," I offered, sitting on the edge of the couch, handing her the book. "Turn off the flashlight. It's right in my eyes." I didn't want her to see me crying.

"Let me read the title first. *Mary, the Second Eve.* I love it. Thank you, Kim." I took the flashlight from her hand and turned it off. In the dark, I hugged my sister with every ounce of being I had within me.

22

The drive to the Indian Lodge was close to five and half hours from Lubbock. A dry, crisp air in the low seventies pushed us along Highway 87, through Odessa and Midland, towns of oil fields and trailer parks, mansions and adobe houses, wind-blown and sand-colored. They were lonesome places, despite the oil field rocking horses and their continuous up and down motion, producing fossil fuel and billionaires at a phenomenal rate. When we drove through the town of Pecos, the chamber of commerce sign greeted us: "Pecos: Home of the First Rodeo and the World's Sweetest Cantaloupes!" Nestled in a valley on the west bank of the Pecos River, that little town caught the imagination of two sisters. We stopped at a fruit stand right outside the town, operated by an old man in a sweat-stained cowboy hat. He charged us fifty cents apiece for the cantaloupes, wrapping each one in a paper towel, soon used as a dining napkin.

"You girls got a pocketknife for those cantaloupes case you want to eat 'em now?"

"No, sir. We didn't even think of that, did we, Kim? All we thought of was tasting the world's sweetest cantaloupes."

"Well, I'll fix you ladies up." He pulled a pocketknife from his jeans' pocket and placed each cantaloupe on a cutting board near the register. I immediately thought the knife and cutting board hadn't been cleaned with hot soap and water since they day they were purchased, but I remained silent, not wanting to deflate my sister's joy or the salesmanship of the old man.

He cut the cantaloupes in half, then cut them again, until there were twelve perfect crescent moons of fruit on the cutting board.

"Just help yourself, girls. Best to eat 'em fresh, just like this."

Kathy Renee helped herself to several pieces, the juices running down the length of her bare forearms.

"You're right. These are the sweetest cantalopes."

The old man and I laughed with her, agreeing. We were back on the road in thirty minutes with watery orange stains on the front of our T-shirts, and the pleasant memory of eating fruit at a roadside stand in a little town called Pecos.

We traveled along the eastern edge of the Chihuahuan Desert, the same route made by the Eighth Infantry of the U.S. Army in its pursuit of Comanches, Kiowas, and Apaches, the last remaining tribes of Indians in nineteenth-century West Texas. I imagined these people were hardy. My view out of the truck windshield was of rock formations, mesquite, and prickly pear cactus. Not much to eat in that terrain. I remember my junior-high history teacher saying those tribes survived on dried deer dung to keep from starving. Her lesson was stopped by the howls of laughter from the students in that Texas history class. Of course, not many of them got the relevant point of starvation, and the slow death of the Southwest Indians and their culture. Menopausal and minimal as a history teacher, Mrs. Martin failed to rise above the crude jokes and laughter of boys and girls, amused by people eating animal crap.

That memory, along with the ones we made that day, floated out the truck windows as I drove toward the one oasis this desert held, Balmorhea, a spring-fed pool and park created by Roosevelt's Civilian Conservation Corps during the Great Depression. We stopped there and ate the peanut butter and jelly sandwiches that I had made that morning. Swinging our legs as we sat on the tail gate of the truck, my sister looked happy, petting Raul and feeding him the crust from her sandwich.

By early afternoon, we pulled into the Indian Lodge parking lot where we were greeted by adobe buildings rising from the soft grays, yellows, and browns of the Davis Mountain foothills. The lodge stood stark white against the liquid blue of the sky. The lodge, created during the CCC program, was made by men desperate for work and skilled by generations doing such work. The adobe walls, the furniture, and interior ceilings were hand-hewed, knotted cedar and pine in colors of warm reds and yellows. Our room included an adobe fireplace and a hand carved rocking chair and desk. I put a pillow on the floor next to the fireplace for Raul, but he chose the foot of the bed after a few minutes.

"Hey, there's a pool. Let's go." Kathy was standing at the window, framed in hand-hewed pine.

"Go ahead. I'm tired. Think I'll read a while."

"Bring your book to the pool."

Why shouldn't I? It was something I enjoyed as a child, all those years ago at the Villa with Granny. Letting my guard down, I smiled at her and reached for my bathing suit in the opened suitcase.

The afternoon beneath the cloudless sky was spent with Wally Lamb's *She's Come Undone.* The antagonist was clearly Mrs. Price, who should have been shot for feeding her daughter potato chips and Pepsi throughout her childhood. I'd occasionally put my book down and watched Kathy Renee in the water. She didn't possess the grace of most swimmers, the rhythmic strength of arms dipping into the water, so close to the left ear and then the right, rising in and out of the liquid blue. She didn't know how to dive but came in and out of the pool with a wild scream followed by a belly buster, a full-bodied thrust into the water. She laughed at each attempt to make the splash larger and larger. She was enjoying herself, even though her cheap, thin bathing suit sagged with water, and the elastic around the butt was about gone. She was happy despite the fact her overuse of zinc oxide across the bridge of her nose gave her a clown appearance. Just happy. And me? I still feared the water, watching everyone interact with life as the calculating observer from the sidelines.

We ate in the lodge's restaurant that evening, a place stuck in time with waitresses in white nurses' uniforms and thick, white ceramic dishware. We ordered fried chicken with gravy, mashed potatoes, and peas. Desert was apple pie with vanilla ice cream. Each bite was worth every sweaty dollar bill I spent from the tip jar.

After dinner I walked Raul among the footpaths surrounding the lodge. I took the leash off, once I saw we were the only ones out that evening. He ran from me, dancing around a covey of quail he caught by surprise near the sage brush. The first of the evening stars appeared in the sky, as I wrapped my sweater closely around me and stared at the orange, red, and purple sinking of the sun behind the mountains as the day became night.

I don't remember falling asleep that night. I shared the double bed with Kathy, painfully remembering our childhood fights of the imaginary border between her side and mine. I rolled over, giving her my back and a faintly whispered good night. The few times I awoke, I saw the beam of her flashlight across the pages of *Mary, the Second Eve*.

When I woke early the next morning, she was gone. Raul and I found her sitting outside with a cup of coffee near the lodge restaurant. On the table next to her was an opened copy of *Our Daily Bread* and her rosary beads. She had completed her morning prayers before I registered sunlight through the motel window, and the simple fact that a new day had arrived.

"Morning." I pulled a chair next to her. "Thought we'd go to McDonald Observatory today. It's got some of the most powerful telescopes in the world. We can see other planets. Not as great as going tonight, but I thought we'd go to Marfa for the Ghost Lights."

"Fun! But I'm paying for supper tonight, Kim. I got a job, you know." She looked away from me at the vastness of the foothills of the mountains behind her. "I don't know about Ghost Lights. That sounds weird."

"It's a legend, mostly. People have seen odd lights near Highway 67, east of Marfa for years. Some think it's ghosts, UFOs, you name it. Might be fun to track some Ghost Lights."

"Never a good idea to mix with the occult. It's dangerous."

"The occult? Really? UFOs are of the occult? Or maybe folklore is of the occult? Come on, Kathy. Step out of the Middle Ages and the Church, a church that murdered thousands during the Inquisition, a church that protected pedophile priests."

Raul barked at me, when my voice became louder and more defensive. Kathy patted him underneath the table, refusing to look up at me.

"My faith is not in men or women in the church. My faith is in God."

"How do you explain it, then? The centuries of greed and abuse?"

"Jesus said to St. Peter, 'Upon this rock I will build my church, and the gates of hell shall not prevail against it.' He never promised life would be perfect on earth, or even human beings could be trusted to do good. I'm not excusing anything, but the Church has also built hospital and schools for the poor. It's supported great scientists and the arts. That church is also your church, Kim."

"There's that ying-yang of good and evil with Satan right in the middle. I've heard all this before. It's not my church. If you thought beyond the convenient answers you've been given all your life, maybe you'd see what I saw."

"Why do you hate me? Why? You call me, invite me here, and insult me every chance you get."

Raul began growling at me. I ignored him and stared at my sister. Her neck and face were completely red; she was on the verge of crying.

"Yes, and you can't return the insult, because of the golden rule, 'Do unto others, as you would have them do unto you.' St. Luke or St. Matthew? I can't remember which, but I learned it just like you when I was a kid, then I had to go out into the world and see what people were really capable of."

"Do you want me to go home, Kim? I can take a bus from here."

I looked at her a long time and thought. I really didn't want her to go home. I wanted her here. I just couldn't stop my mouth, knowing full well it was a waste of energy to argue faith with her. She was unmovable.

"No, I don't. Look. I'm sorry. Forget what I said. Just words. Don't take anything I say too seriously. I'm not used to being around people and making small talk."

And just like I thought she would, she jumped up from the chair, threw both arms around me, and said, "I love you, Sissy." Raul finally stopped growling at me.

After a long, morning walk with Raul, I came back to the room and showered. I decided to leave him here while we visited the observatory. I'm sure dogs weren't allowed; besides, I wanted to participate in the Solar Viewing Program with live telescope images of the sun. I couldn't let my sister have all the fun while I sat outside the observatory holding Raul's leash.

She was waiting on me, sitting on the bed, scratching Raul's belly.

Dressed in a tank top with shorts, Kathy's attire matched perfectly with the hot-pink hibiscus exploding on her shirt and shorts. On her lips a hot-pink gloss shimmered. I had to look twice, because I hadn't noticed her wearing make-up before, but there were two perfect ovals of pink blush on each check and smeared mascara underneath her eyes. She completed the look with a black fanny pack.

We rode to the observatory, talking about the different telescopes used there, as she read to me from the brochure I picked up at the lodge. She was painstakingly slow, and I occasionally gave her a side glance, watching her moving lips, as she practiced the enunciation of words, before speaking them out loud. I felt a pang of guilt, realizing how effortlessly it was for me to read.

It was a beautiful spring day in West Texas, the thistle, black-eyed Susan, and the Indian paintbrush dropped colors of yellow, red, and pink against the backdrop of the desert. Our hair whipped around our faces as we rode in the opened-widowed truck. It was probably the highlight of our day. When we arrived at the observatory, the parking lot was filled with school buses from Val Verde County. Once we stepped inside, we were ushered into a whirlwind of activity jammed packed of schoolchildren, laughing and talking through every exhibit and tour given. Kathy took it in stride, enjoying the children and the nervous teachers trying to corral them. For me, it was a reminder why I chose to be a librarian with the most quoted words of the day being, "Quiet, please."

After completing the observatory tour, I drove back to the lodge to pick up Raul then on to Marfa for chili rellenos at Mando's Drive-In, where we were greeted by chickens foraging in the parking lot. Inside, the décor was informal with cement and tile floors, so bringing Raul in was not a problem. I fed him crumbles of cotija studded with chorizo from our appetizer plate.

"We'd like to order margaritas on the rocks made with your best tequila," Kathy Renee said to the waitress. I was shocked.

"Spoken like a pro, sister."

"We are of legal drinking age."

"Dutifully noted."

It was a beautiful meal and I forgot for a while of my need to put her in her place or perhaps, my need to feel superior to her. We ordered another round of margaritas.

"What kind of tequila are you using?" I asked the waitress.

"It's made from a 100 percent Tequilana Weber Agave. Good quality, out of the Jesus Maria region of Arandas, Jalisco, Mexico."

"Sounds like serious tequila, almost biblical," I laughed.

"Yes. It's really a sipping tequila, not meant for margaritas," the waitress clipped in a snotty tone. Absolutely everything in life had a class system. I was glad my sister didn't catch that remark nor possess the very human ability to keep tabs on one-upmanship. Licking the salt off the rim of her glass, she was elated to be drinking a tequila made in the land of Jesus and Mary.

"Let's head out to the Ghost Lights when we're done."

"Just for a little while, Kim. I'm not so sure this is a good thing."

"Don't look at it as mixing with the supernatural and the devil. Look at it as observing an atmospheric phenomenon, much like the observatory today minus the screaming brats."

"They were cute. I didn't mind them at all."

"Of course, not. That's the difference between me and you. I mind every-thing—a lot."

With Raul sitting on Kathy's lap, we parked the truck among five other cars in a field east of Marfa. This is where it was supposed to happen. I waited ten minutes, before opening the truck door, taking Raul and walking around. The night sky was on fire with a million stars, the Orion Constella-tion, the brightest among the others.

"Come on, Kathy. Let's try to find the Seven Sisters. Remember Dad showing them to us after that hurricane?

"Okay." She reluctantly left the sanctuary of the truck cab, following me and Raul as we walked farther out into the dark field.

"What's that constellation called?" I stopped, pointing to the sky, where three stars gathered next to Orion.

"It's part of Orion. Orion's Belt with those three stars. Also called the Three Sisters."

"That's right. We were reminded of that today at the observatory. The names are Alnitak, Alnilam, and Mintaka."

Suddenly, there was a swirl of lights before us. Raul made a low, guttural growl. I petted him, trying to calm him, noting the hair on his back was standing straight up.

"What's that?" Kim cried, clutching my arm.

Those same bright lights that seemed far away now hovered near us, changing colors from white to gold, then red. Just as quickly, they disappeared. Kathy ran to the truck. I heard the door slam behind me. She whistled for Raul to follow her, but he didn't. He wouldn't leave my side.

Patiently we waited in the field for the lights to return. I turned to walk back toward the truck, after waiting several minutes with Raul panting by my side. The lights returned, this time moving closer to me, then encircling Raul. Around his head, then his torso, swirling brilliant white, gold, and red ribbons of light. The red light touched Raul's head, creating an aura of his animal spirit, noble and fierce as the West Texas sun. I pulled Raul closer to me, and the light went out, the remaining ribbons of brilliant red and white moved toward the open sky, then disappeared.

I stood with Raul, waiting until the unison of car motors started, followed by their headlights igniting the field. Raul barked at the cars and trucks, as they began moving onto the paved road. I wondered what the people in those cars and trucks thought. Did they see what I saw? Maybe I saw what I wanted to see. With shaking hands, I reached down to pet Raul, assuring him before walking back to the track. I was only a few feet from it, when Kathy Renee began pounding on the horn.

"I want to go home, now," Kathy Renee shouted from the opened window.

"We're leaving. Stop blowing the horn."

I started the truck and backed out of the field, driving along Highway 90. I looked over at her as she pulled a Rosary out of her purse and began silently praying; her fingers moving quickly over each well-worn bead.

"You shouldn't be afraid of what we saw, Kathy. It could have been a number of things."

She didn't answer; she was praying. I waited quietly for her to make the sign of the cross and put her Rosary back in her purse.

"There are just as many demons as there are angels in this world. Demons are fallen angels. You know that. We shouldn't invite them into our lives."

"I didn't send an invitation to Satan and his minions to join us, Kathy. I'm just a tourist doing a local attraction. Nothing more. But think about it, before answering me with some rote memorized explanation you were given as a child—did you ever think this is all there is?"

"What are you saying?"

"That what is before you and me, right now, is all we get as humans. There's no hell, no heaven. This is it."

"I don't have to think about it. There is a heaven and hell."

"Heaven and hell are right here. On earth. We live it every day."

"Kim, how can you not believe? You only have to love someone with all your heart to know there is something greater than us that can't be explained or seen. It's the Trinity. It is the perfect definition of love."

"That's a convenient explanation, but why should I torture myself with a philosophical conversation with someone working on sainthood? Here's the truth, little sister. This life. It's all we get. There's nothing more. No guardian angels watching over our sleep. No virginal mother whispering to Jesus to answer our prayers. No merciful, forgiving Father."

"There is, Kim. I pray every day you come to know this."

"Save your prayers for yourself."

"Tell me. What have I done to cause you to feel this way toward me? I really want to know."

"Okay. It's simple. You changed all of us. You. Your birth, your poor health and learning disabilities, made everyone anxious and unhappy. Mom and Dad were never the same. You took Mom away from me, and even Dad. Maybe I'm jealous, you had their attention, apparently God's, too."

It was out now. Never to be taken back again as it echoed off our hearts and into the cab of that truck. I was crying, but I wouldn't let her know that. I also stopped myself from revealing our mother's dark secret, biting my lip until the words tubal ligation and sterilization were evaporated into the night air.

"I didn't ask for this body, or this mind, that doesn't work like yours. What do you think it was like to have you as a sister, beautiful, intelligent, and there I was still confused by my multiplication facts in high school, but I accepted it. It was neither lucky or unlucky, it is how God made me."

"How can you believe in a God who does that to babies?"

"God gave me loving parents, a good home. I'm not bitter. I have peace. That's something you don't know about, Kim. There's no peace in your life. You don't like yourself or people. Why kind of life have you made?"

We rode to the lodge in silence. The last thing I heard her say was good night, followed by the rapid, breathless speech of her evening prayers. I rolled over and turned out the light.

The next morning, we drove back to Lubbock. I put her on a plane that evening.

23

"What did you tell her?" Lionel asked me as I refilled the salt and pepper shakers from the dining room tables.

"I saw something very strange out in that field. The Marfa Lights or Ghost Lights are what the locals call it. Unexplainable. That light followed me and Raul, coming in close, then suddenly spinning, then moving quickly away from us. It touched Raul. At least I think it did. I don't know. Maybe I imagined it all. Maybe it was what I wanted to see. The only spinning of lights I've ever heard of is the spinning of the sun in Fatima, a Marian pilgrimage. I do believe that happened, thousands upon thousands of people have seen it. My sister couldn't handle Marfa. I still don't know if she saw anything or not, but she thought the whole scene was evil. We got into a big fight."

"What did you say to her?"

"She wanted out of there. She said to believe or even seek something like that was evil, against the teachings of the Church. That led to an argument about religion, then family. It got personal and ugly."

"Were you having a decent time before the light show?"

"We were. I don't know, Lionel. She's been a burden my entire life. That shadow following me since I was a kid. Her needs. Her health. I've always resented it. We're total opposites personality-wise."

"If she's the total opposite of you, maybe you notice something in her completely lacking in yourself. She's a true believer, while you believe in nothing." Lionel began emptying the dishwasher, stacking silverware onto the prep counter.

I didn't respond to that remark but changed the subject completely as I grabbed an apron off the hook.

"What are we reading this week? There's a ton of books out about Princess Diana. We can explore more Catholic drama with Patchett's *Patron Saint of Liars*."

"Did you forget our conversation about the healing powers of nature?" Lionel slammed the dishwasher door closed.

"No. You don't understand or you're just not listening. You're an only child. Sibling rivalry can be bitter. I've always resented her. Always. My entire childhood was about Kathy Renee."

"Yeah, you're right. I'm an only child, but one thing I get really well is being an outsider looking in. Like your sister. I know what it's like for people to sum you up before you even open your mouth. My affliction in this world was being born black. Hers was being born too early. It's the luck of the draw. Sounds like she chose to make the best of it. What about you?"

"I don't put my insufficiencies on other people."

"Yes, you do. Your withdrawal from the world says it all. You're aloof, which most people interpret as you feeling superior to them. Come on, Kim. I mean, who the hell do you think you are?

Why, I'm a Blue Bird, I thought to myself, but Lionel didn't wait for a response from me. He walked out of the kitchen and out the delivery door, leaving me to prep for the lunch crowd by myself.

I didn't see him again until the night before graduation. I walked over to Mama's to get my paycheck, and the graduation gift he promised me. My parents were at my apartment with Raul. My sister didn't come, which didn't bother me in the least. Of course, she sent a graduation gift of a year's supply of holy cards and a liturgical calendar with a saint of the month theme.

Graduation weekend was one of the few times in my life I had my parents to myself. It was a short visit; they flew out that Sunday morning. Mom kept complaining about how tired she was, so I promised to be back from work in less than an hour.

When I walked into the restaurant, a twenty-by-thirty-inch frame covered in brown wrapping with a red bow was waiting for me at the hostess station. My name was spelled out in calligraphy across the paper. The letter *i* was accented with a heart. Apparently, our feud was over.

"Come on in the kitchen. Bring the painting," Lionel called out.

He was standing in front of the oven with both hands on his hips.

"It's my best work, Kim. You inspired it. Open it."

Behind the simple brown paper, a portrait of light exploded across the canvas. Yellow. Red. Orange. Purple. It was the Texas sky aflame in the desert. Below the kaleidoscope of hues sat a barefoot girl and her dog. Above their heads was a nimbus, painted in the Byzantine style of early Constantinople during the Middle Ages. Its effect with ethereal. I cried when I recognized the girl as myself with Raul.

"I've exhausted every approach of light you can find in the desert, sitting with a sketch book in my hand for hours at dawn, noon, and dusk. I've waited every hour for the colors to change, so I could find something new. I found it, and I put you and Raul in it. I couldn't stop thinking about the beauty of the desert, and your love for that dog. I dreamed this painting."

"I can't accept this."

"Accept it, Kim. You've been a good friend and employee. I'm painting another one with some slight alterations in the sky."

We hugged briefly, and I was the first to break away from his embrace, because I felt embarrassed by his generosity. Mostly, I felt I didn't deserve such a gift.

Six months later, Lionel's *Portrait of Light II* was purchased by a retired oil man at Ghost Dance Gallery on Texas Avenue. When the oil man's wife, the heiress to Halliburton saw it, she commissioned Lionel to paint a series of landscapes with alternating seasons and light. Lionel quit Mama's Pizza and moved to Santa Barbara, California. I got a postcard from him his first week there. On the front was a picture of a dog on a surfboard.

> *Dear Kim,*
> *Bring Raul and come live with me. Libraries are on every corner, and the ocean is beautiful. No undertows. No mean people.*
> *Love,*
> *Lionel*

24

I didn't move to California, but I finally got out of Lubbock, following the humiliation I endured as a bridesmaid at the wedding of Cindy Jones and Josh Giles. Wedding bells were ringing on the Morning Star Ranch, thirty sections of God's country located ten miles west of San Angelo. The ranch house was staged for the ceremony with Cindy, former Rattle Snake Queen, descending the iconic staircase, for acceptance of a new title, Mrs. Josh Giles. That very average and predictable man slipped a ring on her finger, one of her own choosing, and added a blue-chip stock to his portfolio. He'd never surpass his glory years as a Texas Tech football player or this day. It didn't matter. Josh was adored by his bride, and she was rich. The very dull Josh Giles was set for life; luck had everything to do with it.

I began enjoying the wedding the moment I arrived, despite my bridesmaid dress of fushia, bordering on Pepto Bismol pink, with its dowdy A-line cut and V-neck. All chosen by Cindy, who would never pale by comparison to her bridal party in her gown of embellished lace, Cathedral length train, and ruched bust. I wouldn't say it was exactly chaste white; dusk was a better description of the cloudy hue.

The "I do" exchange was about two minutes in length, followed by six hours of eating and drinking. Behind the main house, men were barbequing sides of beef with the celebrated cabrito on a rotating spit. My stomach did little flips with each interval of the spit.

Carrying a massive wooden plank with a roasted pig resting on top, four men in white chef coats signaled the commencement of overindulgence. Tables of salads, vegetables, pinto beans, pickles, onions, jalapenos, and flour tortillas surrounded the trinity of pork, beef, and goat. On the left-hand side of the food gauntlet were three kegs. A reserved white-clothed table stood behind the kegs, loaded with liquor and wine bottles. Next to it was a margarita machine the bride purchased for her husband with the repetitive wedding day refrain, "You just put in tequila, lime daiquiri mix, and ice. Flip it on, and you've got yourself a margarita!" Yes, life should be that simple every day. It certainly was for Cindy.

We two-stepped, three-stepped, and staggered the evening away to Sammy and the Midnighters underneath a cloudless Texas sky. I learned early in life that men think they own you if you dance with them. Ben Mullin was the first man to teach me. Tonight's selection was Roy. After the second dance, I asked him if his last name was Rogers.

"Who's that?" he mumbled in my right ear. I actually felt his words, a combination of spit mingled with beer on my ear lobe.

"Well, Roy, if I have to explain everything, it doesn't make it much fun for me." I excused myself and headed to the margarita machine, so I could drown my disappointment in the male species. He followed me.

"I can show you a good time if that's what you mean."

"Roy, our conversation is over. I've got a big headache from a lack of mental stimulation."

"What are you talking about?" He grabbed my hand as the initial notes from a fiddle began the "Cotton-Eyed Joe," luring wedding guests from their food and liquor, to link arms and kick their way through a song with the resounding refrain of "Bullshit." *Ah, such cultured pearls, these people were.*

But why question the culture? When in Rome, be a Roman. These people ate goat and cursed while they danced. There was some entertainment value in that. Roy held tightly to my waist, and I grabbed his belt loop as we moved in a choreographed circle on the dance floor. I was giving in, but I knew I would as I mentally counted all the football players who had wooed or punished me for being a girl. Add Roy to the list. I entertained the thought for why I saw football players, exclusively. It was my own choosing. Luck had nothing to do with it.

I allowed Roy to take my hand and lead me to the stables. Among horse dung, hay, and pitchforks, I succumbed to the last dance of the evening. The neighing of horses were within earshot and, for a moment, I thought I was in danger of having my head bashed in by a hoof.

I watched the St. Michael medal on a silver chain, swing from Roy's opened shirt. I thought of my sister, as a wave of sadness washed over me.

The sordid mess lasted less than five minutes. I emerged from the barn, in full site of the wedding guests, with hay in my hair and a rip in the back of my fuchsia gown.

Forever, I would be remembered as the slutty bridesmaid at Cindy and Josh's wedding, while Roy remained a celebrated member of the 1992 Texas Tech Raiders Football Team.

It was the perfect time to leave Lubbock for good. I got what I came here for—a library science degree. Never found a husband, unlike most of my friends, so I moved back to Pasadena. Things were happening there that I needed to see for myself.

Mom wasn't feeling well, something she and dad had alluded to for months. Even Kathy Renee mentioned it on our trip to Marfa. I needed to see for myself. I needed to see my mother.

I gave away most of my belongings to the staff at Mama's Pizza, which amounted to a box of rusted kitchen utensils and chipped dishes. I packed my clothes, the *Portrait of Light* from Lionel, and books in cardboard boxes I had picked up from Pinky's Liquor Store. The truck bed was lined with boxes, except for the *Portrait of Light*, which rested in the passenger seat with Raul, next to me. I drove home, stopping in Waco overnight.

The fifty-five-bucks-a-night motel sat next to a taxidermy and U-Haul rental business, all owned by the same woman, Juanita Frazer, a brute with dyed midnight black hair cut in a burr. I watched from the motel window as she moved U-Haul flatbed trailers by grabbing their metal tongues and pulling them to their final resting place in the parking lot. Occasionally, a skinny white man, who reminded me a lot of Jughead from the Archie's, emerged from the taxidermy business to assist her. The entire compound, motel, taxidermy shop and U-Haul Rental store reeked of embalming fluid.

Raul and I didn't get much sleep there. He whimpered in the night, while I tossed and turned with visions of Granny playing cards with the cigarillo-smoking Poco. Animal hides and heads decorated the walls of the room they played in.

We awoke with a start about 4 a.m. I turned on the bedside lamp and made sure the *Portrait of Light* was still resting against the TV stand. I made the effort yesterday to move everything out of the truck bed and cab inside the motel room. They were the only things of value I owned. In that dim light of dawn, my treasures were still in the room.

We went back to bed with the light on, as an uneasiness spread across the room. It was easy to lose your mind in an environment like this, and that's what happened almost a year later when a young man who thought he was the Messiah got sideways with the ATF, FBI, and the Texas National Guard. In the height of the fire fight, the self-proclaimed Messiah preached to the 911 operator about the Seven Seals in the Book of Revelation. Over seventy men, women, and children went out in a blaze of glory in that argument of separation of church and state. Raul and I left Waco without complimentary coffee at 6 a.m.

We arrived in Pasadena a few hours later. I pulled into the driveway, amid the early morning rush of a garage sale next door. Before I had a chance to get out of the truck, an older woman, rotund in shape and short in stature, was at the driver's window. She was wearing a Garanimals ensemble of matching shirt and capris imprinted with parrots and palm trees. I stared at her, until she began knocking on the glass. I slowly let the window down.

"You must be Kim. I'm Bunny. Your folks told me all about you. Now, get out of that truck and let me give you a hug. I'm a hugger. Hope that's okay." I opened the truck door and Raul leaped out in a smart move of escape.

I allowed Bunny to hug me and emitted a "Hi" when she squeezed the air out of my lungs in her strangle-hold.

"Oh, look at your puppy-dog. He'll just love it here. You know my son is a veterinarian, best one in Pasadena. I'll give you his number later. I got to run, lots of customers this morning!"

We both looked over into the yard next door, where at least fifteen people were scattered about the driveway and garage, picking up, putting down, and turning over in an assessment of the goods she offered.

"I do these once a month. Helps supplement my Social Security. Well, I know how glad your folks are to have you home. We'll visit soon. Promise!" Bunny bounded back across the yard with a final wave of goodbye.

"Welcome home, Baby." I turned around and there was Dad. His appearance shocked me; he had changed so much since last I saw him. Exhaustion rested in the hollows beneath his eyes.

"Daddy." We hugged for a while with Raul jumping on both of us. Dad broke away first, looking into my face with tears in his eyes.

"I don't want you to be surprised when you see your mom."

"I just saw her at graduation."

"She's started the chemo."

"I didn't think she'd have to start chemo right away. Both of you were nonchalant on the phone. Tiny tumor she called it."

I put my head in my hands, thinking this was typical of my parents. Hide the facts as long as you can.

"What else are you not telling me?" I began to cry, then realized Raul was still running around the front yard, sniffing his new territory. "Get over here, Raul."

I walked back to the truck and got the *Portrait of Light* out of the cab and a suitcase.

"Kim. Listen to me. Now is not the time to show emotion. You'll just upset her. She wants your return to be a happy one. She sees this as a chance to reunite you with your sister."

"What does Kathy have to do with Mom's cancer? What?"

"Your mother wants some peace. That's all. Give her that. You stayed away for four years without really talking to any of us. It hurt her. Look, we'll talk later. She's knows we're out here. Let's go on in."

I picked up the bottom of my shirt and wiped my face with it, revealing my bra. My dad watched me, embarrassed and sad. That look, just like Kathy's that night in Marfa. I had alienated him, as well.

We walked into the house together, Raul following closely behind. Mom was in the recliner, still in her night gown, something I had never seen her in past seven in the morning.

"Hi, honey. Hope you had a good drive home." She got up to kiss me. I offered my cheek and stepped away from her.

"Let me get a shower first, Mom. We'd stayed the night at a creepy motel in Waco. Didn't bother showering this morning."

I left my parents standing side by side in the living and walked to my old bedroom. Nothing had changed. My Nancy Drew altar was still by the window. I put the *Portrait of Light* against the bookcase and sat on the edge of the bed. Raul jumped on the bed next to me. I could hear my parents talking about me through the closed bedroom door. My sister's name was repeated twice by my mother, then their conversation stopped.

Just like the prodigal son, I returned home after sleeping with pigs and squandering what my parents had given me. Kathy Renee truly deserved to be the favorite.

25

The first month back in Pasadena Raul developed an ear infection. In fact, both of us did. Moving from a climate with zero humidity to one of ninety percent on average was wreaking havoc with our sinuses. This made the job interview process horrific for me, but nothing was as bad as seeing Raul constantly swiping his paw across his right ear. After a few days, I removed his collar, as the ID charm jiggled with every swipe, keeping us both up at night. One month home, and we were sick and tired.

I eventually called the vet, the son of Bunny, the hugger. When I asked Mom for money for the office visit, she didn't flinch. I immediately became suspect.

"Just pay me back when you can, Kim. Do wear something nice to the office. Bunny's son is quite successful and a decent young man. He's about your age."

"Mom, I want the guy to treat my dog, not propose to me."

Mom gave a nervous laugh that seemed to exhaust her, like most things these past few weeks. She was slowly slipping into another world, day by day, fading from this life, becoming thinner and thinner. It grieved me, but I didn't show it. It wasn't because I didn't love her. I did, more than I ever showed or took the time to tell her. The best I could do was to humor her, like my father.

"I've got the cutest red dress in my closet. Polka dot. Vintage clothes are all the rage now. You'd be adorable in it with a pair of red high heels. Let's look in my closet."

I followed her into the bedroom, where she swung opened the double-door closet, taking dress after dress out of the back of the closet, mumbling to herself and laughing. Twelve dresses, sprinkled with polka dots, lay discarded in an exhausted heap on the bed, before the search was over. Holding a red and white polka dot dress with a tiny, red belt around the waist and a full skirt, my mother proclaimed, "Here it is!"

"Mom!"

"Oh honey, you'd look great in this. A woman's best color is red. Now, try it on, so we can see if it fits."

I pulled off my jeans and T-shirt, painfully aware I didn't have on a bra, knowing how much it would disappoint her, even embarrass her because of my lack of discipline and femininity. I was not the matching panty and bra girl she once dressed. "Where did I go wrong?" registered in her eyes.

"Well, it fits. Does it really matter what I wear? I'll do it for you, Mom."

"Yes, it matters. There's nothing wrong with looking your best."

"Okay, okay, but I draw the line with a red, plastic headband you may have hidden in the dresser."

"That dress got your father, a long time ago," she said, sitting on the edge of the bed. "He's been a good husband and father. I've had a good life."

"Don't talk in past tense. I hate it."

"I'm dying, Kim. I'm not afraid, so don't be sad about it. I'd just like to know the family will be all right when I'm gone. You and Kathy Renee will get along and look after your dad."

"It's ridiculous to have this conversation. You're going to get better. M. D. Anderson is the best cancer facility in the world. Besides, I get along with my sister, even if I don't always show it. I love her if that's what you want to hear."

Raul jumped on the bed, breaking the moment of intimacy between us that I knew would never come again.

"I really don't like him on the bed, Kim." She stood up, picked up the dresses, and began hanging them back in the closet.

"Don't forget the red shoes, Mom. It completes the look."

She smiled at me, then reaching back into the closet, she pulled out a shoe box.

"I love the pointed toes on these."

I took the box from her and gave her a kiss on the cheek.

"We'll be back in an hour or so. I'll help you with supper. Why don't you rest while we're gone."

"Be nice to that man, Kim. Just smile and say something nice."

"Sure, Mom. I'll say something nice."

Bayview Pet Care was located off Red Bluff, nearly forty-five minutes from the house. I was late for the two o'clock appointment, which kept Raul and me in the waiting room for an additional hour. It wasn't easy refraining him, as he sniffed every dog in there, while sending the cat owners and their felines scampering for the exit or complaining at the front desk. When we were finally seen by the vet, my patience was gone. The thought of saying anything nice, as instructed by my mother, left my mind hours ago.

"Kim and Raul Hodges. Good to meet you. Wayne Williams, but everyone calls me Wayne-O. Mom has told me all about you."

He was wearing brown penny loafers with a matching brown belt and a brown and tan plaid shirt tucked into brown pants. The last man I saw dressed in earth tones was my dad when I was twelve.

"Why?"

"Why what?"

"Why does everyone call you Wayne-O? What does the O stand for?"

"I don't know. Never really thought about it. Just accepted it. Why does everyone call you Kim?"

I tried not to roll my eyes, as I was entrusting him with the care of my dog.

"I remember you from junior high. Though I was a few grades ahead of you. My reading class met after yours. I was a Red Bird."

The minute he said Red Bird, I knew what the O in Wayne-O stood for. Ordinary. Not only were the Red Birds ordinary, they were very aggressive, especially the boys. Those older Red Bird boys were entertained for months by stomping on ketchup packages from the cafeteria, squealing with laughter when the ketchup splattered on the floor and walls. They even targeted the back of girls' pants with exploding ketchup packages.

The Red Bird girls tortured me in the bathroom that night during the

133

junior high dance. Red Bird girls and boys struggled reading *The Outsiders,* while the Blue Birds sailed through *Great Expectations* with Pip. The thought of this man, this Red Bird touching my dog, made me cringe. It was just my luck that Bunny, the hugger, retired next door to my parents and reintroduced us.

Wayne-O bent down to pet Raul, whispering "Good boy," as he began examining his eyes, then his ears.

"Lot of irritation in this right ear."

"Yes, it's driving him crazy."

"Has he changed his eating habits?"

"Wait a minute. I'm a little confused here. Are you a real veterinarian? You're just a few years older than me, so how could you have finished a doctoral program already?"

He stood up and looked at me carefully.

"I've got one more year until graduation. Working here is part of the program. I'm qualified to treat your dog. The senior vet will come in afterward, review my notes, and prescribe the antibiotic Raul needs to clear up the ear infection. Is that all right with you?"

He wasn't asking my permission. He was telling me to shut up and let him do his job. Wayne-O Williams was still the aggressive Red Bird.

"Got it, Wayne-O."

"Dr. Stevens will be in here shortly." He turned around before opening the door to leave.

"That's a great dress, Kim. Haven't seen a woman wear polka dots in a long time. Guess you're into that whole Americana, Minnie Mouse thing. I'll pick you up this Saturday at eight for dinner. No need to write down the address. I know how to find the house next door to my parents."

Raul barked at him before he closed the door. Wayne-O Williams was sarcastic, which does require some wit. I accepted the mental challenge of going on a date with him. Besides, it would make my mother happy knowing I was dating a man with a future. She and Bunny, the hugger, could ponder our families joined in holy matrimony and what to serve at the wedding reception. It was better than discussing chemo appointments and garage sale dates.

26

Mom and Bunny, the hugger, staged the entire scene. Twenty minutes before Wayne was to arrive, they set up a spread of seven-layer dip, Fritos, with rum and cokes on the dining room table. The hugger's contribution was a plate of pecan bars, strategically arranged on a doily. Trivial Pursuit, one of Mom's favorite educational games, was spread out next to the food. Dad and Wayne Sr. dutifully sat at the table, determined to polish off the dip, since the women had no intention of serving anything else that night.

"That looks terrific on you, Kim."

I was wearing her white pumps and a polka dot shift, sunny yellow and white, she placed on my bed earlier that day.

"Mom, has the hunting party been assembled for my date tonight? Should I be expecting my sister any minute?"

Bunny giggled. The men never looked up, challenged by the layer of avocado in the dip.

"Thought we'd enjoy our Saturday night, just like you and your date."

I made myself a cocktail and sat next to Dad.

"Nice dress, honey." He was balancing a Frito, tipping to the left side with a disproportionate amount of dip on it.

"I don't think there's an easy way out of that, Dad. Just go for it."

He put the entire thing in his mouth, as I got up to answer the door bell.

"Hail, hail, the gang's all here," Wayne-O announced, wearing a brown plaid shirt, Khaki pants, and loafers. An actual penny, shiny and new, highlighted the inserts on the loafers. He almost matched my dad's attire, sans the pennies.

"You want to play, Wayne? Got your favorite here, pecan bars."

"No thanks, Mom. I got a date with a girl in polka dots."

My father stopped eating and looked at us.

"I love polka dots," sang Mom. And for a moment she and Dad looked at each other, as if they were still young, and the love of his life wasn't dying of cancer.

"You two don't need to hang around the old folks," Dad said, getting up and shaking Wayne's hand.

"We might pick up a game when we get back, if y'all are still up," Wayne-O promised as I cringed walking out the front door.

We drove east on Preston Road in Wayne's red Ford truck with a camper top.

"Nothing sexy about my ride but got a place for dogs and cats with the camper top. Keeps them out of the rain. You'd be surprised how many rescues I do. Can't stand to see abandoned pets roaming the streets. Takes months, sometimes years to rid them of fear and anxiety. January's the worst month, after Christmas, when people decide the new puppy is too much effort."

I sat on my side of the bench seat, listening to Wayne, somewhat surprised at his sensitivity toward animals.

"Do all the animals you rescue live with you or at Bayview?"

"No, I've been volunteering at an animal shelter for years. Bring them there."

He reached for a roll of antacids in the opened ashtray. Without taking his hands off the steering wheel, he removed two from the package with his teeth and began chewing.

"Barbeque okay? Buster's got the best."

"Yep," I replied, as he turned into the parking lot.

He didn't open the truck door for me as he ran to the front door. I did my best to keep up in my mother's forty-year-old white pumps. Surprisingly, they were spotless. Knowing Mom, she applied white shoe polish annually, whether they needed them or not.

"I hope they're not out of sliced beef this late in the day. Can't stand that chopped beef stuff. Just left overs from the prime cuts and mistakes on orders."

"Are you a barbeque connoisseur?"

"Yes, I guess so. I try to be an expert in all things of importance, like food and women."

"I'd hate to ask what a connoisseur of women is." I sat down at our table in a heap, pulled my dress over my knees, and braced myself for the answer.

"I learned a lot about women by observing animals, especially dogs. You want a girl who doesn't run when you call her. One who will get along with kids in the house and guard the family. But the biggest similarity I see between the female dog and the female human is that they just don't like other females. Don't know if it's a threat to mating potential or a natural protection of their own, but they are overly aggressive to each other and to the offspring of their rivals."

"Sad, but true, about women getting along. I can't get along with my own sister. Just a fact I don't know whether to laugh or cry about. But, you're right, Wayne. That's some theory you got. How about the male species? It's only fair."

"You should already know that; you've been out in the world. It's fairly simple. Food, sex, and play."

"Is this a come-on line, this entire theory?" My voice rose, causing the other customers to turn toward our table in hopes of hearing more.

"Nope. Just an observation as a vet and human being," Wayne offered, without aggression or apology.

"Why don't we order?" I suggested out of exhaustion, trying to reason if he was a creep or an honest man, even tempered and unfazed by social norms in dating. Perhaps he took me as just another rescue animal, sensing my fear but downplaying it with directness and patience. No chills or thrills, Wayne-O.

"Knock yourself out. I'm switching gears on the sliced beef. Getting a rack of ribs. Haven't eaten all day.

I shuddered for my mother's little yellow and white polka dot dress and ordered sausage, something you didn't have to eat with your fingers or gnaw with your teeth.

Wayne ordered sides for us, potato salad and pinto beans, as I surveyed the dining room décor of deer heads mounted on wooden plaques and a large sign above the register, a quote from Buster himself, stating, "A vegetarian's worst nightmare."

While we waited for the order, he asked about Lubbock.

"Mom said you got a degree in Library Science. Did you like Tech? Seems isolated out there in Lubbock."

"I see you and Bunny have been chatting about me," I quipped. "I liked Lubbock. It took a while. Worked a lot. Really only got to know a few people. I got Raul in Lubbock. Actually, I got him by default and that's a long story. Just think of Raul as a rescue dog, multiple times. The original owner stitched him up himself after he was hit by a car.

"Good man. Did he become a vet?"

"No, he didn't become anything."

"Was this guy your boyfriend?"

"For a while." I looked down at the plastic checkered table cloth, searching for the next words to speak. "Now what about you, Wayne? What have you been doing besides being a vet and recovering from junior high as a Red Bird?"

He face didn't register resentment on my last comment, as he opened a cellophane wrapped package of crackers with his teeth, then rubbed margarine over it.

"Went to school, met a girl, and gave her an engagement ring. She gave it back."

"Just like that?"

"Yeah, just like that."

Our food was served, and Wayne dug in, tearing the rack of ribs apart with his hands, then ripping the charred flesh away from the bone with his teeth. He did make a nice pile of bones on his dinner napkin, placed on the table. *Why reserve it for the lap, when you can lick your fingers clean?*

I wanted to know more about the returned engagement ring, but I didn't ask. Reaching across the table, he picked up two moist towelette packages, tossing one in my direction. He wiped his mouth, then placed the used towelette on top of the bone pile.

"Dessert? They got a nice peach cobbler here."

"No, thank you."

He ordered one for himself with a side of vanilla ice cream without pausing. In between bites, he asked about my job prospects, even offering to recommend me as an assistant at Bayview Pets.

"I do like animals, but I really love books, probably more than the average person." I wondered if he thought the word average was insulting in any way but, before I could answer, he pushed his chair back and got up from the table.

"That's fine. Let me know if you need any help later on."

He paid the bill at the register, then wheeled the toothpick display, putting the first one in his mouth, while offering me one.

"No, thanks."

We drove back to my parents' house with him singing to the radio, moving the toothpick from side to side in his mouth. The one he offered me was resting behind his right ear lobe. He continued singing solo until pulling into my parents' driveway. He got out of the truck without opening the door for me. Following him to the front door, he leaned into me and placed a kiss on my check.

"I'll pick you up next Saturday. Same time."

"Okay."

I watched him back out of the driveway, the truck headlights making a straight path for him through the darkness. When I turned the door handle to walk in, the door jerked opened.

"Hey, honey, how was your date?"

"Mom, you didn't have to wait up for me."

"I know, but I wanted to, besides no one wanted to play Trivial Pursuit after the dip was gone." She looked me over, then pulled me into the living room by the hand. "Just love you in that dress. Now, tell me, where did he take you to eat?"

"Buster's Barbeque."

"Your dad and I ate barbeque on our first date," she said, then turning away, she looked down the hallway, where Dad was asleep.

"Mom?"

"I guess I'm just tired. Well, the important question is, do you like him?"

"He's comfortable."

Part III

Houston, Texas
Friday, September 13, 2013

27

I ate the leftovers from the Friends of the Library luncheon while watching CNN Friday night in the first home I owned, located minutes from my first promotion in decades. Officially, I was assistant director of the Jesse H. Jones Central Branch Library, in downtown Houston. The cake carved by Missy Barnes, president of the Friends of the Library Association, said so in pink frosting. I received the first slice, a large corner piece. Noting my lack of couth, my boss, Sue Hudachek, frowned at me when I licked the frosting off my fingers. Wayne taught me a long time ago pretense was the waste of a good time.

It had been a quick month of moving and promoting. When I finally got the promotion to move downtown, I left my one-bedroom apartment in the Westchase area I had lived in for years, along with my job as circulation supervisor for the Robinson-Westchase Branch. I found the 1940s-era bungalow on Pease Street in a week. The money I inherited when my parents died, plus the sale of the family home, served as a generous down payment. The first thing I did was place Raul's urn and my parents' portrait on the oak mantle above the working fireplace. The *Portrait of Light* hung above them.

Wayne-O had moved inside the loop years ago, opening his own practice, Williams Veterinary Care. If we didn't go out Friday night, we went out Saturday night. Predictability and comfort remained the reasons we held the world's record for longest years in dating. Buying the house raised the issue of whether or not we should marry and be a normal, middle-aged couple, but I didn't want him moving in. Why get married? I was too old to have children, and I liked my time alone in my own home, even during that first month of getting use to a new place.

After living in apartments for years, where pest control was included in the rent, I found pest control in east Houston not only necessary but expensive. After the initial spraying, I kept the living room windows open all day to filter the stench from a lethal foam ridding my domain of American roaches, German roaches, sugar ants, silverfish, and spiders. Oh, the great irony of modern life. There's better living through chemistry, if it doesn't kill you first.

The opened windows invited the smell of brewing coffee from the Folger's plant located on the East End, a few miles from me. I could hear the children next door playing on their swing set, followed by the command of "Higher, higher" and the squeal of satisfied laughter in return. Ocassionally, I'd hear a mother's warning, "Y'all are going to knock that swing set over. Don't push your sister that hard."

Life was predictable for that moment I stood near the opened window, inhaling all that was familiar in my neighborhood. Once my hair became limp, I closed the windows against the humidity, sat on the couch, and returned to the evening newscast. Just as quickly, the predictability of an afternoon in a working-class neighborhood was replaced by images of the outside world.

Video clip after video clip rolled of flash floods in Colorado, protestors in New Delhi, and Putin, shirtless on horseback, but one clip stopped the world for its forty-five second duration. Men and women were in waist-deep water in Lesbos, Greece, with lifeless children cradled in their arms. The final image of the evening news was of a Pittsburgh convenience store as the location of the winning lottery ticket flashed across the screen. Soon, fourteen million dollars would be delivered to the lucky winner.

I turned off the television, walked into the kitchen, and opened the refrigerator freezer. Standing in front of it, I ate chocolate ice cream from the carton with a metal cooking spoon. I couldn't fill the emptiness fast enough. Trying to retain some self-control, I refrained from eating the last spoonful, put the lid back on, and shoved it in the back of the fridge. For added precaution, I put a frozen bag of winter vegetables in front of it. Out of sight, out of mind.

I showered and retired to bed with wet hair at 8 p.m. On the nightstand was a dog-eared copy of *Seven Houses in France,* a bestseller set in the Congo during the nineteenth century. My boss suggested I read it and participate in the Wednesday afternoon book club that met at the library, but I couldn't concentrate on the corruption of men and imperialism in the nineteenth century. Not when I was living it in the twenty-first century, a front-row viewer, thanks to cable news.

I simply couldn't stop thinking about the children and their parents on that beach in Greece. I dog-eared the book one more time and placed it back on the nightstand. Staring at the ceiling, I knew the world mourned those images, but that empathy only lasted as long as the sixty-second sound bite. Then, pragmatism set in, followed by questions. *Who were these people? Who were all those young men, travelling with those families?*

At 11 p.m., blue babies and blue dinghies circled in my mind, until I patted my stomach bloated with ice cream, sighed to the silence of the room, and rolled over to set the alarm.

Tomorrow was my date with Kathy Renee. After Mom and Dad died, we called a truce delivered in a monthly lunch date. So far, I only talked about work, while Kathy waxed poetically about the Church, occasionally slipping a holy card underneath the tip for the lost soul cleaning the table.

I made a promise to be polite to her. Being kind was still something I had to practice. It never came naturally as it did to Kathy Renee. Perhaps wisdom and maturity persuaded me not to argue with her, but the real reason was because I was tired. At forty, I was diagnosed with rheumatoid arthritis. It was a progressive disease, as I watched my fingers become those of a witch, bony and crooked. At forty-three, I watched my right hand swell and the joints in my fingers produce nodules. Rheumatoid arthritis humbled me, once I realized I no longer had control over my body.

I was prescribed a drug historically used to treat malaria. There was one catch, though. It could cause blindness if taken for extended periods. A popular drug for treatment, it was often featured on slick commercials with an auctioneer voice, announcing in warp speed the crippling side effects. I liked being able to see, so I chose a homeopathic approach to treatment, two crushed aspirins blended with caffeine and delivered in powder form. Comfortable Wayne-O and Saint Kathy Renee were also part of that treatment, providing predictable evenings and low maintenance relationships.

I ended tonight with my usual remedy of camphor and menthol lotion, then turned off the bedside lamp, lying in the dark. My eyes filled with tears from the overwhelming smell of the creams. I couldn't wipe them for fear of getting the cream in my eyes, and I was too tired to get out of bed to wash my hands, so I lay there, thinking of Lesbos, Greece.

I hadn't dreamed of Granny or the cigarillo-smoking Poco in a long time. Just as I tried to forget about Brian and all the men I once knew. Sometimes I'd dream of Raul or Dad. Lately, I dreamed of being in a wheelchair, my hands curved in upon themselves, useless within a nursing home. On occasion, Wayne-O and my sister would stop by to play Yahtzee.

28

I sat underneath a massive oak tree, its branches brushing the wooden deck of the Hobbit Café, while I waited for my sister. Twenty minutes later, she appeared breathless in a pair of white skinny jeans, a pink and white striped shirt, and pink Ked tennis shoes. Twisted around her lopsided ponytail was a pink scrunchie. The entire ensemble exhausted me.

"Kim, Kim, hi, sorry I'm running late. The traffic was horrible." She hugged me as I remained sitting under the tree. "Might be fun to eat outside. Should we?"

"No, let's go in. It's starting to get hot out here."

She followed closely behind, clutching a small gift bag. She always brought me a gift when we met for our monthly lunches. I wasn't as dutiful as her, but I'd occasionally picked up a book I thought she'd enjoy or a potted plant from the grocery store.

"This is such a cute place. Very Irish or maybe English with the little tea pots everywhere?"

"It's Middle Earth. This restaurant is making a homage to Tolkien's *The Hobbit*. Did you read it?"

She put down her menu and looked at me thoughtfully. "No, I don't think so. Oh, here I got you something."

I sighed and accepted the gift bag she handed to me across the table. I didn't peer inside, while placing it on the floor by my purse.

The waitress appeared. "Ladies?"

"I can't image Gandalf eating a shrimp roll but sounds delicious," I answered as I read the description in the menu. "That's my appetizer. Bring me the Balrog Burger for the main meal. I'm hungry."

"I'll have a Baggins Banana Smoothie with that same burger," Kathy Renee offered. "That's two meat patties, right? No onions, with ketchup, please."

"It comes with a chipotle mayonnaise dressing, Kathy."

"No, I want ketchup on mine," my sister smiled back at me.

"Then why aren't we eating at McDonald's?"

The waitress gave me a dirty look, while my sister continued to scan the room, chatting about the tea pots.

"What do you want to drink, ma'am?"

"No ice, no lemon, no fun, water."

The finality of the order got me another dirty look from the waitress.

"How's your friend, Wayne? The new job?"

"Wayne is Wayne, as he forever will be. The new job is a bit of a challenge. I think I got the correct pronunciation of everyone's name down, but the paperwork and new computer system are keeping me up at night." I wiped the back of my neck with my paper napkin.

"Are you feeling okay? We can get this to go if you're not up to it. I made you wait in the heat too long."

"No, I just didn't sleep last night. I made the mistake of watching the news before going to bed. Footage of the refugees drowning in the Aegean Sea, many were children."

"Our prayer group was talking about the refugee crisis last week. People from Syria, Afghanistan, Sudan, Somalia. Everything they own in a little bag and off they go in a flimsy boat. Very sad. You know Jesus was a refugee, too, fleeing to Egypt with Mary and Joseph."

"Do you think they're all refugees, running from militant jihadists?"

"I haven't kept up with the news, but I'm sure they are hoping life will be better somewhere else. War has given them little choice but to leave, if they can. In many ways they're lucky to get out. Many can't."

"A lot of people think they're terrorists, coming to wage jihad in Europe and America."

Our waitress placed the yellow smoothie in front of my sister. She took a thoughtful, long drawl from the straw, all the while looking at me, those eyes, those huge brown orbs of compassion, never thinking evil could lurk in the faces of others. I took a bite of my shrimp roll and an explosion of sweet pepper Thai sauce filled my mouth with happiness, and for a while I forgot about war and refugees. I suppose that's what happened in the land of plenty, once we were fed, watered, and put to bed with scented talcum powder and a lullaby, we quickly forgot about others.

"I can't take responsibility for who is good or bad, Kim. I'm not big enough, but God is."

"How can God let those babies drown?" I found myself crying. I hid it, though, behind the paper napkin and in complaints about the heat.

"This is not our home; this isn't what God intended for us, all the suffering . . . the sick, refugees, orphans, widows, all the things war brings."

The waitress served our burgers. I began eating, all the while, those orbs, looking at me, unflinching in her faith, her delivery of the current world and the world to come, golden gates and a body rid of disease for all the believers.

"How's your burger?" I asked her, because for that moment I cared that her food was enjoyable, and she was comfortable with me.

"Delicious."

We ate in silence, until she began fixating on the tea pots again. I told her the story of Bilbo Baggins, the hobbit who lived quietly in his Hobbit-hole, enjoying cups of tea and routine. What I left out was Tolkien's genius in creating a world based on good and evil, and how the least likely of all the characters, becomes a hero. It was a world where good won.

When Kathy Renee hugged me goodbye outside the restaurant, she promised to read *The Hobbit*.

"Get it at the library. I'm sure there's quite a few copies." I watched her walk away from me, thinking how small she looked. She never really got taller. The same height from junior high with some extra pounds around her hips. She hadn't aged. The glasses were bifocals and the hearing aids more advanced, but Kathy Renee stayed the same little girl from Pasadena.

On the way home from lunch, I stopped at the Super Mercado on Wayside Drive for groceries. I thought of buying bananas after watching my sister enjoy her smoothie, until I remembered *The Houston Chronicle* story of a woman bit by a poisonous brown spider lurking in a banana bunch in a nearby grocery store. Lucky for the unsuspecting shopper, the antivenom was readily available and delivered in the emergency room. I chose the predicable bland taste of picked-too-early Red Delicious apples, instead.

I filled the cart full of superfoods in the fight against rheumatoid arthritis, a guilty choice considering the shrimp roll and burger sitting in my stomach. After checking out, I got in line for an aqua frescas, served from a large, barrel-shaped glass container by a Mexican woman holding an aluminum ladle. I made my choice by pointing to the jar, embarrassed by the fact I was not bilingual simply because of my own ignorance and arrogance. *Why should I learn their language? In a world of six thousand languages, I choose to know only one. Forever, a Blue Bird.*

The woman smiled at me, with the corners of her mouth turned up, revealing two missing front teeth, before pushing her ladle through the sweet drink. *Why am I on this side of the counter in Super Mercado? Was it luck or God?* I didn't think about that more than a minute, as I remembered I had a date with my predictable boyfriend. He was taking me to a new restaurant, where the lamb was flown in from New Zealand and the wine was corked in Spain. It took months to get that reservation, but he was a Red Bird and I was a Blue Bird. Birds of a different feather *sometimes* flock together.

29

I officially met Sean Callahan after my third month on the job, although I noticed him on my first day. He was a regular at the library, our most loyal patron, arriving when the door opened and leaving when the door was locked for the night. Sean was a veteran of Operation Iraqi Freedom, a lover of sci-fi, and homeless. I figured he lived where most of our homeless patrons did, underneath some overpass near Sam Houston Park on Buffalo Bayou.

Sean was a big man, over six feet, with stringy blond hair worn in a ponytail pulled tightly on top of his head, until it stretched the skin from his forehead and eyes into a surprised, youthful expression, although he was middle-aged. What aged him was the cocktail mixture of antidepressants and antipsychotics he took, creating soft rolls on his torso and giving him the gait of an old, confused man.

"I used to play Chopin on the piano when I was a kid. Now, I couldn't even pound out 'Chopsticks.'"

This was the first thing he said to me when he found the courage to introduce himself. It was followed by his eyewitness account of the toppling of Saddam Hussein's statue in Baghdad's Firdos Square, as if he were creating a visual timeline of his mind before the impact of PTSD, its arrival, and the aftermath with a giant playing "Chopsticks."

There were days he was talkative, and there were days he withdrew from the world, sitting upstairs in the library with a stack of Isaac Asimov paperbacks in front of him, with his head cradled in his hands. Those were the days of migraine headaches. The patrons and staff knew to leave him alone on those days. On good days, Sean read his paperbacks in the comfort of the library, with its flushing toilets, running water, and central air and heat. At closing time, he walked less than a mile to get to his home underneath the overpass.

Most of our patrons were homeless. For the most part they were quiet and read or surfed the internet. Occasionally, we'd get patrons who worked in one of the high-rises downtown, doing research or simply browsing during the lunch hour.

My job was predictable and a far cry from the dreams I had long ago of overnight events, marathon reading parties, and endless book giveaways as door prizes. In time, I came to love the predictability, even Wayne-O, and the transient, homeless patrons. Many of them were seasonal patrons, moving with the ice of winter or the heat of summer, but Sean was the most rooted.

Chasity and her girls first appeared for an author-signing event on a Saturday afternoon. Part of my job was to provide a table of light refreshments, as well as a table for the author to sign and sell books. It took a few hours to arrange everything, including the angst of the author, because no one had showed up to hear him read or buy his book.

"There's only homeless people here and those two kids with their mom."

"Mr. Spallers, I can't always predict who will come to our author events. We did advertise it on our website and through social media. I expect someone will show in just a few minutes. You are scheduled for two hours."

"I'm giving this an hour. If no one shows, I'm gone."

"Please stay for the watered-down lemonade and store-bought cookies, Mr. Spallers." I never once looked up from my task of arranging food and books to make eye contact with the author. It was typical of every author-signing event. No one wanted to come downtown for the weekend. By Friday evening, the working stiffs fled the high-rises for the suburbs and the weekend. But we kept booking these authors anyway, and it always turned out the same—the authors were mad, and Sean ate the refreshments.

I turned around and looked at the mother and two children Mr. Spallers pointed out. The girls were dressed in matching short sets with white plastic sandals. They could have been twins. Mom was dressed in a skin-tight leopard print onesie. With no zipper in the center pulling it together, I imagined her to be quite the contortionist to get into that thing. There was something not quite right about this mom and her daughters. I kept staring at them, while Mr. Spallers played on his cell phone, ignoring the books in front of him, while Sean ate all the cookies.

"Now, y'all get a cookie and something to drink. I'll be back in a second. Ain't no need to be bored with all them computers and books in here." She turned around and headed toward the entrance doors.

I didn't know if I should follow her. What were the rules of parents dropping off their underage children at a library? I was dropped off when I was a kid, so I left them alone for the first two hours they were here. Charles Spallers came and went; the folding tables were returned to the closet for the next disastrous author signing, and Sean wiped out the remaining lemonade.

At thirty minutes before closing, I began to panic. Where was that mother? Her daughters didn't appear scared, as if their mother missing was nothing out of the ordinary. They moved from the children's section, lounging on the sofas with books in their hands, to being in the restroom for over thirty minutes. I watched that bathroom door and the wall clock, waiting for them to reappear. Nothing was happening, so I went in. They were both playing at the sinks, splashing water on each other. The hand dryers were blowing nonstop in the background. I immediately slammed the knob to turn them off, only to have them repeat their cycle. I imagined they had been blowing for the full thirty minutes the girls were in here.

"Let's not do this, girls."

They looked at me and walked out of the bathroom. I turned the faucets off and followed them.

"Girls, we'll be closing soon. Is your mom coming back?" I hated myself for asking. Of course, they were wondering the same thing, too.

Both shrugged their shoulders. The sister with the green eyes returned to the *National Geographic Kids* magazine she was thumbing through, while the other sister picked up a paperback copy of *The Secret Zoo* and pretended to read. I left them alone.

At exactly three minutes before I began setting the alarms and locking up, Mom showed up. She stood in the entryway of the children's section with both hands on her hips. "Let's go." The girls ran to her. I felt like approaching her, but what right did I have? Why was I even mad? I didn't know her story.

After a month of Saturday afternoon visits to the library by the two sisters, I finally learned their story—the mother's version of it, anyway.

"I'm Chasity. My folks gave me a hippy-dippy name, 'cause I was conceived during a Sonny and Cher rerun. My girls, Lou-Lou and Pixie," she said, pointing to her daughters. "Sure 'ppreciate you being nice to them. I got to work on Saturdays. Ain't got no babysitter."

I never asked her where she worked. I never asked where Lou-Lou and Pixie's daddy was. I never asked where they lived. They were my patrons, like Sean. They weren't Blue Birds, Red Birds, or Ravens. No one cared enough to put them in a group.

Eventually, Syda joined Chasity's family, showing up with the girls in late October. A shy Guatemalan teen, her brown face and black-blue hair were covered most of the time by a purple hoodie. She didn't talk to Lou-Lou and Pixie. The girls had a set routine by then, spending most of the time in the children's section, reading paperbacks or watching a movie, wearing headphones. Syda looked at magazines and slept.

In time, I learned Syda's story, too.

"She don't speak much English. Just enough to get by," Chasity explained, looking at Syda sleeping in the children's section, when she picked up the girls on a rainy Sunday afternoon.

"That girl was sleeping on the streets when I met her. Brought her home. Not much of a home, but better than the streets. Her story ain't that unusual these days. A coyotaje made a deal with some teens in her Guatemalan village. For $15,000, Syda and her friends were smuggled into the U.S. with false documents for jobs. The raw deal they got was to work off the $15,000 debt with slave labor and sexual favors. She ran away from a chicken farm in Ohio over a year ago and has been trying to make her way back home ever since. She talks a lot about the green mountains in Guatemala and her family. If I got the money, I pay her for babysittin'. If I don't, at least she gets fed. Been with me two weeks."

"There must be some social services that can help."

"Now why you gonna turn her in? She don't trust people, especially white people. Best to leave her alone. She'll get the money to go home. Right now, she's safe where she's at."

"I'm not giving you any money, Chasity. Don't want to hear if you're a druggie or an alcoholic. Not my business. I don't even know if you're telling me the truth about your life, even Syda's. But I'm bringing some clothes for her, a little something for the girls and you. If you're hungry, I'll buy you groceries, but I'll never give you cash. Don't advertise that to the other patrons, or I'll never do it again."

"I know how to keep my mouth shut. Hey, ya know what's so funny about it all. Her name, Syda, means a gift from God. Looked it up on the computer. Now, that ain't even right. Seems like God would of taken better care of his special gift."

I walked away from Chasity and her family, for the simple reason I didn't want to hear any more stories. I turned my head when Sean put everything he owned in a plastic bag and used another one for a rain bonnet when he left, just seconds before the doors were locked. When the workday finally ended, I sat inside my car watching the hypnotic dance of the wiper blades across the windshield, while my cell phone screamed for attention. Wayne was trying to call. When I didn't pick up, he began sending texts. I ignored it. I ignored everything, but the rain falling in front of me.

I finally pulled the seat belt across me, deciding to drive by the overpass near Sam Houston Park before making my way home. In the gray dusk of a rainy night in Houston, the homeless of downtown made their beds with black and brown yard bags, stuffed with discarded clothes from strangers, stolen toilet paper and paper towels from public restrooms, and other items no longer of value to the people driving on the overpass above them. Some of their neighbors lived in olive-colored pup tents or underneath cardboard boxes reinforced with duct tape. Everywhere white plastic buckets served as toilets, when the public restrooms were locked. Somewhere among that plastic, cardboard, and vinyl lay Sean Callahan, a man who many lifetimes ago was a boy who played Chopin on the piano.

"Good night, Sean."

30

Kathy Renee accepted my lunch invitation to What the Pho, a Vietnamese noodle house in the Little Saigon section of Houston, near Louisiana and Milam. Despite several texts fraught with fear of traffic and crime inside the Loop, she decided to come. This was only after a hard-fought compromise. I promised to have Thanksgiving lunch with her at the Villa Maria. When the word *yes* was released by my fingertips in the final text message, I immediately pictured a long afternoon filled with blue hairs and walkers, craft hour featuring Styrofoam egg crates, and loud Christmas music piped throughout the building. I hadn't stepped foot in that building since Granny died.

We met at the restaurant on the Saturday before Thanksgiving. Dressed in an orange sweatshirt with an applique turkey, its feathers fanned in kaleidoscope colors, Kathy Renee sat at a front table near the hostess station, playing with chopsticks, picking up and putting down a plastic straw. When she looked up, she began waving me over to the table with the chopsticks still in her hand. *After all this time, I just couldn't stop judging her, her actions, her clothes. Why did being kind to her become such a job for me? Maybe if she'd stop bringing attention to herself in public places. When was she ever going to grow out of this?*

"I'm fighting a cold. This food is really going to open up my sinuses and help me breathe," I announced, sitting down.

"Oh, I'm sorry. The waiter already brought the menus, but I haven't looked at it." She offered me a one-page paper menu with Hoisin sauce spilled on it. "Let's not order squid as an appetizer. It's like chewing on a car tire."

"There's no calamari here, I can assure you." I just had to put her in her place. True to her nature, she smiled at me as if my sarcastic remark was said out of concern for her. I felt a pang of guilt, so I suggested the spring rolls with chili sauce. "You'll love 'em," I said, smiling back at her.

"How's work going for you, Sis? Is the library doing anything special for Thanksgiving?"

"The children's section will have an arts and craft event. We rented a turkey costume for one of the assistants to wear. The usual. I'm looking forward to a day off."

"You'll have a good time at the Villa. Please invite Wayne. He's just as welcome. We've got all kinds of things planned for the residents and their special guests."

By the way she looked at me, I could tell she considered me her special guest—I was the only family she had. With the appetizer on the table, I began the hand-to-mouth marathon with an occasional dip into the chili sauce. Kathy Renee joined me, followed by a "Yummy" from her first bite.

"You never talk about work much. Don't you like your new job?"

"I like it okay. I still haven't figured out why people read what they read. Someone came in today and asked why Kim Kardashian's *Selfish* wasn't on the shelf. How can a library keep up with celebrity books?"

"Is that like *Keeping Up with the Kardashians*?"

Before I had a chance to reply, Kathy Renee started laughing. She made a little joke, sophomoric, at best, but I found myself laughing out loud.

"I never understood the whole celebrity thing. It's crazy. People are obsessed with it."

"People like an escape from life. That's all it is."

"Where's the waiter? I need to order the main course, before I get into a discussion about celebrities and the meaning of life."

Kathy waved at him with her chopsticks. Dressed in black with a long black apron, the waiter was probably doing double time as the cook.

"Let me order for us. Trust me. You loved the spring rolls, right? Okay, bring us P53 with steak, shrimp, and meatballs. No soy. Just Hoisin and Sriracha. Taro milk tea to drink."

Twenty-minutes later he was back with two steaming bowls of Pho with rice noodles swimming in a rich broth. In separate bowls were chopped green onions, cilantro, and jalapeno peppers. One chopstick full and all my sinus cavities opened.

"Now, where were we? Oh yeah, celebrities. I tell you there are some very sad things that stick in my mind about the life of celebrities. Namely, Michael Jackson and Elvis Presley."

"I know. They had such sad lives, but I still like their music."

"Michael Jackson had it all, except a good night's sleep. Crazy money, but he couldn't get a full eight hours. His doctor gave him anesthetic propofol the night he died. Apparently, he took it quite a bit to help him sleep."

"What killed Elvis?" Kathy Renee asked, working her chopsticks like a pro as they moved from dish to dish, adding herbs and peppers.

"The King died on the toilet. Well, maybe not on the toilet but inches from it. He must have been crawling for help, poor man. By that time in his life, he was very overweight. I'm sure he had high blood pressure. There was always talk about drug abuse, but the cause of death was a heart attack. Like MJ, Elvis had it all, crazy money, great career ... it doesn't make sense they went the way they did."

"Michael Jackson and Elvis had everything but peace. Money and fame don't give you that. They kept searching for it everywhere, and in everything the world offered. The more the world gives you, the more you want, and the more desperate the search becomes for getting even more. True peace is not of this world."

"Please, let's not go there."

"We're not going anywhere, Kim. I'm just saying . . ."

"I know exactly what you're going to say, before you even say it. Look, I think Kim Kardashian was very happy the day she took that photo with a champagne flute on her butt."

"I don't know what you're talking about."

"Oh, forget it. We've given her and every other celebrity out there enough of our day. Time for dessert. Get that waiter over here with your chopsticks."

After licking the last of the Chè chuối from our spoons, we sipped tea, returning to the conversation of Thanksgiving and the Villa.

"Please don't be late, Sis. We've got scheduled activities. Arts and crafts, a sing along, and cupcake decorating. Wayne would enjoy it. He's always so nice to me."

"Wayne-O has his moments."

I knew it! My only day off would be spent singing songs with strangers in wheelchairs. But I kept that nasty thought to myself and promised my sister I wouldn't be late. I grabbed the check before she had a chance to. When we stood up together, she wrapped her arms around me.

"Get better, my Sissy. I don't want a cold to keep you from enjoying Thanksgiving."

I didn't know who I hated more—myself for being so cruel to her, or her for being so kind to me.

I left the restaurant, as a light drizzle fell from the November sky. Not wanting to go home, I drove through midtown looking for a gallery, a boutique, anything different from the same things I saw and heard every day. I didn't want to think about work, the patrons, or my sister. Blue Mesa Art Gallery, a burnt-orange building on the corner of Louisiana, with a violet-blue front door was open. Although I paid to park in a garage nearly four blocks away, the walk in the rain to the blue double doors was uplifting. Inside the cool darkness of the gallery, with single pendant lighting over each painting, I found a tranquility I hadn't felt in a while as I eased into this world of perfect quiet. I thought of Lionel, and for a moment I regretted never going to California. But relationships and people were messy. We had left on the best possible terms of our friendship and that was the *Portrait of Light*. We could never top that, so why jeopardize it with wanting more. I couldn't stand the expectation of making someone happy. I didn't ask it of Wayne, since I learned a long time ago to make my own happiness. I had my books and a decent job.

My boss mentioned Blue Mesa Gallery to me several months ago. She was a collector of watercolors by Nancy Parsons. Now that I was standing in front of her work, I knew why. The subtle colors and images, both ethereal and soothing, lowered my blood pressure and slowed my breathing. I particularly liked *Reflections at Day's End* with its mirrored image of a red and beige rowboat against the blue water. I stood there mesmerized until I heard my name called.

"Kim? Kim Hodges? Is that you, Kimberly Ann Hodges?"

I turned around and there stood Jennifer, Jennifer Blue Bird, from Parks Junior High. Last time I was this close to her, I had thrown a waded-up bologna sandwich in her face. Jennifer at midlife was an attractive woman. She also had an extensive dye job with at least ten different variations of blond highlights in her hair. Once I closed my mouth in surprise, I gave her a quick hug. I certainly didn't touch her back or squeeze her hand, just a noncommittal, quick hug of recognition.

"How have you been? I had no idea you're an art collector. I'm here all the time, but I haven't run into you until now."

She was sizing me up, the way only a Blue Bird could, by measuring the quality of my speech, clothes, hair, shoes, and make-up. Her final check was observing the whiteness of my teeth. Were they professionally bleached or done by a cheap kit from the grocery store? I could almost hear her thoughts leaking from that highlighted head of hers. Because I didn't bleach my teeth at all, I decided to respond to her without revealing my teeth. This wasn't easy, because I was so accustomed to being au naturale in the world of libraries that served as child and adult daycare. My teeth were clean, but no one in my world cared if they were ultraviolet white.

"I'm doing great, Jennifer. Work and live inside the loop." That measured response gave her few details, but just enough to let her imagine I was a corporate tax attorney working at 609 Main at Texas, sleeping every night in my gated River Oaks mansion. No need to tell her I was a state employee, sleeping every night in a neighborhood void of gentrification.

"How nice. I'm not seeing a ring. Married?"

"Career girl, I'm afraid. My job has me travelling quite a bit." Jennifer could just assume I was flying to Paris first class for negotiations with world-class corporations. "How about you? That's quite a ring you've got."

"Tommy and I have been married for twenty years," she smiled, looking at her wedding band, an eternity ring circling her finger, with a multi-diamond count of at least five carats.

"You remember Tommy? He was in our Blue Bird reading group. That little boy, I'm just so proud of him, went on to be head of the cardiology group at Methodist Hospital."

I nodded as she continued listing their achievements—city house, lake house, beach house—and the forever separation between me and her, two bright and healthy children.

I became a mute before her, realizing how average my life was compared to hers, an actualized Blue Bird. It was my choice to live a mediocre life. I had no one to blame but me.

"Who's your favorite?"

I came up for air with her question.

"Sorry, my favorite?"

"Who's your favorite artist here?"

"Oh, I like them all."

She laughed out loud, giving me a noncommittal hug, in return for the one I gave her. Then, Jennifer, the Blue Bird fluttered away.

She didn't ask about my mother, father, or my sister. She didn't ask, because she didn't care. The same reason why I never asked about her family.

On the walk back to the parking garage, I called Wayne.

"Could you use some company?"

"You're up late tonight, Kim. It's almost 8:30."

I ignored the sarcasm.

"I had an event downtown."

"Please don't tell me you're in the neighborhood, and you thought you'd drop by.

"No, I won't tell you that. I'm on my way to your house. I'd appreciate a glass of wine when I get there."

"Got a bottle of your usual."

"That's exactly what I need. The usual."

"You know, Kim. You could marry me, and then you don't have to drive across town when you're feeling lonely."

"Yes, I could marry you, but not tonight."

It took me thirty minutes to drive to Wayne Williams's house. I didn't spend the night.

31

The Christmas season immediately began on Thanksgiving Day. Perhaps a week earlier if you wanted to consider the two holidays and the amount of decorating that was done. Thanksgiving was always bypassed for Christmas. I counted one Thanksgiving decoration at the Villa Maria, the cardboard head and extremities of a turkey attached to a bright orange tissue-paper body. That's it. In fact, Thanksgiving Day ended with a singalong in the formal living room with hand holding around the Christmas tree. On the wall near the tree was a plaque and picture of my sister, in recognition of twenty-five years of dedication to the Villa Maria. Below her picture was a bronze nameplate announcing her as Employee of the Year, followed by multiple years she was honored.

"Before we begin our tradition of singing carols around the tree, I'd like to say a prayer."

Red-faced and nervous, she removed a piece of notebook paper from her smock pocket, cleared her throat, and began reading.

"Heavenly Father, help us to begin this holy season in the spirit of love for others, finding mercy and understanding for all people," she concluded by making the Sign of the Cross.

I heard an enthusiastic "Amen" from somewhere in the living room, then Juanita Cooper, director of the Villa, asked us to hold hands around the Christmas tree. Wayne and I stood next to Kathy Renee, her hand firmly gripped in mine, as she sang with passion, "We Three Kings of Orient Are." Her voice quivered to a higher octave when the refrain began with an extended holding of the letter, O, "Ooooo, star of wonder, star of night, star with royal beauty bright."

I mouthed the words, wondering if it was politically correct to sing of kings from the orient. Perhaps "kings from Asia" was the better term. I looked out onto the patio with its covered swimming pool, closed table umbrellas, and upside-down patio chairs. Summer was gone. Fall was gone. Christmas had arrived on Thanksgiving Day. That simple fact was neither politically correct nor incorrect. It was just stupid. Why did everything have to be a race through life?

"Let's sing "Away in a Manger," my sister offered, squeezing my hand. I squeezed hers in return, as I began mouthing the words of the song, looking out the windows for a sign of Granny and Poco. They were gone, too.

The singalong concluded with coffee and pumpkin pie in the cafeteria. It had been remodeled over the years, but it smelled the same, an unusual mix of disinfectants, french fries, tomato sauce, and sauerkraut. There was no sign of a bar for afternoon cocktails by the pool. I'm sure some health code ended that years ago. Maybe that's why Granny and Poco weren't here. There just wasn't that much joy in a cafeteria that served canned pumpkin pie and nondairy whipped cream. That was a clever way of saying it was imitation whipped cream, which made me wonder what the substitute for milk was.

Kathy Renee was happy in this environment. It was clear by her interactions with the residents and staff, she was loved and well respected, a criterion I never looked for in a job. I had whittled my job expectations down to a few things: patrons must read, and I must get paid.

Wayne made his exit after the first serving of pumpkin pie.

"Thanks for having me, Kathy Renee. I enjoyed it, but I've got one more Thanksgiving meal to attend. It's the volunteer banquet at the animal shelter on Canino Road. I serve turkey and dressing every year to the volunteers as a thank you for their service."

"What a wonderful thing to do, Wayne."

Kathy Renee smiled and gave him a hug, patting the embroidered turkey on the front of his brown sweatshirt.

"I got a shirt almost like yours," she said, smiling at him.

"Bye, Wayne-O," was what he got from me without a hug, pat, or giggle.

"You want seconds, Kim? There's plenty." My sister's words buzzed in my ear, and I returned to reality, dismissing Wayne, and the ghosts of former Villa residents.

"No thanks. Probably should be going, too. It's been a nice day. Appreciate you inviting me."

She immediately looked disappointed, so I delayed leaving.

"Is it too early to plan for Christmas? I mean, I feel compelled with the tree up and all those carols. Any thoughts? We can have it at my house this year."

"Let me help with the residents for a second, and I'll join you by the tree with coffee."

It was hard enough to swallow the first cup of monkey sweat, without thinking of another one.

"Sure."

Kathy Renee smiled at me, then began unlocking the brakes of two wheelchairs and pushing their inhabitants toward the corridor, exiting into the individual patient rooms. Her job was physical, and I wondered how many more years she'd be able to do it. Unlike me, she never complained about aches and pains, though I did notice she began to limp on her right foot. Suddenly, all the years of corrective shoes and orthopedic doctor visits with her and my mother came back to me. I saw myself, reading a paperback in the car, reading in the doctor's waiting room, reading when Kathy Renee and my mother were talking. Reading and avoiding everything in front of me. The only solace was Granny, here at the Villa Maria, all those years ago.

I couldn't stay another minute in this place, so I wrote my sister a note on a paper napkin.

Upset stomach. Overate! So sorry! Call you during the week.

"Can you give this to Kathy Renee?" I asked a woman in pink scrubs, wiping off the cafeteria tables with a tired dish rag. I didn't even fold the napkin. I could care less if the woman read it.

"Wouldn't you like to stay for cupcake decorating? Look at the little decorations we have for them." She pointed to a stack of toothpicks with little turkey and pumpkin flags glued to them.

"Not really."

"Not a problem. I'll get this to your sister as soon as she returns." She folded the napkin in half and put it in her pocket. She obviously cared a lot more than I did.

On the way home from the Villa, I went through a McDonald's drive-thru and got $200 worth of coupon booklets with a snowman and three children ice skating on the front cover. These would serve as Christmas gifts for Sean, Chasity, Lou-Lou, Pixie, and Syda. Maybe I'd buy a little something extra for the girls.

I put the coupons in my purse and patted it. Now, I could sleep without feeling guilty. My sin of not waiting for my sister self-pardoned with an indulgence paid to McDonald's and America's homeless.

Before my head hit the pillow, I listened to my sister's voice mail.

"I hope the food didn't make you sick. You should have said something! We've got everything here to cure a bad tummy. Praying for you, Sis. Call me if you need anything. Be right over!"

At 2:15 a.m., I awoke to the sound of dominoes sliding across a wooden surface. Throwing a robe on, I walked to the kitchen aware that the only weapon in my hand was my cell phone. I could always throw it at the intruder, which would give me a few seconds to run out the front door to safety. I turned on the kitchen light and found Granny and Poco playing dominoes. An unlit cigarillo rested behind Poco's ear.

"He no longer lights up but loves 'em as a wardrobe enhancer."

"Granny?"

"Sit down, Kim. We need to talk."

I sat next to her, leaving an empty chair next to Poco. I remember thinking I must be sleepwalking and hallucinating. *Is it possible to do both at the same time?*

"Count her in, Poco." The dog slid twelve dominoes toward me.

"I really don't want to play, Granny."

"You need to play and you need to listen. Now, take your dominoes and don't let anyone see what you've got."

I took my dominoes and wondered why she was using that tone with me.

166

"I've been watching you, Kim. I know how you talk to your sister."

"Are you my Guardian Angel?"

"I am, even though you don't believe in Guardian Angels."

"I miss you, Granny. Why did you leave me? I've tried, but I've never been close to anyone since," I cried.

"Honey, you need to get over yourself, and look around you. You can be close to Kathy Renee. She loves you. So does Wayne, even if he is a bit on the ordinary side."

"I know that, but it's been too long, too much has been said and done. I can't deal with giving my heart away and then that person dies on me. It hurts too much. It's better if I'm alone. You know, Granny, I don't even have a dog anymore."

Poco took the cigarillo from his ear and lit it with a match, behind the other ear.

"Look, you're making him nervous. Put that down, Poco."

Granny reached across the domino pile and held my hand. "How do you know Kathy Renee will die on you? Or Wayne will kick over? You could get sick tomorrow and lie in some hospital bed, waiting to die, regretting the life you threw away."

When I woke up, I remembered dreaming of my grandmother and that crazy dog from the Villa. *Regretting the life you threw away* stayed with me throughout the morning. Maybe I just needed a vacation or some retail therapy.

I joined the hysteria of Black Friday, looking for the perfect gift for my sister, hoping my generosity would keep the dreams of Granny and Poco from invading my psyche. By the time I exited Westheimer, I knew it was a mistake. The traffic was ridiculous, but not nearly as bad as parking. I circled the parking lot for forty minutes looking for an opening, stalking unsuspecting shoppers leaving the entrance at Saks Fifth Avenue and following them to their coveted parking spot. Once I parked and grabbed my purse, I registered complete exhaustion and hostility for Christmas.

I browsed in Prada, hating the women buying multiple pairs of shoes and handbags. With complete contempt for the human race, I window-shopped at Tory Burch. I uttered "Ciao!" as I breezed past Miu Miu on my way to an overpriced, overhyped national chain jewelry store. Spending an entire paycheck on a fourteen-carat gold crucifix and chain for my sister, I celebrated my guilt-free moment with sushi at the Kona Grill. With not a single table open, I plopped down at the bar, next to two middle-aged men. *Please, no conversation. I'm here for the sushi.*

I never got a sideglance from the two "boyish" men next to me. They had that look – great tan, white teeth, expensive yachting clothes with signature sunglasses pushing back sun-kissed blond hair. Their boat shoes were classic navy, only wannabes wore brown or tan boat shoes. Chip and Hunter were so deep into conversation and beers, I garnered little attention. Besides, I was too old, weighed too much, and dressed in no distinction to register with them. I ate my spider roll, tuna tower, and shrimp tempura, listening to them.

"I'm feeling lucky tonight."

"Really, what's the occasion?"

"I'm finally divorced. No more drama and no more paperwork."

"I kinda liked Abby. I know she never cared for Houston. That was a tough trade, Newport for Houston. The blue Atlantic for the brown Gulf."

"It was good for a while, although Mom never liked her. I begged her, reminding her of Abby's many attributes, like owning a J22 and participating in the Volvo Ocean Race. That's where I met her, in Newport. I was selling resin for a New Orleans firm and wanted to connect with sailors and sponsors. The family home was on Bellevue, eastern blue bloods without a drop of Catholic Portuguese blood in their veins. What's not to like?"

"It wasn't your world, man. It's like being from different planets."

Both men laughed and took a draw from their beers.

"Mom said she didn't shave her arms pits or wear lipstick. Granted she wasn't much to look at, she did have a great body. We had a few good years."

I put my chopsticks down on that last sentence.

"Excuse me."

Now, I had their attention. Chip and Hunter's shared expression of bemusement wasn't lost on me. I became the crazy middle-aged woman wearing a Texas Tech T-shirt, black running pants, and dirty tennis shoes, sitting next to them.

"Wait a minute here. I'm trying to enjoy my food. But the more you two drink, the louder you get. I can't help but overhear your conversation."

Their bemusement immediately went to fear, realizing I was crazy, and I could easily put their eyes out with my chopsticks.

"I guess I wouldn't mind so much the loud talk. Free country, right? People shopping for Christmas. Everything merry and bright. But you started with the prejudice remark about Portuguese Catholics then quickly followed with 'not much to look at but a great body.' Really? What if I said that about you? What if I reduced you to nothing more than what your body looked like and what it could do for me?"

Both men stood up at the same time. Chip withdrew some cash from his wallet, two twenty-dollar bills, and threw them on the bar. Neither one of them acknowledged me with a reply or a look.

"Good riddance. Now, I can eat in peace," I said to their backs, as I popped a shrimp into my mouth with my multipurpose chopsticks.

32

"Good morning, Sean. Did you have a nice Thanksgiving weekend?"

"Went to the Salvation Army to eat. We each got a little stocking full of soap, a razor, toothbrush, and toothpaste. Kinda like Thanksgiving and Christmas rolled into one holiday."

He was sitting upstairs in the research library with a biography of Stephen Hawking in front of him. Next to it was a paperback edition of *The Physics Companion, 2nd Edition.* I could only image the conversation at the Salvation Army over the weekend if this was how Monday was shaping up. Freshly shaven, Sean was also wearing clean clothes. His eyes were clear, and his hands didn't shake.

"Yeah, mine was a lot like that, too. But Christmas doesn't have to go away with Thanksgiving. Here. I got you this as an early gift." I handed him several of the McDonald's coupon booklet.

"I haven't had a Big Mac in years. Thank you, Kim." Sean didn't hug people. I didn't expect to be any different than anyone else. He did smile at me.

"I have some coupons for Chasity and the girls, Syda, but I haven't seen them."

"They're late afternoon people." He opened his paperback on physics and began to read. Our conversation was over.

Two weeks passed and still Chastity, Lou-Lou, Pixie, and Syda hadn't shown. It was late Thursday evening when the first cold front blew in. Outside the glass entry to the library, leaves, Styrofoam cups, and newspapers blew along the sidewalk, as a light rain began to fall. The temperature dropped from seventy-one degrees to forty-one degrees in two hours.

Where were those girls? I couldn't help but whisper a little prayer they were in a warm, dry place with good things to eat. Safe and off the streets.

As I made my final walk through the library before closing, I saw Sean asleep in one of the overstuffed chairs near the main lobby. It had been a bad week for him, and I didn't want to wake him. He got in a knife fight near Freedom Park with another man. With twelve stitches in his forearm, he kept his McDonald's coupons, the object of desire for two homeless men and the reason for the knife fight.

I waited another ten minutes after closing, then I touched his shoulder.

"Closing time, Sean. We'll see you tomorrow. Be careful out there. It's raining."

He didn't say a word but began packing his plastic Kroger shopping bag with toilet paper and paper towels from the library restroom.

"Here, you can have these. Maybe keep them in your shoes or socks, so no one can see them." I handed him the McDonald coupons I bought for the girls, still in my purse from the night I bought them.

He took them from me without saying a word.

"I don't think they're coming back, Sean."

He shook his head and walked out the door into the December night. I was right behind him, and I even considered giving him a ride, but I wanted to look for the girls. I drove the streets of downtown Houston for about an hour. I thought about going to the different shelters, even the police station on Travis. Then it occurred to me. I didn't know their last names. I never bothered to ask them. Where could they be? People didn't just vanish into thin air, or did they?

Beginning that night and every night of December, I dreamed of Granny, Poco, and Chasity. We were sitting together at the Kona Grill bar. Chasity was the bartender. While Granny nursed a Mai Tai and read a paperback, Poco played "Tiny Bubbles" on a ukulele. I kept trying to talk to Granny, then I'd question Chasity.

"Where are the girls? Why didn't you come back? I have McDonald's coupons for you."

Her mouth opened, her lips moved, but I never heard her. I saw everyone's mouths open, but I never heard her.

On Christmas Day, I drove to my sister's house, a shrine to the Advent season. She cooked all the favorites from our childhood, homemade macaroni and cheese, pistachio salad with pineapple, sweet potato casserole with marshmallows, and corn straight from the can. I had no reason to judge a meal made from cans, boxes, and cellophane packaging. I brought the turkey and dressing, straight from Kroger's deli.

We exchanged gifts after eating. Of course, she was thrilled with the necklace. I put it on her, and she immediately ran to the bathroom mirror to look at it.

"Kimmmm, I just love it!" She squealed from the bathroom.

She returned, gave me a bear hug, forcing me to sway with her back and forth for several minutes, then she ran to the Christmas tree, where a gold envelope with my name on it was sitting beneath it.

"For you!"

I opened the envelope and found a Delta travel voucher for $500.

"That's a lot of money. I don't think I can accept this."

"No. It made me so happy to buy it. Please, keep it. I can't remember when you took a vacation, Sis. I think you deserve one."

I put the envelope in my purse and got up from the couch.

"Thank you, Kathy. I need to run by Wayne's and give him his gift." I hugged her and put my purse on my shoulder.

"Oh, no, please don't go. You're always doing for others, never taking time for yourself. Your unselfishness reminds me of St. John's words, 'At the end of our life, we shall all be judged by charity.' Jesus will know your name, Sissy."

After another bear hug, where we swayed from side to side, I left her in her tidy little home in Pasadena. I left her in the home she owned with all the dishes to wash from our Christmas meal.

33

I flew nonstop from Houston to Copenhagen in May. It was my first vacation abroad. Copenhagen was an easy choice for two reasons. *Forbes* ranked Denmark as one of the happiest countries in the world. Those zero-body-fat Danes and their symmetrical faces also possessed the Little Mermaid, a small, bronze statue honoring the fairy tale written by native son, Hans Christian Anderson. I loved her since I was a child.

With multiple dog-eared pages and one emory board marking the city map, my guidebook to Copenhagen remained open during most of the ten-hour flight. The overweight slob next to me was bent on consuming as much free liquor as he could hold, so I punished his gluttony by taking the shared arm rest when he got up to use the toilet. Sound asleep after the consumption of the evening meal with his mouth wide open and a puddle of saliva forming at the corners, he woke once and asked me to turn out the overhead light. I pretended not to hear him as I read among a sea of blanketed people.

The Danes were among the most civilized people on the planet. Their health and education systems were world class, with citizens enjoying one of the highest standards of living coupled with the smallest wealth caps on earth. Where did the homeless of Denmark live, under overpasses and in libraries? Did women with children roam Denmark cities, searching for food and shelter? It was a small world, after all.

An hour before landing, the smell of coffee woke me up with the guidebook in my lap. Jethro Bodine was still snoring away. When the flight attendant asked if she should wake him, I shuddered. Did she think I was married to a guy like that? Why not play the role of a good wife as I smiled at the flight attendant and whispered.

"Let him sleep. He had a rough night."

"Should I leave the tray?"

"Oh, no. He never eats breakfast."

I ate my croissant with Irish-made butter, lavishing organic boysenberry jam over it. I packed the yogurt, bottled water, and biscotti cookies in my purse. Designated as lunch, I could now splurge on a cab to the hotel.

The Admiral Hotel, located near Copenhagen's city center, was a short walk from the Little Mermaid. That is the only reason I justified paying that much for a hotel room. Picking up fruit, bread, and cheese at a local store would also save some cash. Besides, I didn't come here to eat. I came to see the demure Little Mermaid, the youngest of six royal mermaid daughters who yearned to see what was above the sea, like her older sisters.

Before I fell asleep that evening in the hotel, I took my childhood copy of Anderson's story and read:

How carefully her youngest sister listened to every word and remembered everything that she had been told . . . then she imagined that she could see the city and hear the bells of the churches ringing.

Kathy Renee held on to every word I spoke, only disagreeing when I insulted her beliefs. There was a time, maybe in junior high, when she followed me. But we were not royal mermaid daughters. We were Sandy's little girls dressed in polka dot bikinis, who once splashed in the tidal pools of South Padre Island. One sister feared the water, suspect of undertows everywhere, while the youngest never knew fear but followed the instinct of a pure heart.

I awoke at 5 a.m., Copenhagen time, while the rest of the city slept. Plugging in the electric teakettle in the room, I watched the boats move in and out of the harbor from my hotel window. Bored, I turned on the television and watched the local newscast. I didn't need a translator to read the numbers on the weather chart. Every Blue Bird was taught how to convert

Fahrenheit to Celsius, feet to meters. I guess there weren't enough Blue Birds in America, so the metric system was abandoned all together.

With a predicted temperature high of nineteen degrees Celsius, I dressed in jeans, tennis shoes, and a light sweater. I was the only guest in the lobby when I left the hotel and began my walk to the Langelinie promenade.

It was a short walk, with many tourist shops and small convenience stores along the way. I stopped in one and bought a container of orange juice and drank it while walking around the store, picking up and putting down postcards, magnets of the new opera house, and cheap imitations of Royal Copenhagen china pieces. I was prolonging seeing her. Since childhood I had been waiting, building years of anticipation for this chance, and now that it was here, I was afraid of the possible disappointment if she wasn't what I wanted her to be.

After finishing the juice, I found a park bench and sat for a while. As the morning progressed, more people entered the promenade, mostly tourists and the people who worked in the little shops. In the distance, I saw a bus stop and what appeared to be hundreds of people getting off buses.

I joined the throngs of tourists, exiting the buses, determined to beat them in the race to see her. Climbing down a pile of rocks on the waterside, near the Kastellet Fort, I was within a few feet of her. So small, maybe sixty inches in height, perfect Little Mermaid staring out into the sea, the sea full of undertows. I looked at her now as an adult, finally understanding the tragedy Anderson wrote, hidden within a children's story.

Beneath the sea, with her mermaid sisters, the Little Mermaid lived without a soul. She fell in love with a human and wished more than anything to live with him. Sacrificing all, including her beautiful voice, happiness eluded her. The prince wed someone else. Oh, unrequited love. Oh, precarious human heart. She drowned in the human undertow, until rescued by the Daughters of the Air.

> She saw the bright sun, and all around her floated hundreds of
> transparent beautiful beings; she could see through them the white
> sails of the ship, and the red clouds in the sky; their speech was

melodious, but too ethereal to be heard by mortal ears, as they were also unseen by mortal eyes.

Within their sisterhood, the Little Mermaid remained with the Daughters of the Air, perfecting herself with good deeds, hoping to be rewarded with an immortal soul.

The undertows of the Gulf and the Atlantic took my innocence, and I replaced it with fear, fear of living, but more hateful than that fear of living was my inability to love. Unlike the Little Mermaid, I didn't want a soul. It only served to torture me.

I stood near her as long as I could stand it, with hundreds of tourists on top of me, shouting and taking pictures. Disgusted by the crowd, I walked back toward the hotel, stopping at the Gefion Fountain, where a young couple were passionately kissing. I was shocked by the openness of their affection, then I remembered the innocence of young love, and the first time Brian kissed me. That day so many years ago, when the sun's rays shone upon the surface of the lake as I felt his skin beaded with water, and inhaled his breath entwined with mine. Those feelings still lived within me, like a jeweled box I could open and close at will.

I thought of Wayne. There were no coveted jewels of his affection in my memory. He was a comfortable man, and that was all I ever expected from him, so that was all I ever received.

Sitting on a bench near the fountain, as the Norse goddess Gefjun drove oxen in a spray of water, I watched a tourist throw a coin in the fountain and make a wish. I wished I could love a prince with the purity of the Little Mermaid's heart, "he on whom my wishes hang, in whose hand I should like to lay my life's happiness."

I dug into my purse and found a quarter and a nickel. I threw it in the fountain and whispered my desire. I laughed to myself thinking what kind of man I could get for thirty cents.

That evening, a steely blue sky and light rain accompanied me as I walked the inner harbor of the city. I passed the Amalienborg Palace, where I took a selfie with a stone-face Danish Royal Guardsman. I thought the image might make Wayne or Kathy Renee laugh, so I posted it on Facebook.

As I walked farther into the central city, I passed many outdoor cafes, full of tourists enjoying wine and food. I was hungry but determined to walk to Tivoli Gardens amusement park and eat there. Founded in 1843, it was the oldest amusement park in the world and a favorite haunt of Anderson's, with its brightly lit rides, puppet shows, and restaurants.

I ate at the highly recommended Grøften, because of its traditional Danish menu and cheerful red and white checkered tablecloths. Eating the entire basket of complimentary bread, I flagged the waiter, who brought another basket, this time with an assortment of jams. For dinner, I ordered herring, pickled beets, and a cucumber and dill salad with a chilled glass of white wine. I completed the meal with Koldskal, a light pudding of lemon, cream, and buttermilk, topped with an oatmeal and hazelnut blend cooked to a golden brown. Slices of strawberries rested on top. I kept thinking with each bite, *Oh, this is how fresh dill is supposed to taste, or herring, or hazelnuts, or strawberries.* After dinner, I strolled around the amusement park, imaging a young Anderson writing in his notebook, while sitting on a bench, watching children laugh and dance in the park. Anderson, alone, always alone with his writing.

The walk back to the hotel took at least thirty minutes with a steady stride in the crisp night air. I felt more alive than I'd felt in years. It's probably why I made a detour from my usual common-sense approach to people and small talk. When I opened the door to the hotel, the bar area was an amber glow of soft light and beautiful people, whom I imagined had beautiful things to say. I was in an enlightened European country, far, far away from the wild west of Houston. The Admiral Hotel Bar could be viewed as a Blue Bird group, intellectually and esthetically superior. I had come to drink from that eternal pool of better than the average bear.

Perched on an impossibly tall bar stool of chrome and leather, I ordered a cognac. A man in a British officer uniform and a woman, sitting next to me, were engaged in a heated discussion. I occasionally heard the words refugee and Syria. I tried not to listen. Looking at the cognac glass, I imagined the gardens again in Trivoli, and the meal I had enjoyed.

"Putin has Europe terrified, especially the Poles. Add the refugee crisis on top of it, and Europe's imploding," the officer explained to the woman, while looking over her shoulder and smiling at me. I didn't smile back.

"Why don't you join us, Yank? We're all here on business, trying to relax before the next meeting."

"Yes, we were just discussing the current refugee crisis in Copenhagen," the woman, also British, smiled.

"How do you know I'm American?"

"Your clothes. But clearly, you must have an opinion about the European refugee crisis. Don't you think it's rather odd that Denmark, supposedly a world leader when it comes to human rights and development, has adopted such austere policies," she said.

I didn't take the bait. She wasn't interested in my opinion, and she obviously thought my clothes were tasteless. She sighed heavily before launching into another diatribe.

"The Danish government placed ads in Arabic newspapers discouraging immigration. Then, they passed a bill restricting family reunification for Syrian refugees. Police were allowed to search and seize their assets."

"Just an example of as long as it's not in my backyard," I offered.

"Excuse me," the woman quipped. Her counterpoint thought it was funny.

"Yes, yes, how right you are," he laughed, touching my back with his open palm. I stiffened, elongating my spine to the chrome of the bar stool. "Well, yes, the Danes have had a time. They try to send the refugees back via planes, but the poor devils defecate on themselves and are returned."

"I'd crap in my pants, too, if I had to go back to Syria," I said, removing his hand from my back.

This was met with another round of laughter by the man and a roll of the eyes from the woman.

"You cannot break the Arabs. That's what Europe doesn't understand," he explained with his hands folded in front of him on the bar. "They're like the Irish. During the bloody Troubles, I was a young officer stationed in an outpost in County Armagh. I beat as many Irishman as I could who were arrogant enough to be out after the curfew. Every time I hit a Paddy, I thought of a fellow officer dying from an IRA sniper shot, ringing through the hills around Crossmaglen. Ah, you couldn't make those people talk. We tried with the children, candy and toys, they took it and ran. We threatened to drop them from helicopters. They still didn't talk. Like the Arabs, you couldn't break them. They were going to survive, no matter how much the rest of us hated them."

The bartender was standing in front of the British officer, looking at him, coldly.

"You're ruining the vibe. Here's the tab. Get out."

"How dare you!"

"I'm a respectable employee of this hotel for many years. Who do you think the manager will believe? A drunken soldier or me?"

The woman produced a credit card and paid the bill. She looked at her colleague, and together, they left the bar without saying another word.

I finished my cognac in one long drink without looking at the bartender. I had joined the ranks of the ugly American abroad, guilty by association.

I dreamed of the Little Mermaid that night. She was rescuing Syrian children in the Aegean Sea.

34

"Come here, Kim. I got to show you something."

Sean was sitting in front of a computer, surfing the net. It was a summer survival game— who could find the coolest picture or video on the internet. The dog days of summer had begun in Houston, and any diversion from the three-digit heat index, such as videos of penguins sliding on their bellies or polar bears diving off an iceberg made the day a bit better.

I moved a cart of paperbacks onto a table for the Friends of the Library Book Sale this Saturday, then walked toward the row of computers near the fiction section.

"Do you really think this will beat the swimming hippos video I showed you yesterday?" I laughed as I approached him, although he didn't turn around to acknowledge me.

"Yeah, this will beat it."

On the screen was a rattlesnake, at least six feet long, dancing in the high branches of a Pinyon Pine Tree, those evergreens growing in West Texas, in Lubbock and Marfa. It looked as if the snake was glued to the pine branch by its rattler, while the rest of his body was undulating in the air.

"This is one of the strangest things I've ever seen."

"It's the devil, Kim. Look at him," Sean said, starting the video again.

"Well, you certainly won with that video," I said with the hair on my arms standing on end.

"It's an omen when animals act strange."

"According to the Farmer's Almanac?"

"No, according to nature. The animals are the first to know something bad is going to happen."

"Like in Macbeth, when the horses eat each other?"

"King Duncan is murdered by Macbeth. An unnatural act causes chaos in the natural world. Maybe that snake dancing is a reaction to Global Warming."

"Now, Sean, that's a bit farfetched."

"It's too hot for June. The Gulf is a dead zone because of fertilizer run-off from suburbs and golf courses. The accumulated plastic garbage in the Pacific is almost the size of Mexico. We humans are the only animals that defecate in our own nest. Why is it so hard to believe nature would take revenge?"

"Double, double, toil and trouble," I laughed, while returning to my work for the book sale.

"You won't be laughing when that trouble hits."

Sean got up from the computer and grabbed his Wal-Mart bag full of clothes, paperbacks, and packaged beef jerky.

"You aren't leaving are you? It's too hot out there."

"Yeah, I'm going to the West Coast, maybe Seattle or Portland. I'm getting out of here before the storm."

"Oh, Sean. Come on. I didn't mean to laugh at you."

"I think we're gonna have a hell of a hurricane season. If you were smart, you'd get out of here, too."

That was the last I saw of Sean Callahan, the back of his T-shirt that read, "Eddie Would Go," with a faded print of a surfer riding a perfect wave in bluer than blue water.

I finished marking books for the sale, returned a few emails, and waited for the clock to end my workday. I felt a prolonged sadness creeping into my heart. Now, I could miss Sean, along with Chasity, Syda, Pixie, and Lou-Lou. The thought of getting a dog crossed my mind before I went to bed that night. I wondered if Wayne-O had any suggestions.

The smell of urine, feces, and bleach met my nose the minute I got out of the car. It was late afternoon at the Harris County Dog Pound on Canino Road. While it was a short drive from the house, it probably wasn't the best the city had to offer as a dog pound. Wayne volunteered his services for years here. His recommendation meant something was what I kept telling myself, while fighting the urge to gag when I opened the front door.

Quite a few volunteers, mostly high school girls and older women were working. I imagined them to be a lot like me, true believers in the simple fact animals were easier to love than humans.

It was a busy Saturday afternoon with dogs being walked in a fenced-in area, while kittens were held by children, pleading, "Pleeeease, Mama, let me keep her." And, of course, there were plenty of animals listless and depressed in a cage.

"Wayne told us you were coming. We love him. Best vet we have," said Hannah, the volunteer assistant, who walked with me up and down the long rows of the kennel, stopping to chat about a particular dog, only to move on shortly after hearing the stories of "not house-trained," "very social animal," "abandonment issues," and other tales of throw away pets. I felt like I was being escorted in a penitentiary, where every inmate was charged with the crime of being unlovable.

I stopped in front of a cage with two mixed-bred dogs.

"Sisters. They were brought in a short time ago. I believe they're part hound dog, maybe even ridge hound, making them athletic dogs."

I couldn't take my eyes off of them. The larger dog, clearly the older one, was very still, while her sibling, a pup, charged the front of the kennel, tongue out and tail wagging.

"Meet Sadie and Ginger. Sadie's the oldest."

"The older one doesn't seem as active, probably the age. She's at least two years older. The younger dog is a bit too social. No boundaries or discipline."

"I'll check up front. Be back in a second with a leash, if you'd like to walk her."

"Yes, I'm curious about Sadie."

Hannah walked back into the office. With her assertive, no nonsense haircut of two inches in length, colored in a mixed hue of lavender and dark purple, I imagined she was the star volunteer. She was strong enough to handle the stench and heartbreak of working at an animal shelter, yet kind. There could be no false pretense with animals. You either loved them or you didn't, and the dogs were the first to sense it.

I walked Sadie in a mud hole surrounded by a chain-link fence behind the kennels. The first thing she did was pee, which made me think she didn't get out of her cage much. She wasn't much of a walker, a few steps at a time, with most of that time spent resting on her back hunches, contemplating whether she should trust me. Hannah's report of her earlier life was one of being chained to a tree outdoors, rain and shine. Sadie was a sad girl. That was all I needed to know about her.

I paid the fees and was relieved to find she was free of heartworms, and her vaccination records were up to date.

"You sure you don't want to adopt her sister? They came in together," Hannah asked me after I handed her my credit card.

"I can't. I want to, but I work a full-time job. Wouldn't be fair to Sadie or Ginger. Ginger's a cute girl. Someone will adopt her."

I called Wayne on the way home. It was probably the best conversation we've had in a long time.

"I'm happy for you, Kim. You've needed a pet for a long time. Give you something to love when I'm not around."

"Are you saying you love me, Wayne, even though it's awkward, at best."

"I'm offering you free vet service for life, as long as you don't replace me with her. That's the best I can do."

"What an offer," I laughed. "I'll take it."

Sadie and I began our life together on Pease Street. Despite the heat of late afternoon, I walked her as soon as I got home from work. I finally figured out she hated the leash and collar. Not so much the leash, but anything around her neck, so a harness for walking made the experience pleasant for both of us. I often thought her former owner used a choke collar on her, yanking it like a reflex, at every move she made.

She also hated the broom. Every time I took it out to clean, she hid behind the furniture. I could only think there was someone out there, living among good people, beating dogs with a broom.

I thought of bringing Sadie with me for my monthly lunch date with Kathy Renee. We were meeting at the Lasker Inn in Galveston for Sunday brunch. The temperatures were in the high nineties, too hot to take her along the sea wall, and I'm sure she wasn't welcome in the Lasker Inn, with its crystal and antiques, adorning the nineteenth-century grand dame of a house. I just hated leaving her alone. It caused her a lot of anxiety that manifested itself in chewed shoes, rugs, and furniture.

Before I left the house on Sunday, we walked at least two miles, taking advantage of the cooler air of an early morning. The stiffness in my right knee and hip kept me from setting a good pace with her, but she didn't seem to mind. Nothing made me happier than to see that tail wag as we walked together through the neighborhood, and nothing made me sadder than to put her in the kennel and hear her cry, as I locked the front door and drove off.

I-45 South careened past Pasadena and Clear Lake, until finally hugging the flat coastal plains into Galveston County. Once I crossed the causeway, the air, salt, and humidity swept through my hair. All four windows of the car were open as I drove to the Lasker Inn on Sixteeth Street. Built in 1870, the inn was a good walk from the beach, but still a favorite among tourists and locals. Like most things on the island, its past was associated with the Great Storm of 1900, the hurricane that drowned the entire area in eight to twelve feet of water, killing over eight thousand and leaving thirty thousand homeless.

Following the apocalyptic hurricane, the Lasker Inn became the home of orphans, where children roamed the halls for decades. During the nineties, a massive remodeling project and a new owner returned the inn to its original splendor with private gardens and a lush interior. Like many of the grand homes in Galveston, people refused to be beaten by a storm. People simply rebuilt what each hurricane season took away.

But I wasn't like those people. I feared the water. I could have easily lived in the historic beauty of this city surrounded by oak trees and hot pink oleanders, if it weren't for hurricane season. Every time I visited, I was reminded of the Great Storm of 1900. The watermarks from that storm were visible everywhere I went. When they began to fade in restaurants, schools, churches, and homes, the people redesignated them in black, thick paint.

The Lasker Inn was no different from any other historic building. Its watermark was in the dining room, not far from where Kathy Renee was seated when I walked in. An elegant silver tea server rested on the linen tablecloth before her. Behind her, a floor to ceiling window was showcased in heavy silk curtains puddling to the oak floor.

"Don't get up. You look comfortable," I said, bending over to hug her.

"Hope you don't mind I didn't wait. I thought it would be so nice to have real tea. Thought you'd enjoy some, too. It's an organic lemon tea." She poured me a cup and set it in front of me.

"I haven't been here in years. Still a beauty," I said, taking in the room with a baby grand in the corner, covered with a fringed scarf and framed photos of smiling brides. "Still a big wedding venue, I see."

I was immediately sad when I said it, realizing neither one of us would ever be a bride. I kept brushing off Wayne's practical proposals.

"Do you want to get the buffet?" Kathy Renee asked, looking at the silver servers loaded with scrambled eggs, bacon, sausage, grits, and biscuits on a side table. "Or we can order from the menu, if you want someone special."

"Are you kidding? It's been years since I've had grits and biscuits!"

We stood in line together, among the flip-flop and T-shirt crowd of tourists on vacation, a juxtaposition of modern life with barbarians dining in a castle.

"If we hurried, we can make it to eleven o'clock Mass at Sacred Heart on Broadway."

She didn't even give me the chance to take the first bite without having to wrestle with my conscience. But that was Kathy Renee, she never missed an opportunity to preach.

"I rush all week. Can't we just relax and enjoy the meal. Maybe go for a walk on the beach after this."

"Sure," she said, but her face was red, and I wondered if she was trying to figure out how to make it to Mass today without upsetting me. I could have eased that for her, but I didn't. I added extra butter to my grits, instead.

"Oh my gosh, look at the watermark."

Kathy Renee pointed to the line of demarcation between life and death in a hurricane, as represented by black paint and a plaque on the wall:

In the Great Storm of 1900, water rose twelve feet in this room.

"You know the water got that high in the Bishop's Palace, too."

I sighed heavily and put my fork down, thinking of Sean's omen.

"I'm surprised you can read that from here. Please don't repeat it. It gives me the creeps."

"Imagine how it was in Noah's time, the flood of the world."

"Do you really think God sent a flood to drown all the evil people on earth?"

"Yes, I do."

"Well, what about the innocents? What about the people who never do anything wrong and suddenly, their home is swept away; their child develops cancer; their dad never makes it home from work. Do you think God does that, too?"

"Oh, Kim. Why must it always be this way? Let's just enjoy this day. I'm not answering that question, because you're purposely looking to find fault in my faith."

"Agreed. No more talk about God, hurricanes, and people drowning."

"Just let me finish with this. There's always hope after devastation. Like Noah's dove returning with the green sprig. It symbolizes God's creation will continue. People rebuild. Following the hurricane of 1900, Galveston built a seventeen-foot-tall seawall to defend itself from future storms."

"I know the oratory-worthy facts, sister. Like among the dead in the 1900 storm were ninety of the ninety-three orphans at St. Mary's Orphanage and the ten nuns in charge. That's it. No more hurricane talk!"

After an uncomfortable silence, Kathy Renee touched my hand across the table. "Hey, let's go to the beach, rent two chairs, and an umbrella. Just like we did when we were kids."

"I'd like that. Leave your car here. We'll drive together. First stop is 7-11 for sun block and bottled water. Still love chocolate malt balls? We'll get some of those, too."

The memory of Kathy Renee eating malt balls, with the little milk carton they came in nestled between her legs, putting as many as she could into her mouth, and licking her fingers, made me laugh out loud.

She looked at me over the rim of her teacup; her eyes smiled in return. We finished our brunch at the Lasker Inn with two flutes of champagne and a healthy serving of pecan pie with vanilla ice cream on the side.

I paid the check at the bar. Wedged between a bowl of peanuts and the register was a battered paperback copy of *Isaac's Storm*. Its cover featured an enormous wave, a wave that drowned an entire city like the Great Storm of 1900 drowned Galveston.

"Ever read it?" The bartender asked, while swiping my credit card. "It's about the storm of 1900 and Isaac Monroe Cline, the chief meteorologist at the Galveston office of the U.S. Weather Bureau. Cline didn't think the storm would be significant. He finally issued a hurricane warning, but it was too late. People were unable to evacuate. His pregnant wife died in that storm."

"Didn't read it. Probably won't ever read it. Hate the whole death and destruction thing, especially when it's nonfiction." I turned around and saw Kathy Renee slip a fifty-dollar tip and a holy card to the waiter.

"Enjoy your day, ma'am. Come back and see us."

I parked near the Pleasure Pier with its enormous Ferris wheel frozen in time until the evening hours of operation. Kathy Renee stopped a vendor for chair and umbrella rentals a few feet from the pier. It was so hot my bare feet were burning on the sand as I ran and cursed my way to the shade of the umbrella. Behind me, my sister was running and laughing. Under the umbrella, we both slouched in the chairs, digging our toes in and out of the sand, while popping chocolate malt balls into our mouths. An hour leisurely passed before we went into the water with our sun dresses pulled above our knees, then tied into a knot at the thigh.

The water was green and clear, so clear I could see my orange toenail polish through the surf. Wanting to cool off, I went back to the chair and umbrella after a few minutes. I sat and watched a bare-chested boy run, then jump on his wake board, skimming the foamy surf-break at the shore-line. Kathy Renee stayed out longer, looking for shells.

I watched the lifeguard climb from his wooden throne, changing the surf condition flag from yellow to red. I wasn't surprised. In the short time we had been here, the wind shifted and became stronger. Forever the Blue Bird, I knew what the red flag meant. Strong surf. Strong currents. Dangerous undertows.

I stood up and waved at my sister in the water.

"Kathy, Kathy Renee. I got to go. Come on. Now."

She didn't hesitate. She was out of the water in seconds.

"What's wrong? We got at least another hour on the umbrella and chairs," she said, dripping water all over my purse and shoes.

"I need to get home. Got a dog now. She's been locked up all day."

"Well, we were lucky to come for even a little while."

"Luck is just a matter of chance, just ask any loser," I said, running and cursing over the hot sand back to the sea wall, where the car was parked.

I climbed the concrete steps from the beach to the sea wall, stopping to let a man and his dog walk past. That dog looked familiar. *Poco?*

35

It began to rain. And it rained. And it rained until Houston became a rapidly shrinking island floating in a sea called Harvey.

We began hurricane preparation at the library as soon as the tropical depression developed into a Category 1 hurricane in the Bay of Campeche. Secretly, I prayed for it to hit Louisiana, but I don't think I'm any different from anyone else in the cone of disaster. The people of coastal Louisiana were praying it would hit Texas. Those days of uncertainty were filled with a gambler's anxiety and hours in front of the television, hoping a high-pressure system would push the hurricane away from my little spot on earth.

If the Weather Channel didn't give me the news I wanted, I changed channels. If the National Oceanic and Atmospheric Administration didn't produce a projected hurricane path I could live with, I followed the Canadian Global-Scale Model or the European Community Ensemble Forecast Charts. It was hurricane du jour in forecasting but, within twenty-four hours of its landing, it was all a matter of luck. The one thing you could always count on, trailer parks were magnets for a hurricane's wrath. Once it landed, it could intensify with tornadoes or simply stick around for days, drowning everything in sight.

Lil' Red Rambo, a fifty-five-year-old homeless woman who took the place of Sean as our daily patron, helped me move books and furniture away from the windows and entry doors at the library. That was the most we could do for storm preparation. Housekeeping and maintenance had the more difficult task of securing the building and its contents. Tomorrow, the library would be officially closed until the dangers associated with the hurricane passed. This would be difficult for our homeless patrons, who viewed the library as a sanctuary from the chaos of the streets.

I'd come to appreciate Rambo's sense of humor and take-charge attitude. A spunky gal, she wore combat boots and kept her thick red hair in a single braid trailing down her back. Her take-no-prisoners wardrobe was accented with a military jacket and camo pants. I don't know what kept her from passing out in the heat with all those clothes on, but I'm sure the tough-girl image served as protection against the streets. Like Sean, she camped near Buffalo Bayou and Sam Houston Park.

"Rambo, are you going to a shelter when the storm hits?"

She looked at me carefully before answering. At first, I was afraid I'd made her angry. Her eyes quickly diverted from the book she was reading to the patterns in the floor, searching for an answer. I knew it wouldn't be easy for her to find a shelter. The tiny nonprofits that provided services to the homeless were the first to fill to capacity during a natural disaster. Her only other choice in surviving the storm was to leave town, like Sean. Leaving was just as hard as staying. There's wasn't any money, car, or friend to make those choices easier.

"Might just hitchhike to Austin. Probably won't make up my mind for another day, though. You know, I was staying in Biloxi when Katrina came through. There was this church group that helped the homeless near Point Cadet. We could go there on certain days to shower, wash clothes, eat. Had me a nice set-up, until Katrina blew that church off the map. Wind and water! We 'bout near drowned. Bad times after that storm. Katrina taught me a lot, like don't take no crazy chances with a hurricane."

"NOAA predicts it will be a rain event. Shouldn't be too bad."

"Miss Kim, I live on the bayou, by the park. That water got to go some-where with all the rain coming."

"Yes, I believe you're right. Wish I could offer you some better sugges-tions than leaving. That's probably the safest choice but do come back. This isn't going to be forever. The library will probably reopen in another day or two."

When I left at closing, I found her reading an Agatha Christie paperback with her boots off, and her stocking feet curled underneath her in a chair. It made me sad, thinking this was the last bit of comfort she would know for several days, maybe even weeks.

"Hope to see you soon, Rambo. Nothing makes me happier than to see you enjoying a book. You're one of our best patrons, so take care of yourself out there." I handed her two twenty-dollar bills and a plastic bag full of cozy mystery paperbacks, all the while knowing I would never see her again.

Before driving home, I stopped at Super Mercado for bottled water and canned goods. People were in a buying frenzy, depleting the supply of Spam, canned tuna, chips, bread, and peanut butter. Only a few gallons of water remained on the shelf. I couldn't remember if my flashlight worked, so I bought a cheap one with extra batteries. I picked up twenty more pounds of dry dog food and a twenty-four pack of paper towels. Who knew when I'd be able to wash clothes again, so the paper towels would serve as napkins, washcloths, and towels. Use and throw away. I liked that concept, a lot.

Teetering on the verge of a natural disaster, I didn't think about my diet when I added several bags of jelly beans, barbeque potato chips, and marsh-mallows. The marshmallow choice was very random, but I couldn't refuse them in their rainbow colors of pink, purple, and yellow. It made me smile just looking at the bag, which may be helpful to my mental health if every-thing I owned floated away.

The day before the storm, I walked Sadie at least four times. The neigh-borhood kids were out playing, after being released from school earlier. At the community park, pick-up games of basketball with shirtless boys sweat-ing and shouting in the humid heat entertained Sadie and me as we walked the wood-mulch track, around and around. We rested at a picnic table, not far from four little girls playing jump robe. One of the girls threw the rope down, when she saw Sadie.

"Hey, little puppy dog." She stroked Sadie from her head to her tail. I crouched next to her just to make sure Sadie wouldn't be afraid. The other girls joined in, petting and scratching her.

"What kind of dog is she? She kinda looks like a mutt and something else," the first girl said.

"Sadie is a little bit of everything, I think," I laughed, standing up and stretching my back, as the girls took turns petting her.

"Well, have fun, girls. Be careful in the storm." Sadie and I walked away, only to turn around seconds later, when we heard them singing, as they jumped in rhythm with a rope skipping off the concrete.

The day seemed so perfect, it was hard to imagine a Category 4 hurricane was heading toward Port O'Connor, a little over a hundred miles from Houston. Even the weather seemed milder with a slight breeze blowing out of the southeast. Later when I was taping the windows and moving all objects off the porch and out of the yard that could become projectiles during the storm, I heard my neighbors next door. They were having a baby shower.

Parked cars rested in their yard, driveway, and sidewalk, with laughing women emerging from them carrying gift bags, pink balloons, and wrapped boxes. That evening I heard them in the backyard, the chorus of voices and the tinkling of wine glasses. Looking through holes in the six-foot privacy fence between us, I watched the orange-red flame of the charcoal barbeque pit cast shadows of the family and their guests on the patio wall. Laughing, the host ran to dampen the flames, as well-meaning jokes from his friends echoed in the night air. The voices, the laughter, the smell of the barbeque, all of it was a vivid reminder: life was all around me the day before the hurricane hit.

With that gut-punch, I took a hot shower, and drenched myself in Ben Gay and night cream. By 8 p.m., I was in my nightgown, calling Kathy Renee.

"You have everything you need to ride out the storm?"

"I was just going to call you, Kim. It won't come onshore until late Friday, so come over here. I got to work the crisis management schedule, but you'll be comfortable at the Villa."

"I'm not riding out a hurricane in a nursing home. Besides, I got to consider my dog. Surprisingly, the weather is mild, a slight breeze blowing out of the southeast. We'll be comfortable here."

"The Villa has higher safety procedures than anyone else, because of our residents' needs. There's lots of food. We can play cards. Bring Sadie."

"No way. I'd rather take my chances with Buffalo Bayou flooding. Look, that storm is not going to be so bad. We're not a direct hit, like Port O'Connor and Rockport. The most we'll probably get is some street flooding and leaves falling from trees."

"Well, if you need me, call the Villa. I'm on for all shifts, with breaks in between for sleeping."

"All right. Talk soon." I hung up and patted the bed, so Sadie would join me. It occurred to me I hadn't spoken to Wayne. Of course, he hadn't called me either. Did it matter at this point in our relationship? I was too tired to keep score, so I tried his cell.

"Hey. You riding the storm out at your place?"

"You were the next person on my list to call. It's been crazy at work. All the animals we have kenneled, we had the owners or next of kin pick up. We just can't risk anything happening to them if we can't get back in the office."

"No doggy day care in the event of a hurricane."

"You got it. I'm also volunteering with the Cajun Navy's Pet Rescue Service. I'm about to head over to our headquarters near Westchase. We thought about staging it near the Medical Center, but that area always floods."

"I'm getting a bad feeling about this. What if you get into a dangerous situation, Wayne? I'm never thought of you as the athletic type, you know, a strong swimmer."

"Typical of you. I can't tell if you're concerned or insulting me."

"Concerned. You know what happens to heroes. They're the first to die."

"What?"

"I knew a boy once. He wanted to be a hero, too. Went noising around in a place he knew nothing about. He drowned."

"I'm not going to drown. Look, why don't you come and work at the staging center? Help with the pets we rescue. Whatever you want to do. Bring Sadie."

"I'm staying home, Wayne. I've got food. We're comfortable. Harvey is not going to be another Katrina."

"Okay. I'll call you when it's over. Be smart, though. If the water starts getting high, get out of there, while you can."

"Good night, Wayne."

I fell asleep with *A Passage to India* on my chest. I wanted to dream of another country in another century far away from the one I lived in.

Friday morning, I fried, baked, and boiled everything in the fridge in case I lost power. There was nothing worse than the stench of rotting food in a fridge. Sadie and I ate like royalty, reserving the canned goods, chips, and marshmallows for emergency purposes. I did all the laundry, even changing the sheets on the bed and washing Sadie's bed. Sadie was next. A scrub in the tub with washing behind the ears and a prolonged towel drying rendered her useless for the rest of the day.

I moved the garbage cans into the garage, put the flashlight and back-up batteries in one location, along with a battery powered radio. Next, I filled the bathtub with water. There was nothing left to do in preparation, except wait. That was the worst part. The Weather Channel was a glow with white noise in my pacing back and forth the longer the day grew.

Harvey made landfall between Port Aransas and Port O'Connor around 5 p.m. with 130 mile per hour winds. I knew those towns as a child: towns of fish camps, bait shops, and oyster shell parking lots. I could almost smell those towns in my memory. Fried fish and hush puppies served with beer and Cokes. They were towns of happy times, fishing, and family vacations. Now, those towns were matchsticks, strewn about the coastal plains. No homes. No jobs. No more family vacations.

By Saturday morning the bands of heavy rain hit Houston, as Harvey was downgraded from a hurricane to a tropical storm hovering above us. The National Weather Service issued flash-flood warnings near creeks, streams, and urban areas with low-lying areas. The weather anchors consistently warned of underpasses, imploring people not to leave their homes. The fear of drowning in your car was real. Pearland, Friendswood, and North Houston were the first areas to flood, as they usually were. First responders were out rescuing people from their homes and cars, despite all the warnings.

In between eating marshmallows and watching the Weather Channel, Sadie and I went for walks in the rain. By Saturday afternoon, the street was flooded with water encroaching the garage door. Occasionally, a large pickup truck drove by, turning the flooded street into a river with currents.

I texted Kathy Renee, but she didn't respond. Then I tried to call Wayne. No answer. After two hours, I called the Villa Maria again. The operator reported she was on duty and could not be disturbed. She reassured me water had not entered the building, and power had not been lost.

That night the storm still wasn't moving offshore, as tornadoes spun in the area, and the water rose to the front and back doors of the house. A swollen Buffalo Bayou began flooding downtown.

I moved everything of importance to me, the *Portrait of Light,* family pictures, medical records, insurance documents to the top of the kitchen cabinets, along with canned food, a Styrofoam ice chest, and bottled water. It was too late to get out of here, except if I swam out. I fought my fear with Sadie by my side. Brave girl, she never barked, not even when the water swallowed the kitchen table. We sat together on the kitchen counter tops, in the dark, as the water inched toward us. I'd occasionally shine the flashlight into the black water.

Two water moccasins, illuminated by the flashlight, swam slowly toward the kitchen countertops, their cat eye pupils in their large triangular heads steadied their gaze on Sadie. Her frantic barking, the raised hair on her back, only served as a target for them. I flashed the light quickly onto the cabinet tops, searching for something long handled, something to push them away if they came any closer. Nothing, only canned goods, bottled water, and paperwork.

One was more aggressive than the other. It came close enough for me to see dark stripes near its nostril and huge jowls. The grotesqueness of its thin neck in contrast to its large head caused my hands to shake as I threw a gallon of bottled water at it. The snake coiled, then exposed its inner mouth white as cotton.

"Get out, get out of here," I screamed into the dark kitchen with a single ray of light shining on both snakes. In return, they hissed and swam away.

Early dawn began to peep through the rain as I stared out of the lone kitchen window. It was a black sea under a sheet of rain, falling from the sky. I reached for the Styrofoam ice chest on the top of the cabinet, where I had stored bread and cellophane wrapped cheese slices. I fed Sadie the cheese and forced myself to eat four slices of bread. Next, I lowered her into the ice chest and placed her in the rising water in the kitchen, holding it with both hands just to make sure she could float in it. I picked the ice chest up with her in it and placed it on the countertop next to me. Next, I got on my knees and eased the kitchen window open. I picked up that ice chest and reached as far as I could out the window and dropped it into the water. She made it! Sadie was floating in the ice chest. I eased myself out of the window and let go of the ledge, dropping in the water next to her. I slightly touched the rim of the ice chest, speaking to her softly, "Sadie, girl, we're gonna make it. We'll be all right." I kicked my feet slightly as we began to propel through the water. I fought from thinking what was below my feet—dead animals, garbage, raw sewage, maybe even bodies. I kicked until I grew tired, then I floated for a while. I set our direction on a utility pole I knew to be the corner of Pease Street and St. Emmanuel. Sadie's little boat was continuously filling with rainwater, despite the frantic handfuls I tried to cup, then splash from the Styrofoam container.

I was getting tired, and I secretly cursed myself for allowing my body to get out of shape over the years. If only, if only, if only began to sing in my head. There was no one else out. I wondered if all of Houston, five million people, had drowned. Where was everyone?

I made my destination of the first utility pole and pushed to the left, with my next destination being the Gulf Freeway. Maybe there was help there. But once the streets became wider, the current became stronger. I tried and tried, but the rain kept falling, and the water became stronger than me. I kicked my feet; I splashed out the water in the ice chest, but it was replaced faster than I could remove it. I cried out to God. "Save me. Save me and Sadie. I can't go any further." I stopped kicking and looked at Sadie. "Don't be afraid, girl. Don't be afraid." I closed my eyes as I let go for the ice chest.

"Are you an angel?"

"No, ma'am, I'm with the Cajun Navy."

I was underneath a black tarp, lying flat on my back. Rain was pelting me in the face. I could hear a motor of some kind.

"You're a lucky lady. We spotted you right before you let go of that ice chest. Now, lie still, ma'am. Gonna get you to a safe place."

"My dog. Where's Sadie?"

"Got her right here. Come on girl. Easy, now. Your mama needs you."

He picked up Sadie and put her underneath the tarp. I held her tightly and began crying.

"I couldn't go anymore. I couldn't fight the water."

"Nothing to fight anymore, ma'am."

I closed my eyes, listening to the hum of the little jon-boat motor, while pulling Sadie closer to me.

Once I was checked out by the medics at a makeshift first-aid station near the Galleria, Sadie and I were brought to a giant box furniture store serving as a shelter.

The first line I stood in was to receive clean clothes. Organized by the St. Paul Methodist Women of Katy, the clothing pantry was an impressive boutique of used clothes on clothing racks, organized by item and size. In bins were unopened packages of underwear and a collection of bras and socks, boxes of shoes, and baskets of brand-new flip-flops.

"What size are you, hon? I think I might even have a little T-shirt for your puppy, too. At least you could wrap her in it, give her a bit of warmth." A woman in her late seventies, dressed in jeans, tennis shoes, and a T-shirt, with bifocals balanced on the top of her gray head, stood smiling at me. She could have been my mother if she were still alive.

"I'm a ten, maybe could squeeze into an eight. A sports bra will work if you have one."

"Sure do. What about the shoe size?"

"I wear an eight. Flip-flops would be nice. I'm embarrassed, ma'am. I've never had to beg for clothes before."

"Honey, you aren't begging. I'm asking you. I'm sure you'd do it for me in a heartbeat if the circumstances were different."

"I don't know about that. I've been a selfish woman most of my life. Now, I'm knocked to my knees."

"Honey." She grabbed my hands and placed them in hers. "May I pray with you?"

"I don't know how to pray. I used to. My parents taught me, took me to church; they were good people, so I can't blame my lack of faith on them." I began to cry, walking away from her.

"Here, now. I'm not going to let you go. Hold on to me. I'll pray for you."

In the middle of that furniture warehouse, in a sea of half-drowned people, a stranger held me as if she knew me, as if she loved me.

"Father, fill my sister with peace, the peace only your love can provide. Amen." She let me go, then stepped back, looking at me and Sadie, smiling. "Now, you two stay here, while I get you some clean clothes."

I was provided with a gently worn, but clean, velour jogging suit, undergarments, flip flops, and a bright yellow knitted afghan for warmth. Sadie got a red T-shirt from Buc-ee's gas station. We moved to the next line in front of the portable shower units. I was never so thankful for a shower and the use of a bar of soap in my life. I scrubbed Sadie, standing next to me in the shower stall. Fortunately, no one ever said anything about her, but I was also careful, keeping her out of sight by wrapping her in the afghan like an infant.

We were directed to the main room of the furniture store, where I found a recliner, threw the afghan over it, and plopped into it with Sadie on my lap. In front of me was a large screen television, tuned-in to local news. The longer I stared at it, the more I was convinced I was imaging things. It couldn't be. It just couldn't be. I grabbed Sadie and moved closer to the television, so I could hear. The screen showed old men and women being evacuated from the Villa Maria. First responders in boats, including the Cajun Navy were carrying them in their arms, moving slowly through the black water. But I didn't see my sister. Where was Kathy Renee?

The next news clip showed the animal rescue center staged at Westchase. Volunteers were taking animals from the boats of the Cajun Navy and other rescuers brave enough to be out in the floodwaters. Rain dripped from their hats, their clothes weighted by water, they continued to work, bundling wet dogs and cats in towels and blankets and placing them in covered shelters. But where was Wayne?

I'd have to find a telephone and call Kathy Renee and Wayne, but it wasn't the right time. I didn't want to bother any of the volunteers. People were still coming in, confused and half drowned. Besides, who would I call? The Villa was flooded. My sister could end up here. I'd just have to wait it out. I wasn't as worried about Wayne.

I stayed in the chair with Sadie, napping on and off, until we were awakened by an overhead PA system announcing dinner. We would be fed according to where we were placed in the furniture store: chairs, sofas, bedroom suites, children's furniture, and finally, dining tables and chairs. I picked up Sadie, covered her with the blanket and got in line when it was our turn. Volunteers were passing out paper sacks with submarine sandwiches, chips, an apple, and bottled water. I was so hungry I could taste the salt on the chips when I looked in the bag.

Sadie and I were headed back to the recliner where we watched television and ate. I took the ham and cheese from my sandwich and hand-fed Sadie. I fell asleep in the recliner with the blare of the television in front of me, wondering if my sister was alive.

The next morning, I asked to use a telephone to call Kathy Renee. Her cell and landline rang, then went to voice mail. I finally found a volunteer who would give me a ride to Pasadena. By eleven o'clock, I was on my way to my sister's house, although the ride was precarious, as many of the roads were closed. We had to follow alternate routes, making the drive much longer. Downtown, Memorial, and the Medical Center areas were underwater. I tried not to think about the library, and all the beautiful books floating in the vile, black water. I knew my house was gone. It was too much, all of it.

As we neared Kathy Renee's house in Pasadena, I noticed all the dead birds on the ground. Everywhere.

"I know. So sad. Try not to look. There were tornadoes in the area. Though, it looks like your sister's house was spared."

We pulled in the driveway, and I saw watermarks and yard debris clinging to the garage door.

"I wonder how much water got into the house?" The volunteer asked as I got out of the car. "Are you going to be all right here?"

"Things don't look too bad. I'll just wait here until my sister comes home. I'll be fine. Thanks for the ride."

I carried Sadie into the house. There was no luggage, purse, or books to bring in. Nothing. I didn't own a thing in the world, including the clothes on my back. A stranger had given them to me. There was about two to three inches of water inside the house. The carpet was ruined, but it could be pulled up and dragged to the road. Carpet was easy to replace. I carried Sadie back into my sister's bedroom. A flowery bedspread covered the bed, made neatly from the day before.

I lay on the bed, staring at the ceiling. Sadie curled her body next to mine.

I don't have a job, a car, or a house. How ironic. I'm homeless. Just like the patrons. I don't think I have flood insurance. I've lost everything. Nothing will ever be the same for me. Bye-bye, Blue Bird.

Turning on my side, I saw a book on the dresser next to the bed. *Nancy Drew's* The Mystery at the Lilac Inn. *I guess Kathy Renee saved all my books. She's the one who cleaned out Mom and Dad's house after it sold. I didn't come to help. I didn't want to.*

I began to cry. Humility was something I was unfamiliar with.

I stared at the unmoving blades of the ceiling fan above my head. No electricity. The room was hot, humid with the stillness of a city completely scourged of its ability. I thought of Wayne. I wondered if I would live to understand the full meaning of not knowing what I had until I lost it. But my final thought was of her. Kathy Renee. I closed my eyes to the perfect silence within my sister's bed.

I love you, sister. Come home.